With fond memories for a
wonderful tour

[signature]

Published by
MOONSTONE ISLAND BOOKS
31-4025 Roblin Boulevard
Winnipeg, Manitoba
R3R 3V5
Phone: (204) 888-5165

Email:moonstonebooks@shaw.ca
http://www.moonstonebooks.ca

Cover Illustration by John Henry Friesen

Printed in Canada by Hignell Book Printing

ISBN 0-9732569-0-7

Tales From A
Town
With A
Funny Name

By
Doug Evans

Note for the Reader:

I grew up during the Thirties in a strange, isolated mining town in Northern Manitoba with the decidedly funny name of Flin Flon. We grew used to explaining the name to strangers.

There was no regular air service then, nor any road. Communication with the outside world was via the thrice-weekly train, the telegraph and a somewhat unreliable long distance telephone.

The town was peopled with a wonderful mixture of adventurers, refugees and just plain characters.It was a wonderful town for children, having as we did a sampling of people from all over the world and the example before us daily of the wonderful spirit of cooperation and creativity that guided them in turning our isolated mining camp into a community. That strong sense of community was reflected in the many organizations and pastimes that people created for themselves.

The recounting of well-known stories was one of these pastimes. Usually the story had some basis in fact or in the characters involved but the verbal 'embroidery' added generally left only a faint trace of the original and most of the time none at all.

These stories are not meant to portray any actual event that might have happened in Flin Flon, or any person that might have lived there. That said, if any of these events had actually happened, or any of these characters had actually existed, they would not have astonished any of the citizens of that wonderful smoke scoured town perched on the hard green rocks of the Precambrian Shield.

These stories might have been titled 'The Rise and Fall of Two Bob Bobdinsky' since they do chronicle some of the events of his municipal career, but on reflection it seems that most of the things that happened could only have happened in the Town With The Funny Name.

I would like to thank all those who helped me accept the fact that spelling, punctuation and grammar are not matters of personal choice. I owe a great debt to friends who plowed through early drafts and offered advice and encouragement.

A special thanks to Cindy Little and to Ron and Sandi Mielitz. Any errors that might have escaped their careful editing are my own.

This book is dedicated to my wife, Lucille, who has learned to love Flin Flon as much as I do.

Doug Evans

Table Of Contents

Two Bob for Mayor

THE MAYOR OF OUR TOWN, CUTHBERT ANARDICE MCSHEFFIELDER, HAD BEEN ELECTED MAYOR WHEN THE TOWN WAS FIRST FORMED. He had never lost an election since and didn't plan to. Cuthbert Anardice was a big man, with a huge round head decorated with a fringe of faded yellow hair and a moustache that was white on one side and brown on the side he smoked cigars on. A puffy florid face, bulbous nose and watery eyes bore witness to his fondness for the blood of Scotland. He always buttoned his paisley vest up to the very top button and his belly was well enough along that his huge "stem winder" watch lay facing up toward him, anchored in position by its heavy gold chain with the moose tooth fob.

Mayor McSheffielder blew a choking cloud of blue smoke down the length of the council table, nearly asphyxiating Robert Bobdinsky, the newest member of the town council, and thus one who hadn't yet learned to come early and get a seat as far as possible from the mayor. There was another reason for putting a little distance between yourself and the mayor, if it could be managed. It was said that the mayor never liked to be without a cigar in his mouth and that he never smoked in the bath. The council room windows were open to whatever outside air could find its way in, but the still air in the street, baking in the sun of an unseasonably late Indian Summer, was at least as hot as that of the council chambers. The grease of many a rib eye steak glistened on Cuthbert Anardice's pink skin as he dabbed a fat finger on a rather official looking letter that lay before him on the council table.

"I don't have to tell any of you that it is Cornelius Swinton Wahtney that is the sole owner of this mine, which pretty much means sole owner of this whole damn town as well. Ain't anybody can't count the box cars of copper ingots, and slabs of zinc and gold bars and rods of cadmium that goes out of that mine and he owns it all. And just to set everything in perspective here, it is such a small chunk of everything he does own that he only bothers to visit it about once every other year or so, if'n he ain't distracted by somethin' important along the way." Mayor Cuthbert dabbed at the letter again, his heavy fingers making a doughy thunking sound - donk donk.

"Have we been informed of the details of his visit, such as where he will stay, or if he is bringing his private train and such like?" This last was Gunther Volkstien, the deputy mayor, who was typically more taken by details than the whole picture.

"Well, he's been here before, and he's got that house over by the main gate, the gold one"

The house that was used when the mine owner or other major dignitaries came to visit was called the "Gold Cottage." It was not really gold, in fact it was white and green like all the other mining company houses. During the King's Jubilee, management had commissioned a big cast copper model of the mine. The model was about six feet long and just under three feet wide, and had its own sturdy oak table to sit on and a glass cover. The smelter and its smoke stacks were at one end; the open pit at the other end and the mill, tank house and mine shafts, were all faithfully portrayed, as were the various offices and outbuildings. The "Guest Cottage" had been made more prominent by painting its roof gold to distinguish it from the other cottages and bunkhouses and it promptly became known as the "Gold Cottage" by the locals.

"But that ain't what the letter is about. What this here letter is advisin' this council here assembled of, (donk...donk) is that this time he is bringin' Mrs. Cornelius Swinton Wahtney with him and that lady wishes, while she is here, to get to meet some of the ladies of the town, and also to go ridin' on our ridin' path. It says here, (donk... donk) "bridle path," but it seems clear to me they mean ridin' path because just below that it talks about horses, about how she loves 'em

8

and is lookin' forward to ridin' on some of our best ones... ridin' 'em on our ridin' path."

"Mr. Mayor, I do believe the term "bridle path" is correct, and it refers to the bridle of the horse not..."

"Gunther, it don't matter a damn at this point, because this town ain't got no such path and it ain't got any of that kind of horse and we don't have all that many ladies either come to think of it."

"Do you think she expects to find a riding academy up here?"

"Hard to say what she expects Gunther, ain't never met the lady but it does look like the mine is throwin' the ball to the town here on this one. One thing I can tell you is that if that lady wants a ridin' path and a horse to ride on it then I damn well intend for there to be somethin' ready for her when she gets here."

"I understand that Mary Boggins, the mine manager's secretary, met the lady when she went along to the annual meeting a year ago. Might be useful to talk to her."

"Good thought, Two Bob. Why don't you just go and do that and then, at our next little get together, which I suggest should be this evenin' since we don't have all that much time, you can get us all on point about this lady and her horses."

Mayor McSheffielder liked the idea of sending Bob Bobdinsky to talk to the mine manager's secretary. Two Bob as he was known to most, had only been on the council for one term but already Cuthbert could sense a threat to his position as mayor. Two Bob had made a name for himself around town, organizing curling bonspiels and ball tournaments and setting up fishing derbies. Sending him off to interview a secretary would underscore just how low his spot on the municipal totem pole really was.

The council assembled again just after seven. The huge red autumn sun was just setting but it was still hot out, and even hotter in, and there wasn't a lot of enthusiasm being displayed by the councillors, who would far sooner have been doing something cooler on their respective back porches.

"Now then, I believe it was Two Bob here who was to have a report for us, wasn't it so Two Bob?"

Mayor McSheffielder managed to put Bob Bobdinsky on the spot in front of the councillors and, at the same time, give just a hint that his report was so unimportant he, the mayor, had almost forgotten who was to give it. This kind of thing was typical of the mayor and no one put too much stock in it.

"I did speak to Miss Boggins and I believe what she had to say may help us a bit. She tells me that Mrs. Wahtney was formerly Miss Margaret De La Peche, the daughter of an English Earl or Count or somethin' of the sort. She confided to me, and I think we should respect her confidence in this, that when C. S. Wahtney came into his millions he had a desire to be accepted into society, high society that is. The problem bein' that in real high society it don't matter, apparently, how many millions you might have, what matters is how old your money is. If it's new money you made yourself, well, it don't count. If it was made a long time ago, like if your great-great-grandfather made it, then it's old money and it counts even if you don't have it any more. The only way for C.S. Wahtney to make his way into the old money society was to marry into it, so he arranged for himself to marry the daughter of Reginald De La Peche, a member of the English nobility." Two Bob cleared his throat and wished for just a sniff of air untainted by the mayor's malodorous cigar. "It seems Mr. De La Peche was a bit short in the pocket at the time this was arranged, but has since done fairly well in some investments he made with Mr. Wahtney."

"And so what's all this got to do with horses, Bob? Seems like a keeper of a deal to me, Lapitch got hisself out of the hole and his daughter got herself a husband can wipe his behind on big bank notes, I don't..."

"It seems Mrs. Wahtney, the former Miss De La Peche, has a passion for horses, spends hours ridin' on the family estate, and even belonged, in England, to the Marley Down Hunt, whatever that is."

"She goes huntin'? On horseback?"

"Foxes."

"Well, I don't care how old your money is or how little you got of it. You can't get more'n a couple of bucks for a fox pelt these days so what in the hell would a rich woman like her want with huntin' foxes for, and on horseback at that, seems..."

Gunther couldn't resist putting in his two cents worth "It is, I believe, a sport followed by the wealthier classes in

England."

"Sport or no sport, Gunther, its a duffer's way to go about catching a fox. Any fox I ever saw would take one look at a hunter on horseback and make a smart right turn across the nearest muskeg swamp and the horse would be up to his ass in loon shit before he could make two jumps."

"I think maybe...," This was Two Bob's way of getting to stick a word in edgewise, "I think maybe the whole point is that the lady likes to ride horses and she wants to ride one during the time she will be up here."

"Well, we got no shortage of horses, in fact that new Clydesdale we got for the water wagons is about as fine a horse as ever you'll see."

"I don't think" said Two Bob, in his best non-challenging voice, "I don't think that would be the right kind of horse."

"Right kind of horse? What's wrong with that horse I ask you? Big Daniel there pulled Arne Finabogasson's sleigh home all by himself that time Arne's team broke through the ice and nearly sank in that swamp. Best damn horse we got around and a fine looking one, gentle as a lamb to boot."

"Well, he might be." Two Bob persisted. "He might be a fine dray horse for pullin', but for sittin' on top of, which is what's wanted in this case, he's pretty wide across and maybe a bit heavy in his gait." Two Bob had no idea what a "gait" was but he thought that throwing that last bit in wouldn't hurt.

"Ah come on, Two Bob, you tryin' to tell us that this high society lady wouldn't be happy on a fine horse like Big Daniel there? Too wide? Not so's you'd notice. Maizie Parminter sat him in the First of July parade just like a queen."

"Well, I don't want to make a big thing of it, but I think that Mrs. Wahtney would be definitely expectin' a more ridin'-type horse than a pullin'-type horse; narrower through, if you get what I mean."

"You don't think she could get her legs around old Daniel there? Maizie ain't all that big and she didn't have no..."

Gunther tried his best to get the conversation back onto a more useful track, " Mrs. Wahtney comes from the English nobility. That is not a large group and they have been in-breeding for centuries, since 1066, I believe. It might be that that class of people can no longer get their legs as far apart as, say, our Canadian farm bred girls like Maizie can."

Mayor Cuthbert was smart enough to know when things weren't going his way and did the political thing, which is to say he changed sides. "Well, you boys know, as your mayor, there's no question of my ever bein' involved in any gamin' and race track bettin' and such like, but I do know a fellow outside of Winnipeg who boards race horses for the folks at the Downs. I'll give him a call in the mornin'. Shouldn't be too much to ask if we could rent one o' them ridin' type horses for a week if we agree to payin' the freight up and back and the feed and all."

"We have nothing named in the budget for that kind of an expenditure."

"Gunther, there are times when a good town administrator's got to look at the realities and make the plans fit 'em, like we got that money set aside for a new snowplow, and I'm proposin' that we take a bit of that money for this horse thing. We can even call the beast "Snowplow," which should look good enough for the auditors in the expenditure column - haw."

"There still remains the matter of the bridle path."

"Well, so there does Gunther, so there does. But a little bit of a path shouldn't be all that much of a problem. I expect she'll want it kind of scenic and all so why don't you and the town engineer go and mark out a nice path, say, startin' by Polkers's Ice House, then alongside the railroad track, through that stand of old jack pines, down along the lake, and then up that little valley by the miners' shacks and back to the ice house. That should be about a mile or so and when you got the route all figured out we can get a couple of good line cutters to clear it out."

"We would have to insist that the line cutters remove the stumps and sharp stubs of the trees and bushes they cut. A horses' foot is a very tender thing I am told, and it wouldn't be a good thing if this horse stepped on the sharp end of a chopped off willow or something." Gunther was a bear for details.

"Gunther, there is every now and then when you think of too many things that could go wrong. Horses were designed by God for runnin' and it stands to reason they would never have lasted this long if they could only do their best runnin' on special tidied-up tracks."

" I think, Mr. Mayor, with all due respect, the problem is that the horse's foot was developed to run on sand in the desert, and on grass in England. It was never contemplated that any horse would have to gallop bare foot through the stubs of willows left by a mining claim line cutter."

The beer parlor closed at eleven in our town and this conversation was eating into valuable beer drinking time, a fact that was making the mayor less and less interested in the finer points of Gunther's arguments. "Well then, have them chop out the damn stumps... but I tell you now, the bill is going to be something you guys are goin' to have to deal with."

"Maybe if we covered this horse path with sawdust."

"Sawdust? Two Bob, what the..."

"Like we do with the corduroy roads: put a layer of saw-dust down all along the path. I would think the most dainty footed horse in the world ain't goin' to grumble about runnin' on sawdust."

"Well boys, there's your answer right there, sawdust. Somebody talk to Loud Raight and get him to let the town's dump wagon haul sawdust for the path from that sawmill he seized from the Digby brothers when they defaulted on their loan last year. I suppose he'll want to bill us for somethin' he would otherwise put absolutely no value on, but that can't be helped, I guess. Anyway, try appealing to his community spirit first."

No one at the table thought Loud Raight wouldn't bill the town for the sawdust and no one at the table thought that he wouldn't be expected to kick back part of the bill to the mayor for the upcoming election campaign either, but no one said anything.

"Like I said, I'll phone about the horse in the mornin'. You all know what you have to do... So, is there any further business?"

No one could think of any business important enough to take into serious consideration against the fact that the beer parlor was closing in less than an hour. Mayor Cuthbert knew his men and knew when he could make a move, but he did add one little bit.

"This here business of Mrs. Wahtney going horse ridin' is important to this town. If she is happy with the way we're doin' things, it wouldn't take much of a whisper on the pillow, if you get my meanin', to go a long way towards gettin' those extra sheets of curlin' ice on the go. I'm takin' full control of this here project myself and no one, but no one, is to do one damn thing without I know all about it. Meetin's adjourned."

Cutting the path was a matter of a couple of days. In those days, the boundaries of mining claims were outlined by chopping out a clear-cut line through the bush along the border of the claim. A whole class of professional "line cutters" had grown up around this legal requirement, and they could clear a line in the bush with their axes whistling through the stunted northern trees and scrub willows like a mowers in a hay field.

The town was forced to lay out an extra bonus to get them to slow down enough to make the path double the width of a normal cut line and to remove all the stumps and little ends of the willows as they passed. But this was thought to be part of a long-term investment. To have the good will of an Old Money English Lady, especially one married to someone who owned most of the world that we knew of, seemed like a sound idea even if she couldn't get her legs as far apart as a good Canadian woman.

The sawdust proved to be a bit more trouble than anticipated. There had been a very heavy rainstorm the previous fall that had soaked the sawdust down for quite a ways and during the winter all that had frozen hard, and deep down it was still frozen. Frozen sawdust is not like other stuff, it won't melt, at least not very fast, it won't break and you can't very easily saw it or drill it or do much of anything with it. For most of one day the town shook to the sound of Powder Phil's dynamite as he converted the still frozen slab of sawdust around the old mill into chunks that the sun could get a grip on. By the fifth day after the decision to build the bridle path had been made, the council assembled near Polker's Ice House where the path emerged from the willows along the edge of the little valley that led up from the shore of the lake. The more the mayor admired the path, the more he began to sound like he had just finished building it with his own two hands.

"Boys, I don't think there's a bridle path between here and Edmonton that'd be as nice as this one. That Old Money Lady is going to prance along here like she was back in the old country tryin' to catch foxes."

Two Bob had managed to position himself upwind of the mayor, but even so, was wishing he was located even farther away than he was. "I hope she doesn't get bored; this trail is a mile long, but a mile isn't all that much for a horse, especially a horse that's been runnin' in races, I would think."

"Don't you worry your head about that, Two Bob, no sir, don't you trouble yourself at all, at all. All it takes is a little organizing ability here. I'm takin' personal and complete charge of this whole fandangle and I aim to see that that ride is not only not borin' but will be somethin' she will be braggin' about to the other Old Money Ladies for the rest of her days."

The new horse, now officially named "Snowplow," arrived at the CN station in fine shape. Mayor Cuthbert Anardice had to lean on the town clerk a bit to get the expenses entered under the town's snow removal budget but that didn't hold things up much. The horse arrived complete with saddle and bridle. The saddle, when it was unpacked, turned out to be not your standard saddle with the high horn in front and form fitting seat that most folks knew, but the flat kind used for horse racing.

"She ain't gonna like that saddle, it's a racin' saddle not a ridin' saddle."

"Well, you did tell them down in Winnipeg that it was for an Old Money English Lady to ride on didn't you? Maybe that's the kind of saddle they use over there."

"I talked to Stimpy Ross who used to work on a ranch out in Alberta and he says he don't think anyone could stand to ride a saddle like that one, except maybe a jockey and they ride standin' up."

"Well, maybe before we do anythin' like modifyin' that saddle we ought to talk to the Reverend Hoaseman. He's from England and he likely could tell you about what kind of saddle those Old Money Ladies usually like to ride on."

As it turned out the saddle was just the thing, and the little black mare that pranced down the ramp from the CN box car was a delight to behold. Long, slender legs, a high arched neck, and long flowing tail and mane made you think of lightness and speed just looking at her. She had been placed at the farm of the mayor's friend for breeding, but as the owner had told the mayor when he was describing the horse, "She warn't in the mood just yet," and so renting her out to the town for a few days shouldn't be a problem.

The riding path ran from Polker's Icehouse, near the end of Main Street, out alongside the railroad track for a ways, through a stand of gnarly old jack pines, then down to the lake. It followed the shore for a bit then turned sharply up a willow-bordered valley past a few miners' shanties on the tail end of Pyrite Road and then finished up by passing to the north of the icehouse to complete the circle. Gunther and the town engineer rolled the walking wheel over it and came up with a distance of about a mile and a quarter. Walking along the soft sawdust-padded path in the warm fall sunshine was a pure delight and it was generally agreed that this was about as close to an England type bridle path as any one could expect and maybe in some respects, better.

They stabled the little mare in the town's stable, right next to Big Daniel. There was a little concern expressed about this because, as the mayor pointed out "Just because she ain't in the mood today don't mean she might not be tomorrow." Indeed, the town's head teamster thought she might be giving her new neighbor the big eye. Big Daniel, lacking as he did some of the essential bits, only gave her one disinterested stare and went on with the process of turning the best part of a bale of hay into horse.

If you were to have peeped in through the skimpy lace curtains on the window of a little tar paper shack near the very top of Hill Street, you would have seen one of the saddest men in our whole town. Pinkus MacDavey was sitting at his little spraddle-legged green painted wooden table, head bowed, and shoulders bent. In front of him, beside the fresh flowers carefully arranged in an old jam jar, lay a full set of bagpipes.

Now bagpipes come in all sizes but these were the real thing: war pipes, capable of hurrying regiments into mass suicide or bringing tears to the eyes of the most hardened border pirates. MacDavey caressed the long tassels that hung from the drones and once again felt the texture of the bag to be sure the honey and beer conditioner still kept the leather flexible and airtight, and sighed.

Behind him his wife Mehgan dried her hands on her apron. "I wouldn't take on so Pinkus, no I wouldn't and well I know how it must be not bein' able to play and all but..."

16

"They aw need the pipes for the bonspiel, and for the fairst of July, and for any damn potbelly the town wants ta impress and all, but there's no anywhere ta practice!"

"It is true then isn't it, yes it is and you kicked out a' the meetin' hall because of the boys tryin' to sleep in the bunkhouse alongside, isn't it..."

"Too cold outside in the winter and in summer the muskitas. How ken a mon bring his full mind ta bear on the cascades a' triplets in the Rant of MacMoorin when there are twenty of the blood suckin' beasts lined up along yer own nose and tryin' ta drain ya dry? No, ya cannot."

"What's needed, Pinkus, is some sort of a community hall. Yes, a fine big hall with room to march up and down, pipes brayin' like the billy oh, it is, and you could skirl away as loud as ever you liked, yes."

"A community hall! Ah, what a fine thing t'would be an' all but it's no likely ta happen while the mayor has his heart set on expandin' the cairlin' rink ta six sheets' it won't. An the mine takes no notice o' the common mon, no, they don't either."

"If we was in the old country now Pinkus, you could send a petition right to the Queen, so you could, but here in this strange and lonely land I don't know..."

"Don't mock me woman, we have no queen here, we don't, unless that high scooted wife ah old Wahtney's might be..."

"Well, she did come from a noble family, Pinkus, maybe you just could make an appeal to her for a nice warm community hall, and, well distanced from the bunk houses wouldn't it be... and other houses as well", Mehgan added as an afterthought.

"An' how would you propose, woman, that I get to hobnob with the likes of the high and mighty Mrs. Wahtney? Go tappin' at the back door o' the Gold Cottage maybe?"

"No, but they did build that new ridin' trail fer her, and she will be a canterin' along there come Thursday mornin' accordin' to the radio, she will be yes." Mehgan's normally soft Welsh voice rose just a little. "Now if you was to set yourself up along the way somewhere and play her a nice reel or the like, why, then I think she might stop to have a word, she might, yes."

"So I'm ta put on me kilt an' me sporran an' me high

shouldered jacket with the gold bars an' me tasseled cap an' march oop and doon alongside the new path a playing a jig or a reel an' hope she'll remember enough a the royalty business ta stop and make a polite enquiry as ta me health an' general outlook? Y'er daft, I should never a married a Welsh woman, always schemin' they are."

"No, an' I ain't." Mehgan was warming to her own idea now "No an' I ain't daft, it might just work and supposin' it don't, well then what's lost? You great lump, get out yon chanter an' smooth the bumps off a nice couple a' foot swingin', toe tappin' tunes an' you might just get a new community hall fer yer troubles, yes, you might do."

Mehgan gave her husband's broad shoulders a good Celtic hug, for she loved him dearly even if he wasn't Welsh. "Go on with ye now."

Mrs. Wahtney was scheduled to take her first ride on the new path just before noon and the council had met in an informal session that morning just to go over the details one more time.

The mayor was in the chair and well into his second cigar.

"So far as I can see everythin' is pretty well set. Horace Onger took that little filly out and walked her around the new path a couple of times last night to get her used to the feel of it. Not a hop nor a skip out of her; happy as a clam on that sawdust."

"I hope there aren't too many curious people jammed along the path, kind of spoil the effect." Two Bob was worried about the gathering of a crowd of onlookers, not only as it would reduce the carefully crafted woodsy look of the new riding path, but also what effect a lot of people might have on what looked to be a pretty spirited horse.

"Two Bob I'm way ahead a ya. I got the radio station to start broadcastin' a general request for folks not to go gawkin' at this Old Money Lady when she's takin' her ride."

"Well, I imagine curiosity will still..."

"Way ahead a ya again, Two Bob. Pendlebury McNeish from the radio station is gonna set up his microphone on the roof of Polker's Icehouse, from which point he will be able to see the whole fandangle, and just so folks won't be comin down to gawk, he's gonna be broadcasting a description of every thing that goes on."

All this seemed to be getting overly complicated to Two

Bob, but there was more to come.

"Seein' as how it's this fine lady's first visit to our fine community here, I'm goin' to personally present her with a little welcome just so's she'll feel at home. Just after that stretch along the track, among those big old jack pines is where I plan to meet up with her, and I'll welcome her official like to this municipality and its new ridin' track."

"You're gonna stand there by the sawdust path and say all this as she rides by?"

"Not so's you'd notice I ain't, I am the mayor after all. Nope I'm gonna be a horseback just like her, and make my little speech face to face. I'll keep it short a course, this not bein' a truly formal occasion."

"You're gonna go ridin' right with her?"

"Nope, my plan is to be settin' right up on Big Daniel when she comes by, and just speak my piece from there, so she'll be reassured she ain't the only one likes horses in this town."

"Not wanting to sound disrespectful Mr. Mayor, but how in the hell are you going to get yourself up on top of Big Daniel? How are you planning to stay up there considering we got no saddle that will fit him, and how in hell are you gonna get yourself down off'n him without breaking your neck?" Phil McCartney rarely spoke at council meetings, but when he did it usually was pretty clear and to the point.

"You're raisin' an excellent point there Phil, the back of that monster is higher off the ground than the top of my best hat, but there won't be any problem. I'm havin' one of the town teamsters lead Big Daniel down to the spot I picked out for the meetin', he's bringin' along a stepladder and I'll just climb up and set there. The ladder can go outa sight back in the bush till I need to get down. As for the saddle, since I ain't plannin' on goin' nowhere a settin' on that horse, I won't need one...Haw!"

"Seems like things are well in hand." This last from Two Bob who had a sinking feeling that, in truth, things were definitely not well in hand at all.

And it got worse...

"Yep, and the problem of her getting bored going round and round that little trail is solved and I might say solved with style. I ain't goin' to let the cat out of the bag just yet, but I can guarantee you that high society lady is gonna go home with somethin' to talk about."

"Mr. Mayor, wouldn't it be better just to keep things sort of simple for the first time around?"

"That's the trouble with you Two Bob, and that's one of the reasons I 'm mayor and you're not. You got to have vision and a spirit of adventure to run a town like this one." The mayor exhaled a particularly thick and rancid cloud of cigar smoke, "No sir, you got to have imagination and some-git-up-and-git type spirit, and don't ask me about the big surprise because I don't want it all over town before it happens."

It was a beautiful late fall morning, as only you get them in the north. Leaves drifted to the ground from the poplars and willows, and the air had that cranberry bush smell that made you think about building up the wood pile and putting the storm windows on. Shortly before noon Mrs. Wahtney stepped out of the company station wagon attired in proper English riding costume: a small, round black helmet, a short jacket with a white shirt under it, very tight, pale beige britches and tall, shiny leather boots. Those ladies who had ignored Pendlebury McNeish's pleas on the radio to give the lady a little breathing room could only peek through the willows at this marvel of sartorial splendor and sigh.

The introduction to Snowplow went very well, although Mrs. Wahtney did enquire about the name and seemed not much enlightened by the explanation. Without help from anyone she mounted up with a long practiced swing and sat firmly and unflustered while Snowplow made a few tentative jumps and twists to test out her new rider. The two of them seemed well satisfied and without any other formalities, set off to explore the sawdust path.

Up on the roof of the icehouse, Pendlebury McNeish was trying to make his report of her progress as interesting as he could, considering that he could only see horse and rider now and then. Beside him, Two Bob Bobdinsky peered through his bird watching glasses, but it wasn't the horse and rider he was looking for, it was the mayor's "surprise" that had him worried.

About three years before all this took place Regine Lapoint had been out doing a little timber cruising in the late spring when he had come across the body of a cow moose that had obviously been in a terrific battle with a bunch of wolves. She was dead, had been for a day or two. As Regine contemplated the fragility of life, he heard a soft almost mewing sound in the willow thicket behind him, and on investigating, found the tiniest little moose calf he had ever seen. It was so weak from hunger it made no attempt to struggle when he picked it up and heaved it over his shoulders. A few times on the way home he wished he had never come across the darn thing, even a tiny baby moose is still a pretty heavy load. But get home he did and when he called his wife, Jeannette, out of the little house he had built on the edge of town her motherly instincts took over at first sight of the poor, wobbly-legged little orphan.

In jig time she had an empty Catawba Port jug filled with powdered "Klim" milk and water, and the little moose did a very satisfying job of downing the whole gallon. They called him Melvin after Jeannette's sister's husband who did resemble him a little, in the face at least. For the first year and a half he was really cute, he followed Jeannette around like a huge puppy and at night would sleep leaning up against the side of the shack. Weaning him was a real problem. The jump from "Klim" milk to willow shoots was too much for him to grasp without any other moose around to set him an example. Regine offered to kill Jeannette dead in her own bed if she dared to tell anyone of the hours he spent with Melvin down by the creek, demonstrating how tasty willow shoots could be. How to teach him to grab cattail and water lily roots from the bottom of the bay was another matter, and in fact, something that still hadn't been worked out.

Melvin was thriving though and just kept on getting bigger and bigger. So big, in fact, that no one really liked to visit the Lapoints in their cabin anymore with Melvin stomping around and cracking his new horns against the side of the wood shed. Last fall Melvin had begun to feel the urge to find a lady moose, or at least had begun to feel pretty uneasy in his mind although, having never seen another moose, it is a question whether he had a very clear idea of what it was he actually wanted. He knew he wanted something though, and what with his stomping, bawling and whacking his horns on anything that looked solid, he had created quite a stir. Already this fall his huge rack gave him a very scary look, and he was making loud chuffing grunts, sounding much like the big steam engine at the sawmill, only louder. "Phooonka... Phoonka," a call he seemed to think would be appealing to a lady moose. A good many people thought Melvin would be better off made into sausages and moose steaks before he hurt someone, but to Regine and Jeannette this was a suggestion not far off boiling the baby down for soap.

When the mayor had appeared at the door with his plan Regine had been very reluctant to entertain any such suggestion. When the mayor mentioned though, sort of off hand, that the town just might see its way clear to gravelling the mud road that led down to their shack, all good sense went out the window.

According to the mayor's plan, Mrs. Wahtney and Snowplow would make one round of the path, then on the second, in the stand of jack pines, she would meet the mayor mounted on Big Daniel and be properly welcomed to our town. On the third round, as she passed alongside the railroad track, she would have the memorable experience of spotting a genuine Canadian wild moose standing in the willows near the section man's tool shed, an experience the mayor was certain would be the high point of her whole visit. On the morning of the ride, Regine was still a bit nervous about the whole idea and Melvin's amorous grunting and ground pawing weren't reassuring him any. Taking no chances, he looped a sturdy rope around the tool shed and tied the free end to Melvin's horns.

No one really knew what to expect of this Old Money English Lady on horseback. Would she stand up in the stirrups and hurtle around the track like a race horse rider? Would she have Snowplow jumping and turning like an English hunting horse? There were a lot of predictions made in the kitchens and beer parlors of the town, and more than a few wagers, but in the end both she and Snowplow seemed content to amble along the new sawdust path, breathing in the warm autumn air and admiring the strange scenery. On the second circuit, sure enough, there was Mayor McSheffielder, mounted on Big Daniel and stationed along side the path. Mrs. Wahtney, sensing something ceremonial, brought Snowplow to a stop along side Big Daniel, received the mayor's welcoming speech most graciously, and rode on.

Up on the roof of the icehouse, Pendlebury McNeish was keeping the townspeople informed of the royal progress, lapsing almost unconsciously into a "race track" style of delivery as Snowplow and her rider moved sedately along the path.

"It's Snowplow around the first turn by the icehouse, Snowplow and Mrs. Wahtney, and there, by the side of the track, it's, yes it is, it's our own Mayor aboard of Big Daniel, Big Daniel and Snowplow. They're stopping, the Mayor is speaking to Mrs. Wahtney, words of welcome to our fair city, and it's Snowplow moving off down the straightaway heading for the lake."

And at that moment, Two Bob, searching frantically with his bird watching glasses, let out an involuntary oath that Pendlebury's microphone dutifully carried all over town. He had spotted the mayor's surprise, and it was Melvin the moose, stepping sedately out from behind the section man's tool shed, his huge frame towering over the stunted willows. He swung his massive horns back and forth and grunted "Phoooaank Phoooank" and then raised his head high in the air, tongue hanging out as if to catch some wayward scent wafting along on the warm fall breeze.

The mayor had briefed Pendlebury well and he followed the script. "Its Mrs. Wahtney, up on Snowplow, past the Icehouse Turn and heading down the straightaway by the rail road, and there he is, it's MELVIN! Oh what a majestic sight he is folks, and what a thrill for our honored guest, all arranged for by His Honor the Mayor, Mayor Cuthbert Anardice McSheffielder himself. Yes sir, Mrs. Wahtney is seeing for the very first time in her life a genuine Canadian moose. What a thrill, what a wonderful memorable day this will be for... wait a minute, it's Melvin, Melvin and the section man's tool house, he's moving now, and the tool house is moving with him, he's heading for the riding path."

Now, you have to understand that Melvin had never actually seen another moose so he had no real idea what a lady moose should look like. But deep down in his primeval brain stem somewhere, there must have been a fallback pattern implanted for just such an eventuality, dim perhaps, and lacking detail, but good enough to ensure the survival of the species. To Melvin in his confused and tormented state that lovely black creature with the four long slender legs looked just the part.

"Phooounk Phoooounk" he called out to her and set out to proclaim his undying love, scarcely noticing the fast disintegrating section man's tool house that was still attached to his horns.

Both Snowplow and Mrs. Wahtney were of the unanimous opinion that this was no place for ladies of either species. Snowplow began to pick up a bit of speed. "Phooouuunk, Phoooounk." Melvin was on the track now, only the doorframe of the shack and a fast disintegrating bit of wall slowing him down and that soon broke off.

A moose is a pretty ungainly looking animal, looking a bit as though God had set off to design a fairly normal looking deer but having found himself with a bunch of nose and leg material left over, decided, "What the hell" and just threw them in. Not a pretty sight unless you are another moose, but those long legs were good for one thing besides standing around among the lily pads. Melvin could run, and he could run fast.

"Oh my God, folks, this is terrible, it's Melvin, Melvin and the section man's shack, moving up on the track. Snowplow is stepping right out now, but Melvin has reached the sawdust, and it's Melvin, Melvin and, wait a minute, the shack is gone, busted to pieces folks, what a sight, and it's Melvin, he's on the track now, and picking up speed fast."

Mrs. Wahtney looked back over her shoulder but she really didn't need to. "Phoooounk... Phooounka." How Melvin found the breath to whisper sweet nothings to the object of his desire was a mystery and an admirable thing considering that he had now developed what the navy would have called "flank speed." Snowplow didn't need to look back either... whatever that creature behind her was, there wasn't too much doubt about his intentions. Mrs. Wahtney was standing up in the stirrups now, somewhere her little black helmet had fallen off and her hair was streaming behind her as they skidded around the sharp turn by the lake and started up toward the icehouse. She still had her riding crop in her hand but there was no need for it, Snowplow was about as motivated as she could get.

"It's Snowplow by about twenty lengths, but Melvin is closing fast. They're around the Icehouse Turn through the pines and heading for the lake again. It's a fantastic sight folks, all brought to you by your own local radio station, Pendlebury McNeish announcing. And there they go, down the straight away for the lake, and now into the Lake Turn, its a sharp one folks, but she's around, Mrs. Wahtney and Snowplow are around the Lake Turn and headed for the ice house, and Oh! Oh! There's Melvin, a bit of trouble for a moment there, went off the track and knocked over a few small trees and got most of Mrs. Fossick's washing tangled in his horns but he didn't lose much, he's back on the track making up those losses fast!"

Pendlebury dragged his microphone to the other side of the icehouse roof. "And there they go, Mrs. Wahtney is yelling something but it's hard to make out what, and it's Melvin closing fast, not a bit slowed up by the unmentionables tangled in his horns. Mrs. Fossick is not going to be pleased about that laundry. Twenty lengths, fifteen lengths, ten lengths, it's an exciting race folks, but it ain't over yet, little Snowplow seems to have put on an extra burst of speed heading down the straightaway by the rail road toward the jack pine stand."

It was under one of those very pines that Pinkus MacDavey had stationed himself, hidden by the long heavy branches. He planned to wait until Mrs. Wahtney was on the open stretch by the railroad, and then step out onto the sawdust trail and play a spirited reel as she rode by. Pinkus puffed up the bag on his pipes to its fullest and as the sound of hooves grew nearer he stepped out onto the track and gave the bag a mighty squeeze to start the drones and launched into the sprightly strains of " Maggie in the Morning."

It was turning out to be a bad day for Snowplow. She could hear the indecent proposals Melvin was making behind her "Phoooonk Phoooannnka" and he was gaining, no doubt about it. And now, a monster emitting the most obscene sounds she'd ever heard had appeared right in the middle of the path. Snowplow did the only thing a maiden in such distressful circumstances could do. She leaped high into the air, sailing over the dragon that was screeching in front of her, sending the Old Money English Lady into an even higher orbit in the process. Landing gracefully without the burden of a rider, Snowplow made one long leap across the ditch to the railroad embankment and took off down the tracks.

Melvin, taken by surprise, was slower to make the turn. Not being much of a jumper he had to wade through the ditch to gain the track but he was soon flying down the right of way right after her.

Two Bob, watching the frantic flight of Snowplow and her rider and the determined, nay frenzied, pursuit of the love-stricken Melvin, could only pray. Then, at the very moment that it appeared that all was lost, Pinkus MacDavey had stepped into the path of the flying racers with his pipes and it seemed as though the gods might have answered his prayers, although in the strange unpredictable way that the gods usually have of doing such things.

Through his bird watching glasses Two Bob could see that Mrs. Wahtney had landed high in the branches of a jack pine. Not a very noble tree, and one given to growing crooked and inhospitable branches. Looking closer, he could also see that the rear seam of her natty riding britches had failed utterly. He grabbed the microphone from Pendlebury, praying that the Chief of the Volunteer Fire Brigade was amongst the listeners following the ride. "Hello Chief Redmond, if you can hear me, send two long ladders and at least four of your best men down to the new ridin' path by the icehouse." Two Bob took another look at the failed britches and added, "married ones if you got 'em." Under his breath he muttered with astonishment, "Them Old Money Ladies can get their legs a lot further apart than we was givin' em credit for."

Two Bob worried for a moment about taking the initiative from the mayor, but that worthy had his own problems. As I said, this whole thing started out in the late morning and now it was noon and in our town the big whistle on the mine power house always blew at noon and it did this day too. No one really noticed it, but Big Daniel did. Big Daniel was not just any horse, he was a municipal horse and as such very sensitive to teatime, lunchtime, and quitting time. He knew the big whistle blew for lunchtime and, without consulting the mayor or anyone else, Big Daniel set off sedately down the path, heading for the barn and his big bucket of oats. He took no notice of the mayor still up on his back, yelling and pounding on his thick hide, and no notice either of the stable hand running along behind with the mayor's step ladder. The loose pine needles from the tree Mrs. Wahtney had landed in had barely stopped falling when Big Daniel made his measured way along the path and under the tree. The Mayor, helplessly born along, looked up at Mrs. Wahtney who was glaring down at him in what seemed a most unfriendly way. There was no stopping Big Daniel, and no way of getting down off his back. Cuthbert Anardice McSheffielder knew in his bones that his political career was in ruins. Even so, the will to survive runs deep, and he tried his best to remember what the English Royalty did in "drive by" situations like this. Looking up at Mrs. Wahtney spraddled helplessly in the upper branches of the jack pine, he waved his hand gaily to her using limp little waggles of the wrist as he had seen the Queen do on the Movietone News. Big Daniel made his single-minded way toward his lunch. Dazed, the mayor continued to waggle his hand bravely to all he passed until Big Daniel scraped him off his back as he went under the low door into the barn.

At the moment that Snowplow had made her desperate leap for the railroad right-of-way, Phil McCartney was standing just below Two Bob's position on the ice house roof. Two Bob leaned over and yelled "Phil, for God's sake, get your ass over to the telegraph office and have them tell Cranberry Portage to flag down the 3:15 from Hudson Bay Junction and warn them there is a horse and a moose comin' down the main line."

Later, after Mrs. Wahtney was rescued from the tree, Two Bob called the section foreman to see if he knew what had become of Snowplow and Melvin.

"Well, Two Bob, I don't know as I can say. If she lost the race she's likely sittin under a tree by the side of the right-of-way about now, kind of smilin' to herself and contemplatin' givin' birth to the first horned race horse to start at the Assiniboine Downs. If she won, I would imagine she's down around Cranberry Portage somewhere by now."

For two days the whole town waited for the wrath of the Old Money English Lady to descend upon them, not to mention the outrage of Cornelius Swinton Wahtney himself.

It was Pinkus MacDavey who got the first call. He was in the change house just getting out of his work clothes after finishing graveyard shift in the mill, when the foreman came looking for him.

"MacDavey."

"There's no a need to shout mon, I 'm not deef."

"You are wanted in the main office, in the personnel department to be exact. You are to go there at once."

There was no love lost between the mill foreman and Pinkus; Pinkus with his unerring eye for the ice had somehow seemed to snatch the bonspiel from the foreman's rink more times than seemed just to that vindictive man.

"If it ain't a pink slip MacDavey, you're a lucky man."

Pinkus hadn't been inside the mine's office building since he was hired, but he knew how to find his way to the personnel department on the second floor.

"Mr. MacDavey." The young woman at the reception desk seemed uncommonly glad to see him and Pinkus could only suppose that the whole community could hardly wait for him to suffer for his causing Mrs. Wahtney's sudden elevation into the Jack Pine tree.

"Mr. O'Groach is waiting in his office for you."

This really looked bad. Usually, if someone got fired they just handed you your pay and asked for your little brass time badge and that was that. Grimly, Pinkus walked into O'Groach's office and took the proffered chair. Over O'Groach's shoulder he could see the mill building through the grimy window and thought to himself that, as bad as it was, he was going to miss working there, and miss his buddies as well.

"I have asked you to come here at the express wishes of Mr. Wahtney himself."

"There was no any intent to cause the lady harm..."

"No, I think you misunderstand, Pinkus. I was asked to convey to you the thanks of both Mr. and Mrs. Wahtney for bravely intervening in what could have been a terrible situation, at some cost to yourself I understand as well."

"Not to me, but Melvin did step on me pipes in passing... the drones..."

"Yes, well that may not be a worry..."

"She's not angry then?"

"Well, when they first got her down out of the tree she was calling for heads to roll in real English nobility style I can tell you, but then she got a phone call."

"From who?"

"We don't know, some woman Mrs. Wahtney thought had a Welsh accent. Seems whoever it was explained about how you risked your life to divert that moose, and why you were there at all and so on..."

"A Welsh accent you say?"

"So Mrs. Wahtney thought, but in any case she wanted me to express her gratitude to you."

Pinkus could hardly believe his ears. "So I'm not here to be fired then?"

"Well, you might have to give up your job at the mill yet." O'Groach's smile was as broad as he could make it, but still Pinkus' face fell so pitifully at his attempt at humor that he at once set out to explain himself.

"Mrs. Wahtney now understands the importance of a community hall, and has persuaded Mr. Wahtney to direct the mine to build one for the community before the coming of winter. No small task, but we will do it of course. She did, ahem, she did specify for some strange reason that it was not be located near any bunkhouse or occupied dwelling."

"Did she now," said Pinkus thinking of the unfathomable mysteries of Welsh women in general "Did she say that?"

"She did, and there is more. She wants you to leave your job in the mill and become the manager of the new community hall."

Pinkus's head snapped up. "Did she now, did she say that as well?'

"She did, and there's more yet Pinkus. It seems that Mr. Wahtney also got a call from some mysterious woman with an odd accent, and he now thinks that the Company should have its own pipe band to represent it when the occasion arises. Bonspiels, hockey games, First of July and the like. He would like you to organize it, lead it if you feel you wish to, and see to the purchase of suitable uniforms and a good class of instruments."

"And would the uniforms include a real tiger pelt for the bass drummer?"

"'Spare no expense' were the words I believe he used."

As it turned out, neither of the section man's predictions about the fate of the horse and the moose turned out to be true. Snowplow had done very well on the gravel and ties between the tracks but a moose's feet are designed for shlupping around in swamps and reed beds. Melvin had limped to a stop after only a quarter mile or so, thought the whole thing over and decided to go off deep into the bush, rethink his whole life, maybe find a nice willow swamp somewhere and go into the moose business full time.

Snowplow was found munching weeds and oat sprouts along the right of way and returned to the municipal barn. At Mrs. Wahtney's express request, she was purchased from her former owner and shipped off to upper New York State to spend the rest of her days romping around on real grass. Mrs. Wahtney knew what it was like for a high bred female to be subject to the gross attentions of a bellowing, foot stomping North American male.

In those days the mining company made a point of never interfering in municipal affairs, and yet it should be understood that the smooth running of the town was very important to them. For this reason, it was the unofficial job of one of the management staff to act as a conduit between the mine and the town's various organizations, including the town council.So unofficial was this job that it didn't even have a name and that good person was simply referred to as "the man from the mine."

A couple of weeks after the Wahtney's private train had left for New York, Two Bob was sitting on the front porch of his cabin when "the man from the mine" came by. Over a couple of jam jars of Five Star and ginger ale, the talk turned to politics and "the man from the mine" gave it to Two Bob pretty straight. If he were to put his name up for mayor in the upcoming elections, he would receive a lot of support.

And so it was that we came to have a new mayor in our town, Two Bob Bobdinsky.

Belinda's Blossoms

WE HAD A FLOWER SHOP IN OUR TOWN, WHICH YOU MIGHT THINK UNLIKELY FOR A MINING CAMP, WHERE ABSOLUTELY NOTHING GREW, BUT THERE IT WAS, AND IT WAS ODD HOW IT GOT THERE.

It was Simple Smith who was primarily responsible, although responsible might not be the right word as he was dead at the time, but if he hadn't of been we wouldn't likely have had the flower shop, so I guess...

Well, to get started at the right place, you would have to go back to Miss Arethema Dalgleish, who was also dead; a bit ahead of Simple Smith, but when you are dead such niceties of timing don't usually matter all that much. In this case though, timing did matter because Simple Smith was the town's undertaker. Undertaking in a mining camp, where dead bodies tend to be somewhat fragmented, was not a calling that appealed to everyone, but as long as he was sufficiently fortified, Simple Smith was willing to do the job and nobody expected too much of him.

To get this story started at the right place, you would have to back to Monday, the day Miss Arethema Dalgleish died of something feminine. The talk over coffee down at Wong's cafe was that it was the pleurisy. It was summer and pretty hot so she was whisked off to Simple Smith's undertaking parlor to be preserved a bit in order that she could be put on the Tuesday train and sent back to her folks in Yorkton.

On Wednesday, her folks phoned the town hall, that being the only place they knew the name of in our town, to ask where she was, since she wasn't on the train when they went to get her. They had checked the baggage car, and the express car, and even made enquiries at the mail car, but there was no sign of her at all. The town clerk couldn't offer any help and since Simple Smith had no phone he couldn't refer them to him either, but he did promise to look into the matter.

George Burton had been a town clerk, it seemed, ever since he was born, and he understood the job perfectly. He buttoned every button of his grey vest, wore black sleeves over his shirt and was obsequious to all the right people, rude to all the rest, and was flawless in his ability to pass on every problem that came over his desk to someone else to handle. The case of a missing lady, even though dead, it seemed to him, was definitely a job for the Mayor if not the Constable of the local RCMP detachment. Remembering what had happened the last time that he had involved the RCMP without first discussing the problem with the mayor, his decision was made for him.

Two Bob Bobdinsky, despite his easygoing manner, was a mayor who got things done. Problems for Two Bob were of two kinds: the ones you solved yourself and took the credit for and the ones where little credit seemed forthcoming and so you delegated. He listened to George Burton's recounting of the strange long distance phone call from Yorkton, thought about it a bit, and much to George Burton's disgust, told him to go around himself to Simple Smith's undertaking establishment and see what the story was. It was near time to close the town office by the time all this got sorted out. George Burton might have occasionally opened the town office a bit late, but he prided himself on never having closed it late. He decided that since it was such a nice hot July day he would put off visiting Simple Smith till morning, drop in on him on his way to the office and then report to the mayor.

It was at a special meeting of the town council called the day after George Burton's morning report, that Two Bob banged his gavel to get a little order. Laura Langmuir, the town secretary, had been called in to take notes and every single councillor had answered Two Bob's call for an emergency meeting. George Burton was sitting where he usually sat, ready to refer to the bylaws or any records required, but it didn't take but one good look to see that he was distinctly not himself. He had gone beyond pale to a sort of delicate green shade and seemed to be trembling just a bit. No one had ever seen George so unstrung before and it was not a pretty sight. Collar awry and generally looking sorely tried, he sat slumped in his chair. The few thin hairs that he always combed carefully across his head were hanging over one ear, and even his gold rimmed glasses were sitting a bit askew.

"Boys, we got a problem here. Now, as your mayor, I've used my powers to take some steps toward solvin' it, but I think we should all be in on this one." Two Bob took a deep breath. He inhaled slowly, as though savouring the sweet air, and took his time about letting it out again. "Early Monday mornin', as most of you know, Miss Arethema Dalgleish died of the pleurisy. Her mortal remains was entrusted to Simple Smith, his job being the usual one of boxin' her up properly, seein' to the shipping arrangements, and, it bein' pretty hot, to takin' the necessary steps to make sure she would keep for the trip down to her folks in Yorkton."

Around the table seven heads nodded in unison. It seemed to Two Bob that Gunther Volkstien was paying more attention to Laura Langmuir's knees than to his statements thus far, but he plowed on...

"Wednesday afternoon, about three, Arethema Dalgleish's folks phoned by long distance from Yorkton. It seems that she never made it onto the train, or at least she wasn't on it when it got to Yorkton. I sent George, here, over to see what the trouble was, but for his own reasons," Two Bob glared at George, but not too hard because it was obvious he was already in about as much misery as a man should have to bear. "For his own reasons, George decided not to go around to the undertakin' parlor till yesterday mornin'. What he found was that Simple Smith was dead on the floor of his own establishment, likely since sometime on Monday. Doc Williston opines that it was the apoplexy that got him, but anyway, once George got aholt of himself, he came here to me, to see what should be done." Two Bob did one of his famous pauses here, the kind he used when he was about to spring something. Everyone sort of straightened up a little and tried hard to look like they could handle whatever it was that was coming. "Now you boys know how hot it was on Monday, (long pause) and on Tuesday,(long pause) and on Wednesday it was even hotter, and by yes-terday mornin'," another glance at George Burton who didn't seem to be listening, "by yesterday mornin' it was still hot when George finally got there and, well, not to put too fine a point on it, old Simple wasn't in the best of shape."

"Good lord, don't tell me he is still there on the floor of the...."

"Nope, he ain't, but I had to get Ole Barstead to go over and roll him into a tarp."

"You got the town honeyman to pick up a..."

"You boys know that Ole's nose quit working years ago. Anyway, you know the usual thing when we got to hold a body over till the next train. The Lucky Leaf Meat Market has been real good about discreetly keeping them cool in the walk-in cooler, but not this time. It was way too much for the cooler to handle, so I phoned Polker's Ice and Coal and got Polker to bring a dray load of chopped ice over. Ole slipped Old Simple onto the back of the dray and they covered him up with it."

"It seems well in hand." This last was Gunther Volkstien who always liked to give the impression that he, as deputy mayor, somehow had the job of passing judgement on the actions of the mayor. It was no secret that he had the may-or's chair firmly in his sights for the next election.

"It was, Gunther, it was, but Ole had had to fortify himself a little to get the job done. Polker was in a big hurry to get that load back to the ice house, so nobody noticed Simple's big old feet hanging out the back of the dray until they turned the corner by the Co-op Store." Two Bob did another pause, not so long this time but long enough to let everyone have a chance to picture the scene. "There was a bunch of lady shoppers waiting for the Co-op to open. (long pause), We're gonna be gettin' a big bill from Polker for repainting his dray so he can pretend it's a new one since nobody will take any ice from him off of that dray since."

"I don't think anyone will object to that if he turns in the bills to support whatever he claims," Gunther was really flying.

"Well, I hope so, but that ain't all. I could see a whole heap of trouble comin' out of all this with us now havin' no undertaker and Miss Arethema Dalgleish with one more day to wait for the train and all. So I took it on myself to phone an old acquaintance in Winnipeg who is familiar with the funeral business. He put me onto a young fellow, young, but experienced mind, who was looking for a town to set up shop in. I invited him up here, and wired him the fare..."

"Was there any stipulation that he pay it back once he gets established?"

"No Gunther, there wasn't, and, on top of that, I'm goin' to ask the council here assembled to waive the usual waitin' period for a business licence and occupancy permit and business tax assessment and let this young man get right to work."

Before any one could get a grip on all this, there was a knock at the door of the council chamber. Laura Langmuir unwound her legs from her stenographer's chair and walked over to open the door. She didn't actually walk. How Laura Langmuir managed to move so many parts of her at once just answering a knock on the door was beyond anyone's understanding except to say that it was pretty obvious that it was intended for Two Bob's benefit. Moments later she returned, leading one of the strangest looking men anyone at the council table had ever seen, and in a mining town like ours the competition for that honour would be acknowledged to be pretty stiff by any fair minded person.

Phineas Makepiece McQuorquedale was dressed in a grey suit, with a high white collar to his shirt, and a grey silk tie tucked into a matching grey vest. He was a tall man, very tall, but no one seeing him ever thought tall, he was so slender that "long" was the only way to get at describing him. His face was long, his chin was long, his, long thin nose seemed to reach past his mouth as if it was trying to join up with his chin. His eyes were a strange, unsettling greeny-grey colour and that little bit of colour was the only part of his face that didn't look like it had been squeezed out of old wax. He wore his thin colourless hair long for those times and kept his pearl grey bowler hat firmly on his head as he approached the council table.

"Gentlemen, since I am unknown to any of you I must introduce myself. I am, sirs, your humble servant Phineas Makepiece McQuorquedale. Most recently in the employ of the prestigious firm of Lount, Blackhurst and Maypenny of Chicago, Bereavement Advisors and Funeral Home to the best families. I have with me, if you care to see them, letters from Mr. Lount, Mr. Blackhurst and Mr. Maypenny attesting to my good reputation with that firm and offering to recommend me in whatever location I settled, as I was forced to seek a drier climate for my health."

Somewhat taken aback by this rush of information, the councillors took a moment or two to get a grip on things, but northern hospitality didn't require documents. If you were willing, you had a place. To a man they welcomed McQuorquedale and assured him that he and his wife, who was waiting in the outer hall, would be welcome in our town and looked upon as valued citizens.

"As you may know, at the mayor's kind invitation I hurried to catch the early train out of Winnipeg. I will, of course, be presenting you with a detailed accounting of our expenses, including meals and seats in the parlor car. We have taken rooms, temporarily, at the Corona Hotel and, I am happy to say, have made some progress in dealing with the unhappy situation that this wonderful community has been burdened with."

"Ah, there are some formalities, of course. We are prepared to expedite the business licence and...."

"Leave it for now, Gunther, let the man say his piece. Seems to me he is getting' right down to it and, as far as I am concerned, and I think I speak for the rest of the council, all the details can wait till later."

"Yes, thank you, I should report to you that the remains of the dear departed Miss Arethema Dalgleish were taken to the railway station late this afternoon just in time for the evening train. I took the liberty of removing the necessary papers from the desk of the late Mr. Smith and I am satisfied that there will be no problems in returning her to the arms of her grieving family. Naturally, as I have had no arrangements with the family, I have made out the bill for my services, including the preparation of the body, a suitable casket and shipping box, to the town. I trust that will be satisfactory...." McQuorquedale stared over the point of his long nose at each councillor in turn. Restoring their nerves with a "rye and ginger" at Spookie Kittering's house later that evening, they agreed to a man that not one of them had ever felt such a chill in their lives.

"Ah, I am sure we can discuss all this later, but there is still the matter of... ah... the... ah... the late Mr. Smith." Gunther wasn't about to let the stranger get right out of control.

"Mr. Smith, yes, well, the little bit of ice that had been rolled up in the tarpaulin with him had melted by the time I was taken to view the remains." McQuorquedale swept the table with his long nose, as though to share with the councillors what that implied. "It seemed to me that the situation could not remain as it was for much longer, in particular as a Mr. Polker was threatening to bring in his bulldozer from the ice house. Knowing that the town fathers, you gentlemen," McQuorquedale inclined himself forward from the waist just a bit, did the thing with his nose again, and went on "would not wish to haggle over minor expenses given the urgency of the situation, I enlisted, on the town's behalf, the services of the Copper Town Plumbing and Heating Company. Once they understood my plan, they produced a fine sheet metal horse watering trough, and delivered it to the ice house yard. I placed Mr. Smith in the trough with all the reverence and respect due to the dead and a workman from the sheet metal shop soldered a sheet of galvanised tin over the top of it. An airtight container gentlemen, rough but serviceable. You will find an item on your account from the Bell Hardware for a pint of black stove pipe enamel which I used to give the trough a suitably funereal appearance."

"Good God, you soldered old Simple into a horse trough?"

"A container that I think would be better referred to as a coffin for the future, but, yes, he is now ready for burial. I would recommend, however, that the service be prompt and not too lengthy, as we have no way of knowing how much pressure might be building up... it is, as you know, quite warm out..."

"A funeral," Two Bob knew when it was time for a mayor to step right into a situation, "a funeral, of course, old Simple Smith was a respected member of the business community even if he was a..." It was hard to keep your train of thought when Phineas Makepiece McQuorquedale was staring at you with those bad ice eyes.

"Yes, good sirs, a funeral, with a church service and flowers, of course"

"Well, now, there's a problem 'cause we got no flower shop here."

"So we understand but by a wonderful coincidence, my good wife Belinda is planning to open just such an establishment in your wonderful and welcoming community, and, anticipating an urgent need, she has brought with her several fine floral arrangements suitable for the occasion."

"It will be necessary, of course, before she opens up her business to...."

"Oh leave it, Gunther, I am sure that will all be done in good time. Now then Mr. McQuokle, I suppose some sort of a wreath..."

"A fine wreath, laurel leaves to show sadness intertwined with white lily of the valley to speak of the City's loss and the hope for resurrection."

"Don't seem like a problem," Two Bob looked up and down the table...

"And, of course, as mayor, you will be wanting to make a personal statement, something in the nature of a trailing spray of lilies that can be placed directly on the coffin..." Two Bob looked up sharply at this, but it didn't seem like the time to quibble. Gunther had only a moment to enjoy Two Bob's getting finessed like that before Phineas went on, "only slightly more elaborate than that of the deputy mayor, of course. This is not a contest, but a solemn occasion. And for each of you," Phineas pointed his nose and his whole chin at each councillor in turn, "I am sure that my good wife Belinda can create very acceptable bouquets of white miniature carnations, arranged to droop just a bit in mourning and garnished with green fern to speak of the everlasting nature of our faith and belief in the eternal spring of life."

With that little windfall, *Belinda's Blossoms* was off to a running start and never looked back. Weddings, birthdays, graduation days, and funerals kept the little store humming. And that was how we come to have a genuine flower shop in a town where nothing grew. As far as I know it is still there, just a hop from the corner of Copper Lode Street and Pyrite Road.

The Uplifting of Paidrech Oin Sheehan

OUR TOWN WAS ABOUT AS FAR FROM ANYWHERE AS YOU COULD GET AND, FOR SOME OF THE PEOPLE THAT ENDED UP THERE, THAT LOCATION SUITED THEM RIGHT DOWN TO THE GROUND. One of those people was Paidrech Oin Sheehan. Paidrech, or 'Irish Paddy' as he was generally known, had arrived in our town in the midst of a very nasty winter. A very small man, he arrived dressed in clothes that once would likely have been judged as fashionable, but now looked much the worse for hard travel. He stumbled through the cloud of steam from the passenger locomotive and tripped over the station steps. He was dead drunk and no one saw him in any different condition during the rest of his short life.

The mine took one look at his delicate hands and diminutive frame and, even if the smell of whiskey on him hadn't been strong enough to knock a fly off a gut wagon, wouldn't have had any use for him. He found odd jobs here and there and when old Findley went through the ice with his team that winter, he took over Findley's old shack and announced he was opening up a coffeehouse. The new constable was pretty certain that there wasn't a whole lot of coffee getting drunk in Paddy's place, but no one ever invited him in to find out for sure, and without an invitation you couldn't get in. You knocked, a little flap in the door opened and someone looked out at you, and, if no one inside knew you and was prepared to invite you in, you could stand outside in the cold until spring.

There was no bar in Paddy's place, just a plank table with some grubby old jam jars on it and a coffee can. If you felt you needed a drink bad enough to drink what Paddy had available, you picked the cleanest jam jar, stepped into a little larder built into the corner of the room and poured yourself whatever you thought you needed. By way of payment, when you had drunk your fill and were ready to leave, you were expected to drop something into the coffee can. Now in terms of modern notions of stock control and accountability this doesn't, on the face of it, look like a grand way to run a business, but in truth, it worked out very well. No one wanted to seem like a piker in front of his buddies. Paddy, who was usually snoring dead drunk in his chair by the airtight heater, had been known to open one or even both eyes for a moment or two, so customers would put in a good sized bill and make a big deal out of not fishing around in the can for change. By the same token if a man came in half blind with the DT's and dying of the shakes, no one worried if his wallet was empty. It was assumed he would make it up when the mine pay-day finally rolled around.

Paddy's place only lasted one winter. That spring a forest fire pretty much wiped out the little town the mine had established by the lake, about two miles from the works. Every one moved up onto the barren rock hills closer to the mine, safer and a lot closer to work. Paddy's cabin and part of the old hotel were pretty much all that was left of the old town when the fire was over.

As much as the guys had come to love the wild little Irishman, who sometimes sang so beautifully and some-times even made long drunken speeches that most agreed would stand up to the best sermons anyone had heard, no one would walk that far to get a drink, especially when con-templating the problem of walking back. Paddy was singing to an empty house.

Most folks in our community had a boat of some kind, some better than others, but all good enough to fish from. Almost all of those boats were tied up to the old government dock near Paddy's cabin or floated in crude boat houses along the shore on the south side of the dock. In those days, all boats were made of wood, none of your fancy aluminium or fibreglass. They were all wood, and as such, they required a good deal of looking after. Most of them leaked like sieves until the wood had soaked up enough water to swell up and tighten the seams. The most notorious of these were the Peterboroughs, "Lakesides" and "Fishermen," whose thin cedar planks could dry out in a few days if left pulled up on the shore. To keep them "tightened up" they had to be left in the water. This wasn't a problem if you were around to look after them, but after the fire everyone now lived a couple of miles from the lake. Running down to bail boats out every time it rained, or to throw on an extra rope when the wind got up became a big problem, or would have become a big problem if it had not been for Paidrech Oin Sheehan.

In another life he must have lived by the sea because the one thing that would bring him out from behind the safety of the wall of whiskey he surrounded himself with was the notion that some boat needed tending too.

It wasn't very long before more or less formal arrangements started to develop between Paddy and the boat owners and, by the end of the summer, Paddy had become an important cog in the wheel of the community. He still could be found snoring or singing drunk most of the time, but the slightest patter of rain drops would bring him charging out of the shack with his bailing can in hand. Some were a little nervous of him because on particularly stormy days he would stand teetering at the end of dock, waving his fists at the lightning and the wind and bellowing long melodic curses in what some who knew about such things swore was Latin.

Things went on this way through the summer and, when Paddy offered to store the boats beside his cabin until spring, pretty much everyone took him up on it. This provided him with a little money for the winter, but not a whole lot. He wouldn't even think of accepting handouts from anyone, although if someone wore an old coat they didn't want any more down to his place and happened to forget it there, he never offered to give it back. With the failure of the bootlegging business he didn't get many visitors any more. In fact he wouldn't have gotten any if it hadn't been for Shamus Hoolihan and old Father O'Brian. It was thought that Shamus might have known Paddy from before, well, maybe not known him, but at least known of him. Strangely drawn to the snarly little potato eater, he was the only one who visited Paddy regularly and seemed ready to put up with his drunken tirades. Father O'Brian was another matter. He knew Paddy was a Catholic, well, what else could he be, being Irish and all. He would gently and patiently tug away at him, trying to get him back into the church, never seeming to give up on the idea no matter how surly and wretched he found Paddy curled up on the stinking mattress in his old shack.

We had two barbers in our town. One of them was a little short Frenchman who talked constantly and waved his scissors around in the air like an artist's paintbrush. He was too short to lean over the barber chair when he was shaving you, so he had a little box that he would jump up on. He would take a few strokes with his razor, jump down, give the box a kick, then jump up and take a couple more swipes from his new angle. He did in the end give a pretty decent shave, but it was an altogether nerve-racking experience. Getting a shave with a straight razor was a test of courage in itself and having the wielder of that lethal instrument constantly leaping up and down behind you was a trial not many could handle.

Big Barney, our other barber was just the opposite. He was a huge man whose idea of fun was to start fights in the beer parlor of an evening. He could barely get his big fingers through the handles of the scissors, but his artistry with the razor was legendary. He somehow seemed to know everything that went on in the town, and besides keeping everyone up on the best of the news and gossip, he could shave you in two minutes flat if there were other customers waiting. He could also draw a shave out for ten minutes or more if there weren't customers waiting, keeping you in the chair so that the shop would look busy. Fast shave or slow, haircut or singe he always seemed to manage to extract whatever information his current customer might have. It was noticed that anyone with political ambitions in our town, who had the politician's usual goals of looking smart and being well informed, had a delicate choice to make. A person could either look shabby most of the morning and get a shave later on when Barney had most of the news gathered, or look slick and get a shave too early to be up on what was going on around town.

The other centre for keeping up to date was Wong's Golden Gate Cafe. Most of the merchants and professional men in town used to gather at Wong's for coffee in the morning. Politics got talked there, news got exchanged, as well as information on the latest action on the penny mining stock market.

One morning late in the winter, a cold morning of the kind that makes the snow squeak, the usual gang was gathering in Wong's back room. Some had not even hung up their coats yet when, to everyone's astonishment, Barney the Barber came lumbering in. Now to say this was unusual would not really give you the flavour of it properly. It had just never happened and no one had ever expected it to happen. Mornings were just not a time Barney would ever leave his shop. No one said a word, though, when Barney came in, blowing on his fingers and brushing snow out of his hair. (*Barney rarely bothered with a coat unless it was really cold, and for Barney, this was sissy weather.*) He plopped himself down on the chair at the end of the table, in fact he plopped himself into the chair that was always left for Frank Schindlemacher. No one said anything to him about that, and neither did Frank Schindlemacher when he came in.

Barney had been barbering so long he even talked barber style when he wasn't in the shop: little bursts of words, followed by a pause where he would do a bit of clipping, then another burst of words while he checked the results in the big mirror behind the chair, another pause for more clipping and so on.

"You guys all know Paddy Sheehan I guess"...clip... clip... "Had Shamus Hoolihan in my chair this morning"...clip...clip... "Always takes Bay Rum"...clip...clip... "Took a telegram out to Paddy's place yesterday."..clip...clip... "Black one."...clip...clip...

Most outside news in those days came in the form of a telegram. Men with green eye shades and black sleeve covers on their arms sat at telegraph machines in a room off the main lobby of the railroad station translating a bewildering stream of clicks and clacks into deaths and births and weddings and rush orders. A small troop of boys hung around in the station and made a decent amount of small cash delivering the messages once the telegraph operator had typed them out on the standard yellow forms and sealed them in a little envelope with a window that let you see who the addressee was. Telegrams that announced someone's passing were put in an envelope with a black border around it. It was thought this was meant to help people get a grip on themselves before they opened it.

Slowly, with many a pause for clipping, the story unfolded, some of it direct quotes from Shamus, some of it embellishments and embroidery of Barney's own. A few verbal flourishes were seen as quite acceptable if it helped to get the meaning clear. It seems that Paddy had come from a pretty high up family back on the East Coast. There was no explanation of his sudden leaving or why he had ended up as he was. Shamus had shared with Barney however, that for the last year, he had been taking letters to the post office for Paddy, letters that told his family of how well he was doing in the west and what a great success he was making of life. And Shamus had also carried the letters that Paddy's proud mother had written him in return back to the squalid little shack on the lakeshore. Then came the black bordered telegram with the news that Paddy's father had died, and that his mother was expecting him at the funeral.

Everyone looked at everyone else. Paddy had never said a kind word to any of them, but he was so consistently rude and surly that even to have him give you the barest of greetings sort of made your day. Even if they didn't each have a soft spot in their hearts for the little man, there weren't many around that table who hadn't known what it felt like to be down on your luck.

It was Mayor Two Bob who broke the silence following Barney's revelations. "Well, I don't think the little bugger will make much of an impression if he goes to some big funeral down east dressed like he was the last time I saw him."

"We oughta do a little somethin', I guess." Mel Storokin owned the pool hall and never put his foot in a boat, but he had as good a sense of community as anyone.

It was Frank Schindlemacher from his unaccustomed place half way down the table who started things rolling. "I got a last year's suit that got scorched a little at the tailor's; customer refused it, but it would come pretty close to fitting Paddy there with a bit of tucking and snipping."

"He's gonna need some decent shoes, people judge a man by his shoes as much as any other blame thing. I might be able to find something. I expect he takes a pretty small size though." Norman Bracenose owned Norman's Shoe

Emporium and had always been a bit upset that Frank Schindlemacher had carried a line of shoes in his men's haberdashery, and wasn't about to let him one-up him now.

It took more than a bit of pushing and pulling to get Paddy into the public bath. Mavis Armberry who owned the Swirl and Curl where the public bath was located, said she was going to have her the bathtub washed out with kerosene before she let any of her regular customers use it again. A good chunk of the mainstreeters were at the station the next morning to wave good by to a partially sober, reasonably well dressed and washed and manifestly ungrateful Paidrech Oin Sheehan.

When he came back from the funeral, he went straight out to the lake and nobody saw him again till spring. Shamus reported that Paddy hadn't spoken to him for a month after his return for shooting his mouth off to Barney the Barber, but after a bit everything settled down and the letters from his mother kept coming so everyone figured it must have all worked out all right. Spring came and the boats were in the water and Paddy was out with his bailing can when needed and all seemed well with the world.

The Catholic Church in our town had started out as a pretty casual affair. There weren't churches for all the different brands of Christians who were trying to make a life for themselves in our isolated little community, and for the first while old Father O'Brian often found himself ministering to a collection of High Anglicans, Polish Catholics and Greek Orthodox Ukrainians. In time, each group managed to get some sort of church for themselves and moved into it. This never bothered the good Father O'Brian, nor did it bother him that the temporary cookhouse the mine had given him for a church was in great need of repairs or that the general finances of the ministry were in even worse repair. His motley flock loved him and were quite content with things as they were. Everyone had been quite taken aback when, with only a couple of days notice, Father O'Brian was recalled and in his place arrived a very different kind of priest.

Father Dollardeaux was from Quebec where a village priest played a very different role from that expected in the west. His first run in was with Mayor Two Bob Bobdinsky when he demanded a seat on the town council, a position apparently that was customary in the villages he knew. It took all Two

Bob's considerable political skills to convince him that this was not customary in our community.

Not long after Father Dollardeaux's arrival, grumblings began to be heard, even among the staunchest supporters of the church. The skim on the bingo had been increased, fees for everything were more than before, the expected donations for candles and medals and prayers rose and rose again. Those casual about attendance at services found themselves being visited by Father Dollardeaux who would remind them in no uncertain terms of their obligations to the church. Tithes were discussed and an ambitious building fund was making serious demands on the incomes of church members. Father Dollardeaux soon earned the sobriquet of "Father Dollar" and some were heard to murmur how nice things had been under Father O'Brian.

Wong was just making the rounds of the table refilling coffee cups, when, to everyone's astonishment, and for the second time in less than six months, Big Barney the Barber came lumbering through the door and with him he had a somewhat embarrassed looking Shamus Hoolihan.

Shamus was something of an enigma even in a town where many preferred not to offer too much information about themselves. He seemed well educated, but had insisted on a labouring job in the mine. He was Irish, but after Father O'Brian's departure was not often seen in church. He made no friends and kept pretty much to himself except for his regular visits to Paddy's place. Having both Barney and Shamus plunking themselves down at the long table was unusual enough to stifle even Three Piece Thompson for a moment or two and Barney got right down to business.

"Paddy," Big Barney tossed out like it was a comment on the weather, "is dead."

"Dead?" No one seemed prepared to believe anything could have killed the little Irish goblin.

"Yep, Shamus here, went out to see him last night and he was cold as a mackerel."

"Well, that is too bad." Frank Schindlemacher could spare a moment's sorrow for the little man, but only a moment. "Wonder what we'll do about the boats now?"

"Now, now, Frank, we can surely worry about that later. The man is gone and he deserves some proper send off I guess..." It was Mayor Two Bob who got the group back on track.

Two Bob turned to Shamus Hoolihan who still hadn't spoken. "Shamus I guess you knew him as well as anybody. Are you going to look after things for him or do you want some help from some of us?" Mayor Two Bob could be subtle at times, but the appearance of Shamus and Barney together at this time of day had his antennae waggling.

"Shamus has already notified McQuorquedale's," Barney put in before Shamus could answer, "and has sent a telegram to his folks. Nope, all that is done and done fine, that ain't where the problem lies." Barney paused...clip...clip... "Nope, it's the new priest, Father Dollar." Barney using the priests nickname in public was a sure sign of the depth of his agitation. "Says he won't give old Paddy a proper send off because he hasn't been goin' to church and, worse still I guess, hasn't been payin' his dues. Says there'll be no flowers or candles and such and that his coffin can't be up at the front of the church by the altar, but will have to sit way back by the door instead."

"So what's the problem, Barney? You need a few bucks from each of us to make up a nice donation to the good Father's church fund so he'll bury Paddy all right and proper?"

"Well, it wouldn't be so bad if that's what it was, or at least all it was, but Shamus, here, has been to see Father Dollardeaux" (Barney finally remembered his manners) "and it ain't no small amount he figures Paddy is behind in his duties to the church."

"Well a buck or two is one thing... everyone deserves a decent send off, but I got fall stock coming in soon and things aren't all that flush, with the mine not hiring and all." Frank Schindlemacher looked around the table and the head nods and coffee slurps reassured him he was speaking for just about everybody. "Just how much is it going to take to push Paddy over the threshold anyway?"

"Well, Father Dollardeaux did hint to Shamus here that it would be nice if Paddy had willed his estate to the church."

"Well, that wouldn't get him far past the front door unless he had something stashed away that nobody knows about." Two Bob looked at Shamus as though expecting something.

"No, nothing I know of, except half a quart of moose milk and about twenty old coats. He did ask me once to see to things if anything happened to him, but he never mentioned any estate."

"So what is the problem anyway? Seems to me there have been lots of other guys popped into the ground without a lot of singing and flowers." Three Piece Thompson was already looking at his watch thinking it was high time he got back to his furniture store.

"The problem is...," said Shamus, "the problem is that his mother is coming to the funeral and she believes Paidrech to have lived a very successful life..." He looked up and down the long table and added, as though teaching a group of unusually dim-witted students, "...very successful, both in the community and in the church." Letting that settle in for a moment Shamus then continued, "Paidrech's uncle is a bishop, and is not the only member of the family who hold's high office in the church."

"Well, you would think all that would be enough for Father Dollardeaux to do things right."

"Father Dollardeaux," Shamus responded in that odd resonating voice he had, "Father Dollardeaux is a Dominican."

Well, there was nobody at the table who had any idea what a Dominican might be but it was plain from Shamus' tone of voice that it wasn't in Paddy's favour.

It was lawyer Loud Raight who broke the silence that hung over the table. Broke the silence was a bit of an understatement in Loud Raight's case; he never spoke under a loud shout. When he was in court you could hear him all over Main Street. Even greeting him in the street could turn heads a block away. People who didn't know him thought they knew all his business because they could hear him so well, but Loud's real secret was that he sometimes spoke softly. When his voice dropped from roar to shout, from shout down to just plain loud and finally to a near whisper, the whole table was straining to hear him.

"You," he whispered down the table to Shamus, "you are the executor of his estate I presume?"

"I can't say, he never did make anything official."

"But he did ask you to look after things?"

"Yes."

"Well, then, it seems to me then that no one would likely object if you took it upon yourself to make a gift of Paidrech Sheehan's estate to the church that loved and cherished him and to which his family have devoted their lives for centuries." When Loud began to wind up you had to listen carefully to sort out the good bits from the freehand verbal flourishes.

" Perhaps," said Shamus, "but he has no estate except, as I said, the whisky and the old coats, unless you count the shack which is pretty much falling down."

"Well now," Loud Raight turned to Otto the Bank, "Otto, didn't you tell me one time that a number of your customers had bought into that East Lake Winnipeg Railroad deal? Without mentioning any names, of course." Loud hastened to add, and then, as an after thought, turning to Shamus and Barney, he whispered, "Perhaps you two have things to do to get ready for the funeral. If you have to leave us I am sure no one would object." Loud waited patiently while Shamus and Barney finished their coffee and left the room.

It should be mentioned here that this was in the days before all this instant share trading. When you bought shares in a company in those days, you went down to the bank and ordered them. You put up your money, and in a few days, the bank would call you and hand you a real certificate for your stake in the company. These certificates were works of art in themselves, engraved with marvellous fine tracings, curlicues and Greek columns and pictures of things related to the company's business all intertwined and shaded in fine engraver's lines. It was generally accepted that, the more shaky a company was, the more elaborate its share certificates would be, and the Great East Lake Winnipeg Railway offering had been acknowledged to be a true masterpiece of the engraver's art. In the same class were the Manitoba Marble and Granite Quarry Company, The Big Gold Dipper Mining Company, Loon Walk Arsenic and Gold and not a few others.

"Well, then, George, didn't you tell me one time that your wife had papered the outhouse walls with your beautiful Great East Lake Winnipeg Railway shares?"

"She did that, Loud, said she wanted to make sure I never forgot where her washing machine money went."

"Do you think George," Loud's voice could barely be heard now, " Do you think that you might be able to get those certificates loose? And if you did, might you be willing to transfer them to the estate of the late Paidrech Oin Sheehan?"

The group around that table weren't university professors or anything, but you didn't have to slap them in the face with a wet moccasin to get an idea across. Drawers were rummaged, old document folders thumbed through, outhouse wallpaper peeled off, and dusty bank boxes searched.

The next day Shamus Hoolihan found himself seated in Loud Raight's second floor law office. It was a nice warm day and the windows were open, allowing Loud's voice to carry nicely into the street and even as far as the Ladies Style Shop about half a block away.

"You are, I believe, Shamus Hoolihan, executor and trustee of the estate of the late Paidrech Oin Sheehan, sometime owner and manager of the Shist Lake Marina and Dry-dock?"

"Loud, you have known me since I came to this town, what are you up to?"

" Well then..."People were stopping in the street to listen as Loud continued. "Well, then, I officially turn over to you this folder." Loud tapped his fat forefinger on a thick folder that lay on his desk. It was a brown paper folder of the kind that is used to contain documents and was bound with a slender piece of blue ribbon. A neatly lettered label on the top left hand corner said simply "Estate of Paidrech Oin Sheehan." It was bulging with some of the most impressive and elaborately engraved stock certificates to be seen anywhere. Schist Lake Copper, Loon Walk Arsenic and Gold, Walcher Mining, Kay's Lake, Great East Lake Winnipeg Rail-road, they were all there.

"Which said folder comprises the full estate and sum of the worldly goods, including title to the building of the Schist Lake Marina and Dry-dock Co. Sign here."

Loud pushed an official looking paper at Shamus, who dutifully signed.

"It was, I believe, the uncontested wish of the deceased that the entirety of his estate be given in perpetuity to the church that was his spiritual home and place of earthly solace and refuge." Loud smiled, a process that involved at least four of his chins. "I would have attached a summary of the value of these certificates but Otto the Bank has gone fishing and so it will be impossible to get an assessment of the current value of this portfolio until Monday when he gets back to the bank. To provide some indication of how generous the bequest Paidrech Oin Sheehan is making to his beloved church, I have included a covering letter containing a list of the original purchase prices."

Shamus took the thick folder under his arm and stood up. "It will give me great pleasure to convey Paidrech's gift to Father Dollardeaux", he said with no trace of a smile.

"Mrs. Sheehan will arrive on this evening's train I understand..." Loud's voice had gone back to a whisper, "arrive on this evenings train, and after the funeral Friday, be departing immediately by sleeper coach back to her family home in the East?"

"Yes, I have arranged for her to stay with the Finnisters, she will leave on Saturday's train."

Well, Paidrech's funeral was one of the grandest the town had ever seen. Father Dollardeaux outdid himself in every priestly line you could imagine. The church was awash with flowers. There were so many candles burning that the fire chief, who was a Lutheran and not used to fire with his ceremonies, was seen to slip out of the church and alert the boys at the fire hall, just in case. Incense wafted, holy water sprinkled and the choir sang, and Paidrech's coffin was so far up the aisle it was just short of sitting on the altar itself. Mrs Sheehan looked around the church with proud satisfaction at the number of obviously prosperous citizens come to pay their last respects to her son. A grand funeral it was indeed.

It happened that Barney's route to work on Tuesday morning took him past the train station and he was astonished to find Shamus Hoolihan standing on the platform, a small club bag in his hand.

"Shamus, you're not leaving us?"

"Yes, I must go."

" You goin' to Trail or Yellowknife or someplace?"

"No, no more mining for me, Barney."

"Never thought you was no miner with those hands."

Shamus seemed to struggle with himself for a moment, sighed, and then set his bag down on the crushed slag of the platform.

"I guess I owe you a little explanation, since it was you who set things going for Paidrech." Shamus' voice seemed to have lost its low class Irish brogue a bit, as though casting off an old coat that didn't really fit. "You see, Barney, I have been a bit dishonest with you and that has always bothered me some. I am not Shamus Hoolihan, well, I am, but my full title would be Brother Shamus. As Paidrech's would have been Brother Paidrech. For the longest time we never knew what had become of Brother Paidrech. He was sent off to study with the Christian Brothers in Boston and the next thing we knew he had disappeared. It took a long time to find him, but the Church has its ways and the good Father O'Brian knew at once who he was. I was sent to watch over him, but my work is done now and I am recalled."

Barney was silent for a long moment. "I hear Father Dollardeaux has been looking for you ever since he took Paidrech's estate to the bank to have it valued Monday morning."

"Yes, I expected he might be." Shamus' twinkling Irish smile belied his serious tone of voice...

"Yes, I expected he might be. I had a few of those East Lake Winnipeg Railway Shares myself."

A Rose By Any Other...

THE SUMMER DAY WAS STILL, AND HOT AS ONLY A NORTHERN SUMMERS DAY CAN BE. The sun had been up since five, along the shore the willows drooped and the bush had that tinder dry smell that makes forest dwellers nervous. In the water beside the dock, hundreds of little black water beetles swirled and turned in a dance that had meaning only for them. Up a short path from the lake a small log cabin sheltered among the pines. It was too small to entertain guests but Two Bob didn't really want all that many visitors anyway; he treasured his time alone in the little cabin on the bottle neck bay. He had put two rocking chairs on the shaded front porch though, just to show he wasn't altogether denying the world outside.

He had dragged one of those chairs out to the end of the dock, where he sipped his warm "rye and ginger" slowly, trying to make it last as the sun slowly inched its way toward the big old jack pine at the end of the bay that marked refill time. A few feet out the bobber of his fishing line jumped and swirled as something deep in the weedy water attacked his bait. There was no need to grab the rod and reel in his catch though; Two Bob was at one with the other denizens of the bay and had long ago removed all the hooks from his impressive collection of lures.

Two days of holidays left and it was back to work and back to the joys and frustrations of the town hall. Two Bob Bobdinsky had a couple of years of being mayor under his belt now and he was pretty sure that the upcoming election would give him two more. Presiding over the affairs of an isolated mining camp with its wild mixture of inhabitants drawn from every corner of the world could be a challenge at times, but he liked being mayor. He had never had a family of his own and had no present plans to start one; the town with all its joys and troubles was all the family he needed.

Our town was a strange place with an even stranger name. Isolated by miles of lake and bush and accessible only by rail, it was populated by thousands of single men, leavened with a growing number of families and children. The mining company had scoured Eastern Europe for miners, and the fame of the place with the odd name had attracted adventurers and refugees from all over the world. Strangers in a strange land, they somehow managed to forget the ancient hatreds of the old country and in a babble of languages were busy making homes for themselves in the hard and unforgiving north.

Two Bob's only opposition in the mayoralty campaign was Gunther Volkstein, the deputy mayor. Beaten soundly in the last election, Gunther was not a man to give up easily. It was the custom for the deputy mayor to become acting mayor when the mayor was absent. That Gunther would take advantage of his position as acting mayor to further his interests in the upcoming election had been a foregone conclusion and something Two Bob felt was just part of the game, nothing to worry about. If Two Bob hadn't been so intent on the progress of the sun toward the jack pine, he might have knocked on wood as this thought passed through his mind, but he didn't. The gods might look like they are not paying attention, sitting in their big leather armchairs in that great club room in the sky, but they don't miss much. Two Bob should have knocked on wood and, when he didn't, his omission did not go unnoticed.

Out in the bottleneck passage into the bay Two Bob had installed a series of reef markers that just about covered the whole entrance. They didn't really mark a reef; in fact, there was twenty feet of water in the channel, but they did help to discourage random visitors to the little bay. Two Bob admired the yellow and black markers bobbing in the wake of some unseen passing boat and then turned his attention back to the sun and the tree and the prospect of another two years as mayor. He was yanked back from his dream of the oddly named utopia on the rocks when he realised with a start that, for some time now, he had been listening to the sound of a boat. Not the sawmill howl of an outboard, but the deep burble and rumble of a powerful inboard. There were a number of inboards on the lake, most of the Carlyles had inboard Grey Marines, but this motor had a completely different sound. There was only one boat on the lake with a Cummins diesel engine. Two Bob sighed with quiet resignation as the mining company's boat, "*Marie*" poked its long white nose around the point, moved with slow confidence right through the nest of fake reef markers and sidled gently up to Two Bob's little dock.

Usually Nick Klimkew or Marvin Saunders piloted the "*Marie*," but this time the "man from the mine" was the only person on board. Two Bob grabbed his glass as the dock swayed against the weight of the big boat. He caught the bowline tossed to him and managed to kick his tackle box shut as he moved forward to snub the line on one of the dock's projecting posts.

Two Bob took a quick glance over his shoulder at the trees along the shore line, the sun was still about one thumb width short of the jack pine that marked his three o'clock drink, but the arrival of the "*Marie*" made routine a bit irrelevant. The "man from the mine" was the person who looked after the relationships between the citizens of the town and the mining and smelting company. The mine made a great point of not interfering in the running of the town, but no one really believed there were not times when the mine's concerns might need to be made clear. By the same token, the town made a great show of its independence from the mining company, but a quiet word with the "man from the mine" was usually all it took to get the mining company and its vast resources behind some needy project.

Generally Two Bob enjoyed his sessions with the "man from the mine." More than once they had shared a bottle of rye and discussed the astonishing town that was under their care. But today was different. That the "man from the mine," who seldom handled the "*Marie*" by himself, would manoeuvre it all the way down Schist Creek, and through the reefs and shoals of Schist Lake to find Two Bob's little pocket bay could only mean trouble, big trouble with the running of the town. Two Bob sighed. He was resigned to the fact that Gunther would stir something up while he was acting mayor but he wasn't ready for the tale the "man from the mine" began to unfold.

It had always been Gunther's firm conviction that the quiet, anonymous support of the mining company was the real trump card in the municipal elections, a card that Gunther never had felt that he held.

Gunther was a European, inheritor of generations of experience in dealing with royalty. If you wanted the king's favour, you did something nice for him, like winning a battle, or painting his portrait or better yet, that of his mistress. You could write a book and dedicate it to him or compose an opera in his honour. Gunther had a pretty clear idea of the sort of thing that should win him the favour and support of the mine, or better yet of its owner. He had been quietly working on his plan all summer, waiting until Two Bob was officially off on his vacation and until he, Gunther Volkstein, was officially the acting mayor.

At the first meeting of the council at which he occupied the chair, Gunther made his move. Waiting until most of the councillors were starting to look at their watches and calculate the amount of time left until the beer parlor would be closing, he tabled a long and complicated motion. He had his sole ally on the council read the motion, all of it, slowly, with Gunther interrupting every now and then for clarification of his own memo to stretch the procedure out even further. By the time first reading was over with, and it looked like Gunther was planning a speech even longer than the motion itself, the councillors were in no mood to prolong the proceedings with debate. Dispensing with any idea of second reading, or a detailed discussion, to a man they voted for the motion, scraped back their chairs and headed out for a well-deserved cool draft.

The motion was really a hodgepodge of resolutions: proposals to beautify the town, to improve the social amenities, (whatever that meant), and a dozen other things. So many other things that no one noticed, as Gunther had known they would not, that one of the sub-subsections included a motion to examine the admittedly odd name our town had, to see whether it might be improved upon.

So certain had Gunther been of the success of his slight of hand with the motion that he had already drafted a press release for Staples Dibson to print in the next morning's paper. It was this paper that the "man from the mine" put into Two Bob's hand as he thanked him for the "rye and ginger.

"TOWN TO HONOUR MINE OWNER AND BENEFACTOR OF THE PEOPLE
........see page 3"

Staples never liked to sell the whole paper on the front page, too many cheapskates catching the news without buying the paper. The "man from the mine" had thoughtfully folded the paper to page three so that the headline article was easy to find. It was to Two Bob's credit that he didn't spill a drop of his "rye and ginger," but the rising tide of red in his normally calm face left no doubt about his reaction to the article as he read on.

"Acting on a motion put before the town council at last night's meeting, the Deputy Mayor has struck a committee to examine the name of our fair town to see whether a more dignified and meaningful name might be found. A name that would carry our town proudly into the future, a name that the third largest city in Manitoba could bear with pride.

Acting Mayor Gunther Volkstein has already dropped hints that the committee is planning to honour mine owner and town benefactor Cornelius Swinton Wahtney by renaming the town Wahtneyville."

To avoid accusations of acting highhandedly, Gunther had added a rider to the proclamation to the effect that everyone was to be free to make suggestions for a new name for the town. There would be a vote on the proposed new names at the time of the fall elections.

The "man from the mine" usually made one "rye and ginger" last a fair while, but this one disappeared in about two gulps. Without a word, Two Bob set the bottle of Five Star on the deck of the *"Marie"* where it would be within easy reach. Cornelius Swinton Wahtney, to paraphrase Queen Victoria, "was not amused." If he accepted the "honour" of having the town named after him, he would be the laughing stock of the upper class society he was trying so hard to break into. No one would ever believe he hadn't ordered the name change himself. If the honour was actually offered to him and he refused it, the bloodthirsty tabloids would have a field day portraying him as a man too proud to accept the... etc. etc. The "man from the mine" was a refined sort of gentleman and, as such, incapable of repeating Cornelius Swinton Wahtney's tirade *verbatim*, but he did manage to get enough of the spirit of it. The "man from the mine" had tried to explain to Wahtney about the holidays and the acting mayor and the upcoming elections and so on, but ended up just saying "yes sir, yes sir " over and over again as Cornelius Swinton hollered over the long distance line that "somebody had better get that chicken-assed town under control."

Two Bob watched the "*Marie*" rumble majestically back out over his fake reef markers, wondering briefly about the new gadgets he had read about in "Popular Science" that were supposed to be able to tell boaters exactly how much water was under the keel and even, some said, tell you if there were fish down there. It didn't seem very sporting if it were true. The fish weren't going to have much of a chance. It was Friday. The "man from the mine" had urged Two Bob to cut his holiday short and come back to deal with the situation, but Two Bob had refused. He wasn't due back in the mayor's chair until Monday morning and it had always been his policy not to interfere. Gunther was the acting mayor until Monday morning and that was that. Besides, it didn't seem much could happen or be done about anything over the weekend.

The sun was well past the big tree by now, but when Two Bob looked around for the rye he realised it was still on the boat. With a sigh he picked up his tackle box and headed up to the cabin, a bit of the shine had been taken off the last two days of his holiday.

On Monday, when Two Bob settled himself into the big green leather chair in the mayor's office with his first mug of coffee, the problem didn't seem all that bad. The whole thing was, after all, only a proposal. There would be a vote, but not till fall, if it ever got to that. He would have a chat with Staples Dibson and get him to cool things a bit in the paper. The proposal to honour Cornelius Swinton Wahtney was quickly spotted by most as a not too subtle election ploy by Gunther Volkstein and, outside of Cornelius himself, no one gave it much more thought.

But it wasn't to be so simple.

The real problem, it turned out, was not in Gunther's plan to honour Wahtney, but in the cover-your-ass part of the motion that said that everyone would get an equal opportunity to suggest other new names for the town and to have them appear on the ballot.

The first hint of what was about to be unleashed on the community came when Laura Langmuir, Two Bob's secretary, popped her head in the door of the office to enquire who was in charge of issuing parade permits.

"Who wants a permit? And for what kind of a parade?"

" It's Father Dollardeaux, he wants a permit for a parade from the railroad station to the church for just after the time when the train comes in on Wednesday."

"A parade?"

"It's about the new name for the town. Father Dollardeaux thinks the town should be named after a saint, the same as most of the towns in Quebec where he comes from. "

"Well, he don't need a parade to put in a suggestion about the town name."

"It's the Saint. He wants it named after Saint Egelian, the patron saint of miners. He has ordered a big statue of St. Egelian. It's arriving on Wednesday's train and he wants to have a parade to take it to the church. Oh yes, and he said to remind you that this is a religious matter as well as a civil one, in case you were of two minds about granting the permit."

"Well, tell George Burton to issue him a permit if he needs one, tell him I said to go ahead and do it"

"And the new constable is waiting to see you."

Two Bob liked the new constable. He was going to take some breaking in, of course. The academy in Regina taught their men how to enforce the law, but it didn't teach them how much of the law to enforce and, in our town, most of the citizens were of the firm opinion that less law was better than more.

"Good morning Mr. Mayor."

"Mornin' Constable," Two Bob noticed that the constable's stiff brimmed hat had a curious stain on it, and that two buttons had been somewhat inexpertly reattached to his uniform tunic. "What can I do for you this fine day?"

"Well, Mr. Mayor, I don't normally like to bother you with

police business, but something has to be done about this town naming proposal. Things are getting out of hand."

"Things?"

"I have asked Miss Langmuir to type up my report, as it is rather a long one and my fingers are somewhat stiff after last night."

"I'll read it."

"Well, it is a bit more urgent than that. There have been seven fights both in and outside the beer parlors that the waiters couldn't handle and had to call me for. One last night pretty much wrecked the Corona and I had to order it closed."

"All that about the name change thing?"

"Seems to have brought out all the old hatred and prejudice and stuff from the old country that people had pretty much forgotten about over here. If this keeps up much longer, I may have to ask Regina for an extra officer to back me up."

As the constable was leaving Two Bob's attention was attracted by a growing hubbub outside the window.

"Laura, what's all that racket down there?"

"It's people who want to get in to see you, Mr. Mayor, mostly people who have some problems to do with the name change and..."

"Well, let them in, everybody's got a right to say their piece."

"I would, but they can't get in, I guess that's what all the noise is about."

"Can't get in? Why not?"

"Its Mrs. Teddy-Keedy, from the Daughters of the Empire Loyalists, she has sewn herself a dress out of the Union Jack and is sitting on the steps with a cane that she swings at people, and shouts, " No socialism in the Empire!" Or something like that. I think she is upset about the union's proposal to name the town Karl Marx Burg."

"Tell her to go home. Tell her it ain't likely that anyone would vote to change a two-part name to a three-part one and, anyway, there's too many Liberals here to vote for a name like that."

"I'll tell her but do you think she will accept that?

Two Bob looked out the window at the gathering crowd in the street, "She might, it's starting to rain."

It did rain a bit but things continued to get out of hand.

Big Barney the barber got into so many fights that his knuckles were all swollen up and he couldn't get a proper grip on his cut-throat razor any more, and the drugstore sold out of the new safety razors starting a trend toward shaving one's self that was never reversed. The last fight he got into was the one that closed the Corona.

According to Taxi Joe who had been there at the time, Ole Thorstienson had been arguing loudly with Toivo Pukanen that there were more Norwegians than Finlanders in the town and that there was no reason why the town shouldn't be named Oslo after the major city of Norway. It would be a better choice, he claimed, than Toivo's suggestion of New Helsinki and besides the idea was to get away from having a two-word town name. Ole claimed none of the great cities of the world had two part names except maybe New York and the "New" part wasn't really part of the name. Big Barney, smelling the makings of a good fight, had leaned over from the next table and said, "There ain't a capital city in the world that ain't a two note town." And Ole Thorstienson had leaped to his feet and started to yell out the names of all the capital cities he could think of that were one word

"London, Moscow, Paris, Cairo, Oslo, Berlin, Madrid...."

But Barney could yell too and right behind Ole he was chanting "Lon-done; Moss-Cow; Pa-ris; Kay-Ro; Aus-Low; Ber-Lin; Maaaa-Drid." Ole poured some beer on Barney to get him to stop interrupting and Barney tapped Ole over the head with a chair and Ole's friend Svein tipped Barney's table over spilling Barney's beer onto Elmer Balcan.By the time the constable got there the whole place was one wild melee that took him over an hour to calm down and left the beer parlor pretty much wrecked.

At the besieged town hall, Two Bob's phone was ringing again. You could tell it was important because, in those days, when a central operator still handled all the phone calls, she also handled the ringing machine and you could read a good deal into the long insistent jangles she was sending to the mayor's office. At that moment, the town engineer managed to push past a distracted Laura. His normally spotless high top leather boots were covered in mud and his prized campaign hat looked as though it had been the same place as his boots had been. Ignoring the phone, he started right in, "Bob you got to do something about this damn town name thing, and you got to do it soon."

Hardly believing that the contretemps over the new town name could even have involved the town's engineering department, Two Bob called to Laura to find out who it was on the phone and waved his distracted engineer into a chair. It appeared that Janish Mitzel who drove the tank wagon that delivered water around the town had been getting his hair cut at Leo LaPointe's barbershop when the subject of the name change came up. Janish had offered the opinion that a good Austro-Hungarian name like New Vienna would grace the town nicely, but Leo LaPointe had been in the French army in the First World War and been pretty blunt about what he thought about that idea.

An argument had broken out and Janish Mitzel had stormed out of the barbershop, still wearing a steaming towel around his neck. Leo LaPointe got out a big piece of cardboard and put up a sign in his window that said "A bas les Austriches."

"Now what the tarnation has all this got to do with ostriches?" Two Bob was starting to lose his sense of reality.

"It ain't ostriches like birds, Two Bob, its some kind of German country I think. Anyway, Janish was so mad that he went and got his water wagon and emptied the whole thing into that low spot in the street right in front of LaPointe's barber shop, people been getting stuck in it all morning and the parades are starting soon. They're lining up now in fact."

"Well, can't you tell em to take a different route?"

"They won't. The Orangemen say they won't give up the right to go down Main Street as long as Father Dollardeaux is goin' down Main Street and Father Dollardeaux says...."

"Hold on, we ain't got any Orange Lodge in this town that I know of."

"We have now. It was formed a few days ago by all the Irish Protestants who are against naming the town after..."

"Wait a minute," Two Bob had no time for details at this point. "Wait a minute, two parades you say?"

"Yes, the Catholics are marching south from the station to the church with the new statue of Saint Egelian, and the Orange Lodge is marching north from the Elk's Hall to the station."

"Both at the same time? Both down Main Street in opposite directions? How the hell did that happen?"

"Well, I guess George Burton had just issued a parade permit for the Orange Lodge when Miss Langmuir came down with your orders to issue one to Father Dollardeaux and..."

Laura Langmuir normally looked as though she had just been starched and ironed but even she was beginning fray a bit. " Mr. Mayor you really must take this call, it's from the "Pee-em-oh" office, whatever that is, and he says he is calling on behalf of the Prime Minister."

"Hello? Who's this?"

The voice on the other end of the line, blurred and muffled by the humming long distance wires had a definite French accent and a definite sound of authority. Two Bob listened respectfully at first but then, losing his temper altogether, began to shout into his end of the line. "No, we ain't got any rebellion here, this is a law abidin' town and no we don't need no army and, of course, everyone has a gun, who ain't? No, I don't care what the New York Times says, there ain't anything like that goin' on up here and if there was we could handle it ourselves. We got our own Mountie here and we don't need any army. Yes, I will, I'll call you if I need you, but I ain't goin' to call because I won't need you. Goodbye, oh, and say 'Hello' to the Prime Minister for me and thank him for his interest." Just at the end there, Two Bob had remembered his manners.

"Now, can somebody tell me what the hell that was all about?"

"Maybe I can." It was Staples Dibson, the publisher of our local paper, *The Daily Staple. S*omehow he had gotten past the crush on the front step and was trying to get past a determined Laura at the door of Two Bob's office."Maybe I can 'cause I just got a call from the New York Times wanting me to do some follow up and a background on the story."

"What story?" Two Bob's voice was becoming uncharac-teristically sharp and seemed to have risen a note or two.

Staples took the question as an invitation. Wriggling past the departing town engineer he crossed the room and, uninvited, plopped himself down in the chair across the desk from Two Bob.

"Seems like Hughie the Movie and Three Piece Thompson were arguing about what the town's new name ought to be and somebody said it couldn't be changed without Ottawa's say so because of the maps and the post office and the census and all that. That got Hughie and Three Piece goin' about that dumb idea they're always on about, you know, that notion of seceding from the other provinces and starting our own province of *Precambria*'."

"The Province Of Precambria" was a kind of local inside joke. Whenever someone got really frustrated trying to deal with a provincial government almost six hundred miles away, or a federal government even further removed from the realities of an isolated northern mining town, some one would propose that the northern parts of the four western provinces should split themselves off and join together as the province of Precambria. The new province would have a fine port on each ocean, Churchill and Prince Rupert, mines producing more wealth than many European countries enjoyed, and a fine grain growing area around Grand Prairie. It would boast more fish and timber than any-one knew what to do with, huge powerful rivers like the Nelson, the Churchill and the Saskatchewan for transport and power; there was even talk of oil around Edmonton. It would also of course be much better attuned to the needs of northerners.

According to Staples, while Hughie and Three Piece were working themselves into a fine frenzy over the "Precambia" idea, an American fisherman had been sitting in the next booth taking the whole thing in. It turned out he wasn't just any old fisherman; he was a reporter for the New York Times. This talk of seceding and forming a new government and so on was just the stuff he needed for a story that could turn his costly fishing holiday into an all expense paid working trip. He didn't stop to hear the whole thing but felt that he knew enough about the planned rebellion to write his story. He had wired it in on Friday and, things being a bit slow in New York, it had made the Sunday Paper.

"INSURRECTION LOOMS IN NORTHERN CANADA!"

But before Staples could get to talking about the follow up story he had been asked to write, a huge uproar broke out on Main Street, the shouting and yelling loud enough to reach the town hall.

"Now what!" Two Bob yelled to Laura to look out the window and see if she could spot the source of the distur-bance. "What's goin' on down there anyway?"

Laura hung as far out the window as she dared. "I can't really tell... it looks like a bunch of men are having a mud fight in front of LaPointe's barbershop."

The two parades had met in the main street, separated for the moment by the sea of mud caused by Janish Mitzel and his water wagon. The statue of Saint Egelian had been uncrated on the station platform. Bigger and heavier than anyone imagined it might be, it was finally manhandled onto Polker's ice dray. For appearance's sake, Father Dollardeaux had insisted that it travel standing up. Wobbling precariously at each rut and bump in the road, Saint Egelian towered majestically over the crowd that trailed after the wagon. Father Dollardeaux hesitated only a moment before commanding the drayman to drive his team right through the mud hole.

Banking on the fact that the mud had only been there a short while, Father Dollardeaux calculated that it wouldn't yet have become very deep. He should have been right, would have been right in Quebec where he had spent most of his life, but this was the north and all that nice, warm, dark water had melted the permafrost in the muskeg that underlay much of our town.

The wagon lurched, and the off wheel sank. Saint Egelian started to slide, the crowd roared, and the men on the wagon struggled against the huge weight of the careening plaster saint.

From his barbershop Leo LaPointe saw the disaster developing and rushed out to help. Everyone's eyes were on the swaying statue and when, inevitably, it did topple from the wagon into the mud, no one noticed that Leo LaPointe had arrived just in time to be caught under its majestic fall and be driven deep into the mud beneath it.

No one in the parade noticed. But Big Barney and Ole Thorstienson who had just stepped out of the Royal after repairing their friendship with a number of glasses of draft saw the tiny barber go down. Both of them leaped into the mud to rescue Leo. The statue was heavy, but for these two giants it would have been child's play, but for the fact that everyone thought they were attacking the precious statue and rushed to pull them off it. On the other side of the mire, the Orange marchers gave a huge shout and rushed into the melee to the aid of what they perceived to be, two loyal anti-papists. It says something for Barney and Ole that it didn't take them very long to clear the area of combatants, roll the statue off Leo and drag him up out of the mud. It was hard to tell what sort of shape he was in, encased as he was in a slippery layer of grey gumbo and he didn't seem to be breathing. Barney lifted him up, put his arms around him from behind and gave him one big rib-cracking squeeze. About half a gallon of loon shit shot out of Leo's tortured lungs, followed at the second squeeze by most of his lunch. He was breathing again, breathing loudly... yelling in fact, with the first breath he drew he was demanding instant membership in the Protestant church and protection from the Catholic saint that had turned on him so ungratefully.

It was obvious to everybody that Leo needed a beer and the whole parade trooped into the Royal, dripping mud and shouting for service. A dozen loyal followers helped Father Dollardeaux get Saint Egelian back on the wagon. The statue wasn't broken but the dark waters of the muskeg had given the saint a deep tan that was to stay with him forever. About the third or fourth round of beer a fight broke out again over the proper name for our town and the con-stable had to clear the beer parlor and close it down.

Two Bob was so thankful when the end of the day finally arrived that he didn't even say anything to George Burton about the parade permits. All he wanted was to get home to his little shack and sit quietly for a spell, but that was not to be. Parked in front of his house, in the company station wagon, was the "man from the mine."

He bid Two Bob a good evening, reminded him that he owed him a bottle of rye for the one left on the *"Marie"* and invited himself in. Two Bob got a couple of jam jars out of the sink and set them on the chequered tablecloth. It seemed only polite to wait until the "man from the mine" was good and ready to talk; the two men sipped their warm "rye and ginger," confident that the right moment would come.

Mr. Wahtney's father had been a muleskinner in the borax mines of Death Valley before stumbling on the gold reef that had made his son a rich man. Some of those riches had been used to set up the fabulously wealthy mine that was the reason for the existence of our town.

As a muleskinner, the elder Wahtney had need for, and had fine tuned the use of, the kind of profanity required to get two dozen mules all moving in the same direction at the same time. The present Mr. Wahtney was no muleskinner but he had learned the words, music and rhythm from his father and was not above using his skills when something seemed to call for it. All this is by way of saying that the "man from the mine" could not give Two Bob a direct quote from the phone call he had received that afternoon because none of it was printable or even fit to repeat. Suffice it to say that Mr. Wahtney was in a fine rage and demanding action.

The *Times* article about insurrection had panicked a country that knew something of civil war. Prices of stocks that stood in any way to be affected by the reported insurrection dropped like the proverbial stone. Shares in our mining company had plummeted, losing four dollars in a single day and likely to lose even more tomorrow. Four dollars didn't sound like much until you stopped to think that Mr. Wahtney was rumoured to own about six million shares, not counting the ones he had put in his wife's name.

Two Bob barely had time to digest all this when the constable came limping up the steps. The buttons he had lost this time he hadn't even bothered to sew back on.

"Mr. Mayor." The formality in his voice caught the attention of both men. "Mr. Mayor, I am formally requesting that you read The Riot Act to this town. Things can't go on like this much longer, somebody is going to get hurt."

"Well, Constable, I sure do appreciate what you're goin' through, but I ain't readin' no Riot Act because we ain't got no riot."

"Something's got to be done sir. You have got to get these people calmed down somehow!"

"I been thinkin' that I might go on the radio tomorrow mornin', talk to people a little, get 'em to back off a bit and start behavin' themselves again."

"Wonderful idea, sir. I am certain Pendlebury McNeish at the radio station can set things up. What will you say?"

"I haven't the faintest idea," said Two Bob, and poured himself and the "man from the mine" another "rye and ginger." The constable was technically off duty, but declined on the grounds that he was as likely as not to be called upon before morning.

At eight o'clock the next morning, Two Bob plopped himself

into his big green chair, still wondering what on earth he would say. The address to the townspeople had been set for later in the morning. Mrs. Teddy-Keedy, wearing her dress made out of the Union Jack, had already taken up her position on the town hall steps. It looked to be a long, hot day. Two Bob offered up a silent plea to whatever gods might be taking an interest. It was going to take the speech of his life to calm the town down and the big clock on the wall reminded him with each tick that his mind was as blank as a lake full of winter ice.

Now and then, though, the gods do pay attention. Some odd prayer might stand out above the streams of prayers passing through their office... some unusual request might pique the interest of a god with too much time on his hands. One never knew what to expect, however, when the gods did decide to take an interest. They were pretty heavy handed when it came to adjusting the affairs of humans, usually either doing too much or too little of something, or getting the original request wrong or, as often as not, being just plain mischievous, but this time...

There was a respectful tap on Two Bob's office door and Laura Langmuir announced with a definite touch of chill in her voice that there was a "woman" to see him. And, indeed, there was. Miss Prestoupoulious was a schoolteacher and, that was all she ever wanted to be. The bright spark of her formidable intellect could light fires in the soggy minds of students where nothing had ever burned before. Miss Prestoupoulious' problem was that her wonderful mind and natural flair for teaching had come packaged in the kind of body that elicited from women the sort of jealous chill that Laura Langmuir was displaying. On seeing her, men tended to forget their home addresses and have difficulty concentrating on what she was saying. Miss Prestoupoulious was not unaware of the effect her beauty had on other people, but it just wasn't part of her life. She was a teacher and her sure certainty in that role was what defined her world.

Firmly she closed the office door on Laura Langmuir and moved with confidence to the chair opposite Two Bob's desk.

"Mr. Mayor, it seems that there is a good deal of discussion, heated discussion one might say, to do with ideas for the selection of a new name for our town."

Mrs. Teddy-Keedy had already whacked someone with

her cane on the steps of the town hall and the noise level outside Two Bob's window was starting to rise. There was no need to comment on the obvious. Two Bob sat still and waited.

Miss Prestoupoulious used the English language much like a skilled artist might use his paints, each word carefully selected, each sentence finely crafted. If there was a flaw, it was perhaps in her accent. Nearly everyone in our town spoke English with a dash of some flavour or other but when Miss Prestopoulious spoke all the "A's" seem to bulk up rounder than called for and the "L's " and the "W's" kind of sidled up against each other.

"I understand you are to address the townspeople this morning, on the radio, at ten o'clock."

"I am and I must admit I don't have the faintest idea what I am going to say, but it sure looks like something needs to be said." Two Bob nodded his head toward the open window and the sounds of conflict rising from the town hall steps.

"Perhaps you would find this interesting in that case." Miss Prestoupoulious handed him a sheet of ruled yellow paper of the kind school children use for exercises.

Two Bob read the paper over several times. There were three short paragraphs, already studded with the corrections and comments of Miss Prestoupoulious' blue pencil. The paper had received a B+. Two Bob looked questioningly at his guest.

"I would have given her an A but her spelling is so bad...."

"Do you think she could come to the radio station and read this herself?"

"I will have to ask the principal, of course, but yes, he will agree and we will be there."

Most of the town was glued to their radio sets as ten o'clock rolled around and, right on cue, Pendlebury McNeish introduced Mayor Robert Bobdinsky.

Two Bob stepped up to the microphone, not at all comfortable talking to a black knob on the end of a chrome plated pole instead of a room full of people. Pendlebury was hunched over his control board watching some gauges whose needles jumped and danced alarmingly with each sound. "Ahem, I, uh, I know everyone has taken a real personal interest in the proposal to rename our town, some perhaps putting their ideas forward a little more forcefully than others, but everyone I am sure having the best interests of our town in mind." Two Bob sidled up a little closer to the microphone in response to Pendlebury's frantic hand signals. "A lot of suggestions and ideas have been put forward to the town hall. For a time, I thought most everyone had had their say, until this morning it was pointed out to me that there was one group at least that we hadn't heard from. And, uh, well, anyway, here's one of them now."

Not being used to microphones, Two Bob didn't think to turn his off and so most of the town listened as....

"You got to let that thing down to where she can reach it."

"It don't go down that far Bob, it only adjusts for about a foot each way."

"Then get her something to stand on, how about that chair out there?"

"Just a minute, okay, now then, you just hop up here and stand with the microphone real close to your mouth like this and just go ahead and talk."

At first the soft young voice was barely audible, but Pendlebury did some things with his dials and suddenly all over town...

"I am not supposed to talk, I am supposed to read."

"Well, you just go ahead and do it then, go ahead and read."

Sophia stood stiffly on the chair and leaning toward the microphone began to read.

"FUNNY NAMES "
by Sophia Mykelnetlicoff Grade Six Tonapah School

Sometimes people say that other people have funny names, but our teacher, Miss Prestoupoulious, who has a really funny name, says that everyone's name sounds strange to everyone else until you get used to it. She says that it doesn't matter that your name sounds strange to other people. What really matters is what you do with your name. If you do things to make yourself proud of your name then people won't think you have a funny name any more.

Our town is looking for a new name and everyone

is talking about it. My Dad says our town has a funny name but he doesn't care. Yesterday he said that the town should be named The Town Where Nothing Grows, because the smelter smoke got his cabbage sprouts again. My Dad is always right, but this time he may have missed something because something is growing here and it is us kids. There are twelve of us now in grade six and Miss Prestoupoulious says that next year there will be many more.

We know that our town has a funny name, and sometimes we get tired of explaining to people how it got named after the first parts of the two last names of a man who never existed, but it is the name of our town. We are growing up here and, when we are all grown up, we will do things to make you very proud of the name of our town and it won't sound funny to you any more.

The end

Well, the next day our ball team, "The Hard Rocks," beat the "Nipawin Buffaloes" nine to five and a few days after that a freak storm washed out part of the road around the lake and then Murray Pilchur's house caught fire, but the volunteer fire department put it out. And every one pretty much forgot about changing the town's name. The "man from the mine" had the company carpenters build a beautiful oak pedestal for Saint Egelian. It never hurt to have an extra saint around, especially one who took a direct interest in the affairs of the men working in the dark, dripping dangers of the stopes and raises deep under the ground.

Robert Bobdinsky was re-elected Mayor.

A Mysterious Loss Of Life Incident

THE TOWN'S BUSINESSMEN MET FOR COFFEE IN THE MORNING AND AGAIN ABOUT MID AFTERNOON AT WONG'S CAFÉ. But there was another group of coffee drinkers who never appeared at the long table in Wong's back room.They preferred to gather in the Gateway Drug Store. It wasn't that they were antisocial in any way, a nicer group of people you would never meet, or that they weren't essential parts of the machinery of the town like the businessmen. They were essential. But people like the town undertaker, the town policeman, the Anglican minister and the doctor were resigned to the fact that a comfortable, easy conversation at Wong's long table just couldn't run with them in it. By mutual consent, they had their coffee at another location. Pretty hard to josh someone about his hangover from drinking moose milk with the policeman there, or rag somebody about his fascination for someone else's wife with the minister listening in and the undertaker was just naturally a damper on any conversation.

The soda fountain in the Gateway Drug was a long, grey marble slab, punctuated by little chrome stands that sported a small paper napkin holder, a glass container of sugar that dispensed a spoonful each time it was tilted over, and some small bottles with perforated tops that contained cinnamon and tiny candy bits and some small black seeds that tasted like liquorice. The long counter started about halfway down the store and ran nearly to the magazine racks at the back where it took a right angle turn in toward the wall. It was at this corner that you would find this other group of coffee drinkers of a morning, about eleven, and in the afternoon, some time around three.

These men really did play an essential role in the town and Mayor Two Bob certainly recognised this, often choosing to join this group for his morning coffee just to keep the bonds of his little community tight. On the morning all this started Two Bob had arrived a bit early at the Gateway and was chatting with Phineas McQuorquedale, the undertaker. The topic of the conversation was our new RCMP constable, a fresh young thing right out of the Regina academy, sent up to replace old Sergeant Brimms.

"You know, Mcquockle, the town policeman is as essential to the good running of the town as... as... well, as you are, for example, or the fire chief. Every one has an important role to play and the town doesn't feel right unless each one does his part and does it well."

"And how do you see the policeman's role as part of the great social system, Robert?"

"Well, you got the Doc there, bringing in new members and there's you, seeing the old ones off in good style, and the Reverend, making sure everyone is resigned to whatever his fate is. Then you got the policeman, kind of like a mechanic, maybe. If some of the parts of the municipal machine ain't doin' what they are supposed to, or are interfering with some of the other parts, well, that's the policeman's job." Two Bob wasn't altogether satisfied with that simile and tried again, "Or maybe the policeman is sort of like the referee in a hockey game, to make sure everybody plays by the rules, like. But at the same time, like a good referee he can't choke up the game bein' too picky."

Phineas contemplated Two Bob's philosophy on the municipal construct for a moment or two, seeming to peer down his long nose at the question as if it was right there in front of him.

"Well, I haven't been a member of this community all that long as you know, but I can see that you have some work ahead of you. This new policeman is pretty much convinced the letter of the law is what defines his job. He doesn't have that fine flexibility that old Sergeant Brimms had."

"There's your problem right there. Old Brimms had seen so much of life, and rough life at that, that he could tell where to tighten up and where to let loose a little. This new guy has all that to learn, but this is a pretty tough town to dump a brand new policeman into, and him sort of still in his original wrappings and all."

"Still, you like him I gather?"

"Yep, got the right stuff in him, you can tell that right off. Up to us to make a good town policeman out of him. He needs time to learn just how much of the law is important to the good running of the community and how much is just stuff that might be needed for a southern community, but isn't necessary up here."

"Like the laws against bootlegging and running houses of ill repute, I gather..."

"Well, some things is essential services in a minin' town and it don't do to push against that too much. Anyway, given a bit of time and some help and guidance from us, he could become a respected policeman."

"I heard he already faced down Big Barney in the Corona the other night. That takes a bit of sand, one would think."

"Well, Big Barney might be a lot of things, but bein' dumb ain't one of them. You wouldn't have to take a jack hammer to his head to remind him that it's bad news to mess with a Mountie, big or small."

"So you think this new fellow has the makings of a policeman of the calibre of the good Sergeant Brimms?"

"Yep, McQuockle, I do, just as long as we can keep him from doing anything stupid till he gets his feet under him, so to speak. We ain't his main problem and he knows that. This is his first assignment and the brass down in Regina will be watching him like a hawk. One mistake and out he goes and we're lookin' at startin' all over with another new one and more'n likely one that ain't got near the potential of this one."

Myrna Pockenbury was one of those women God built on a Monday, getting the parts mixed up and generally drifting from the blueprint. Myrna had a bosom designed for a much, much larger woman, a fact that brought her a lot of unwelcome attention, which in turn sent her husband Tyndal Pockenbury into absolute fits of jealousy. The situation would have been bad enough, but Tyndal worked shift work as a dobe tapper in the smelter where he had far too much time on his hands between slag trains, time he often used to imagine all kinds of things. It didn't help matters any that Myrna had a job as chambermaid in the Corona Hotel, a job that Tyndal was certain brought her within grasping distance of every eight-armed travelling salesman that passed through town. That Myrna was as proper as a preacher's wife and would not even give these weasels the time of day cut no ice with Tyndal; he was jealous anyway and often imagined their leering faces in the dobe plugs he smashed with his big tapping bar.

Room 6 had been in the hotel about a week and Myrna had already been forced to swing her mop at him on more than one occasion. On Tuesday morning when she came to clean the room there was a "Do Not Disturb" sign on the door. Myrna thought nothing of it; mining promoters often needed a little extra privacy.

The next morning however the sign was still there. Myrna tidied up the occupied rooms on the third floor and about eleven o'clock returned to check Room 6 once more. Thinking he might have forgotten to take the "Do Not Disturb" sign down, Myrna tapped on the door, and tapped again. Finally she opened the door with her pass key and peeked in. Myrna was not a big woman, but the scream she let loose stopped motion in both the cafe and the beer parlor downstairs. It was even heard in the fire hall across the road. The volunteer fire brigade tumbled out of their chairs and scrambled for the truck, propelled as much by that scream as the fact that Myrna, doing the only thing she could think of in her utter panic, had pulled the fire alarm.

Except for the Chief, our town's fire department was entirely volunteer, so when the big siren over the fire hall started its mournful bellowing, barbers dropped razors, butchers abandoned sides of beef and truckers made u-turns. All over town the volunteers would drop whatever they were doing and answer the call, guided to the scene by the local radio station which would begin announcing the address of the fire as soon as it was called in. The radio station would also begin pleading with everyone listening to the fire location announcement not to go there so as to leave the firemen room to do their job, but half the town would go anyway, there not being all that much excitement available most days. By the time the new constable arrived on the second floor of the Corona, the hallway was full of firemen, as well as some general gawkers who had managed to get up the back staircase before the fire chief had time to post a man there. Some of the firemen were even in the room itself, but it was pretty evident that they weren't going to be able to do the occupant much good. Trying to regain control of the situation and preserve the scene of the incident as best he could (while desperately trying to recall his training in investigative procedures), the constable used his best Mountie voice to shoo everyone out of the room. He also urged all present to say nothing of the details of what they had seen, advice that in the end didn't do a whole lot of good.

The alarm had been sounded just around eleven and, by the time the volunteer firemen realized they weren't going to be needed, it was close to noon. The whole crew of volunteer firemen went to their various homes for lunch, and there wives and landladies subjected each one to a grilling that soon pried out the details. By the time the women had met over the back fences later in the afternoon, there weren't many left in town who didn't know that Room 6 had died a pretty horrible death. Murder without a doubt and a nasty one at that.

It was a big shock to our town, our first real murder. You shouldn't get the idea that nothing in the line of a mysterious loss of life incident had ever happened in our town. There was the time, for instance, when Curly Martin accidentally shot his brother-in-law. Mistook his scrawny, 150 pound frame for a sixteen hundred pound moose and put a bullet square in the centre of his red plaid hunting coat with that old thirty ought six of his.

That Curly's brother-in-law had a bad habit of beating up on Curly's sister and her kids whenever he got drunk, which was pretty often, was not mentioned after the accident. Old Sergeant Brimms had been called to Curly's sister's house to intervene in scenes of domestic violence more often than he liked to remember. He had decided pretty early on that it was one of the more useful accidents he had come across, and closed the case after only a day or two.

But this loss of life incident was something completely different. The first that Mayor Two Bob heard about the murder was a hurried phone call from the desk clerk of the hotel. The desk clerk often felt it his duty to keep Two Bob informed as to who was doing what to whom in his town. Two Bob didn't get many details in that first phone call, hearing only that someone was prematurely dead in one of the hotel rooms. Given that we had never had a real murder in our town, it might have been normal to entertain the hope that this would be another one of those useful accidents like the Martin case. Two Bob, however, had a sinking feeling that the new constable was not yet ready to make a seasoned Sergeant Brimms type evaluation of the situation. Worse yet, the new constable would not likely let go of it until he had shook it and chewed it and worried it to a rag. As it turned out, the case was much more complicated than the simple settlement of a marital problem.

The deceased, as Phineas McQuorquedale would refer to him, was one Pilchard Wilbur, mining promoter and general all around scam artist with a penchant for other peoples' wives. Altogether a man that almost anyone in the North American mining community, and a good ball team worth of husbands, would have paid someone to relieve the world of. Mining promoters in general have a reputation just a bit lower than lawyers or pawn shop brokers and Pilchard Wilbur was thought to be a pretty low example of even that derided group.

The Wednesday morning after the discovery of the body, Two Bob made his way down to the Gateway. Phineas McQuorquedale was already there and Doc Williston came in just behind Two Bob.

"Well Doc, you finished the coroner's inquest I guess?"

In those days it was necessary to have what was called a Coroner's Inquest if someone shuffled off this mortal coil without reporting in to a doctor or a minister or some other official on the way out. The Coroner's jury was made up of whoever happened to be standing around when the Coroner was looking for members. Six good men and true, they would listen to the Doc outline his findings and then were required to bring in a verdict. The verdict could simply say that the death seemed to be from natural causes, or could say that the causes were not known and suggest an investigation or, as the jury did in this case, say that the person had died at the hands of person or persons unknown.

"Yep, pretty straightforward, poor fellow died of strangulation, a rope around his neck, dug in so deep I had trouble getting it loose. Died sometime Monday night or early Tuesday morning from the look of it."

"Any chance he just hung himself?"

"No, not a chance, unless he could somehow have managed to tie himself up hand and foot and then put a rope around his neck. No, it was murder, no doubt about that."

"And our new constable? I guess he's getting right at it?" This last, with some trepidation in his voice, from Two Bob.

"I'll say. Pretty much got the whole thing figured out, he says. Left this morning early with Ivar Helgason's boat."

"Ivar's boat? What..."

"Well, and Ivar too. They have gone down the big lake to look for Tyndal Pockenbury. Apparently several people heard him threatening to kill this Wilbur fellow during a dust up in the Corona beer parlor Monday night."

"I think if Tyndal killed everyone he has threatened to kill this would be a pretty lonesome town, but you say the constable has gone after him in a boat?" Two Bob was still having trouble with this idea.

"Yep, apparently Tyndal told a few friends that he was sick and tired of trying to fish spots that the 'Youalls' had already fished out. He was taking a few days of overtime compensation to go way down to the East End to look for some new fishing holes. That's where the constable's headed, I guess."

"When did Tyndal leave?"

"Early Tuesday morning apparently. The constable thought that was pretty suspicious, but hey, I have to get to the clinic, see you all."

After Doc Williston had gone Two Bob ordered a refill for himself and for Phineas McQuorquedale, and sat staring glumly at the coffee stains on the old marble counter.

"I think one would be quite safe in guessing that you are worried about your new constable."

"Oh I am, I am. McQuockle, I'm the first guy to admit Tyndal has got a bit of a jealous streak in him and maybe shoots his mouth off a bit more than he should, but murder just don't seem..."

"I should mention to you, I guess, that I put all the knots in the town hall vault for safe keeping in case they are needed as evidence at some future date."

"Knots?"

"Yes, I cut them from the body to preserve them and put

them in envelopes sealed and initialled by me."

"But knots? What knots?"

"I guess things have been happening so fast no one had really described the scene of the crime to you."

"No, I just assumed he was hangin' from a rope or something from what the chief said."

"Well, he was hanging alright but in a way most bizarre. You know the steam pipes that run along the ceilings of the rooms in the hotel? "

"Yes sure, they feed the radiators on the floor above"

"Well, he had his two arms tied to that pipe, wide apart, and one ankle tied to the bottom of the steam radiator on the floor, suspended so that only the tip of the toes of that one foot touched the floor."

"What about his other foot?"

"Well that's the really unsettling thing. His leg was pulled up behind his back, one end of a length of rope tied around his neck with a slipknot, then his ankle tied to that rope with another slip knot. When he could no longer hold that exaggerated position the weight of his own leg strangled him."

"And the constable wanted you to save all these knots?"

"The knots used weren't just any old knots. There was a different knot at each wrist and on the ankle tied to the radiator. A completely different kind of knot tied to the ankle pulled up behind his back and the slip knot, according to the fire chief was a special knot called a Carter's knot, one that will slide along a rope one way, but will never go back."

"Good lord, and what did the constable make of all this?"

"Well, I don't think he has really looked at all that yet; oh yes, and the long end of the slip knot, that was trailed across the floor sort of pointing toward the door had a strange ball-shaped knot at the end of it."

"But now he's gone off after Tyndal as his main suspect?"

"Yes, and from what I am told, he likely won't get back much before tomorrow afternoon, even if he does have good luck finding Mr. Pockenbury among all those bays and islands at the East End."

"McQuockle, we got us a big problem here."

"You think the constable is about to do something that he will regret?"

"Somethin' we all might regret. Damn, just when we got

us the makings of a good town cop! But, well, you remember that time, summer before last, when Paddy Sheehan got so mad at Tyndal he refused for a time to look after his boat any more?"

"Yes, I remember, but what…"

"Well, think about those fancy knots, McQuockle, because the reason Paddy got so fed up was that Tyndal can't tie knots worth a damn, not even good enough to keep his boat from getting loose every time it got a little windy. Oh lord!"

"Well, it seems to me, Robert, that we have a day and a half, two days at the most to find out who the real murderer is, and have that information ready to hand to the constable when he returns with Mr. Pockenbury. Before he can do anything that might jeopardize his career as this town's constable."

"The trouble is, McQuockle, I can't hardly bring myself to the job because there ain't a soul in this town that I would want to see hang for the removal of that shyster."

"True, and laudable, but consider that Tyndal might well hang for it even though he must be innocent."

"Oh lordy lord! Well, I guess we got us a job, but I'm darned if I know really how to go at it. Like I said before we don't get any murders here… But hey, I seem to recall it was Chicago you came from. You must have seen your fair share of murders?"

"Certainly a good many of our clients at Lount Blackhurst and Maypenny came to us sooner than they had planned to, but usually assisted by Mr. Thompson's new gun rather than an elaborate rope trick."

"I hate this, McQuockle, somebody in this town is never goin' to vote for me again and likely none of his relatives neither."

"Well, it's the price of assuming the mantle of leadership, Robert. Now then, suppose we make a list of those who might have had a good enough reason to do away with Mr. Wilbur. Then we will endeavour to eliminate them one by one until we have the murderer or at least a very short list."

"Well, if that's the way to go at it, well… hmmm, let me see. Last year Shaky Stefanovich hired Pilchard to evaluate some claims he had been holding for years down by Rocky Narrows. Pilchard told him they were worthless and when

Shaky dropped them Pilchard staked them up for himself the very next day and sold them to the mine."

"An excellent...."

"But Shaky's got the sleeping sickness so bad he can't tie his own necktie for shaking let alone a bunch of fancy knots on a guy who certainly wouldn't have been making it easy for him."

"Let's just make our list and then work on the elimination process. Who else?"

"Well, old Good Rock might make the list. I don't know if he knew Pilchard personally, but he sure hates mining promoters in general. There was some talk that the reason he's so strange now is because of a terrible experience to do with some promoter down around Pickle Lake, where he came from."

" Is he the one who just sits in the beer parlor with that large sample of good ore in front of him until some curious soul buys him a beer to find out where it came from?"

"That's him, chunk of high-grade gold ore so big he can't even put it in his pocket. Has to carry it around in a leather bag. Grew that big beard after he came here about four years ago. Never talks to anyone, just comes into the Corona, takes that big chunk of high-grade out of that leather bag and sets it on the table and waits for a sucker. Been drinkin' beer off'n that chunk of rock since day one."

"And they fall for it?"

"McQuockle, that chunk of ore has more gold in it than Fort Knox. Nobody knows where Good Rock got it from, but whoever does manage to get that old bird to talk has found himself maybe the richest gold play ever."

"Should we put this Mr. Good Rock on the list?"

"Might as well, anybody hates promoters like he does has got to be considered even if only to eliminate him. Babbling old fool doesn't know who he is himself half the time let alone murder anyone, specially as fancy a job as this one."

"Excellent, and who else?"

"Well, Pilchard was chasin' Hughie the Movies' wife for a while. Rumour had it that he was catching up to her from time to time, but Hughie has got sort of resigned to that over the years."

"Nevertheless we'll put him on the list. Think hard now, it

is just the one that barely seems likely at this point that might be our man."

Moishe Fineberg had come down the counter wiping slowly and listening closely. When he got to Two Bob and McQuorquedale he made no pretence of not listening and in fact joined right in. "Two Bob, you remember that dust up last summer when Angus McNeil went after this Wilbur guy right in front of Osprey's Grocery?"

"Was that the time that he found out that Wilbur was tryin' to convince Mrs. McNeil that he would finance her ballet dance class just out of his love of the art?"

"Yep, well, old McNeil found out that ballet wasn't all this Wilbur was interested in."

"That man has got more folks hatin' his guts than you could imagine."

"I only mention it because of what my wife told me about what they found when they got to the murder scene this morning."

"You mean all the rope and stuff?" It was no use pretending about the evidence everyone in town knew all about anyway.

"Well sort of. More like what the rope was doin'. You think about how he was, Two Bob, just think about it. Never dawned on me either till my wife pointed it out. She has some experience with the arts, that one. No, you got to look past the ropes and stuff and get the big picture. That man was standing in a perfect ballet pose, arms up, balanced on the points of his toes with the other leg up behind him."

"Lordy, lord! Never rains but it pours. What do you think McQuokle?"

"Near the top of the list, I would suppose."

"How many more guys out there might have had a good reason to nail this guy anyway?" Two Bob thought for a bit. "Or woman."

"Oh yes, 'the woman scorned'... Was there anyone who thought that Mr. Pilchard's advances were serious in anyway?"

"Well, Morty Ferguson had to lean on him pretty heavy last fall when his daughter began to think Pilchard was her ticket to the big city. When he got the message and dumped her she was pretty cut up about it, but..."

"Never mind the 'buts' just yet. Remember, we agreed not to exclude any reasonable suspect until we found some evidence to exonerate them."

"McQuockle, we got half the damn town on our list already, it seems to me, and we ain't eliminated any strangers who might be stayin' in one of the hotels or anyone who might have left on the train Tuesday mornin'.'"

"I suppose we should try to find out who might have been on the train."

"Well, Staples Dibson is your man for that. Never misses a train. I'm goin' back to the town hall to make a few phone calls."

"I have to go right past the *Daily Staple* office anyway, I'll stop in and see what Dibson can tell us."

"You know McQuockle, there are some things about all this that don't seem to make a lot of sense to me. Like, you said that the slip knot around his neck was done in such a way that his leg sagging down would pull the noose tight around his own neck?"

"So it seemed when one examined the arrangement of the ropes."

"Well then, at some point the rope must have been loose, or sort of loose until he just couldn't hold that leg up anymore. So, for a time at least, he could still get some air into him. Why didn't he holler out? No matter how dumb he would have looked to anyone he got to come to help him, it would have seemed better than having his own foot strangle him."

"Maybe he did and nobody heard him."

"Nah, the walls in that old hotel are so thin that when Maizie Montgomery got pregnant there last spring, travelling salesmen three rooms away knew about it before she did."

"Ahem, well, yes, I see. Then that must mean that he didn't, or couldn't, raise a cry for help."

"And there's gotta be a reason."

"I think, Robert, that there is a reason for everything here. Whoever did this terrible thing went to a lot of trouble. That ballet pose, the complex knots, that long bit of rope with the knob braided into the end laid out along the floor, it almost seems as though we are meant to find out who did this."

"I see... You figure whoever did this wasn't just having fun with old Pilchard but was leavin' us a message. One we might have to work on a bit to figure out?"

"Exactly."

"Well, damned if I know what the message is, or could be."

"At least part of the message may be in the knots themselves. Do you know anyone who is a real expert on knots? Knots have names as I recall from my distant youth, maybe the names might tell us something."

"Well, then, old Baldy McMellon is your man. Been a Boy Scout leader for about a hundred years or so. I would guess he maybe even invented some of those knots."

"Perhaps he would come down to the town hall and look at the knots and offer an opinion."

"I'll call him right away, but we do have one problem there."

Phineas McQuorquedale looked down his long nose at Two Bob and waited.

"You yourself sealed all the knots up in envelopes and initialled the flaps."

"They were my envelopes and my initials. There could be more envelopes and more signatures if some accident befell those."

"You ain't half bad, McQuockle, we're gonna get along. See you at the town hall, lets say right after lunch."

Back at the town hall Two Bob brought Laura Langmuir up to date on what they were trying to do, on the theory that she could be more help if she was in on the process. That idea was not long in proving itself. He had started by describing his attempt to talk to Angus McNeil. "And then, Mr. McNeil apparently heard that Wilbur was back in town and went down to the Corona on Monday night and threatened him with no end of mayhem if he wasn't gone out of town the next morning."

"I do hope he has an excuse or, what do you call it, an alibi?"

"He might have. But you know McNeil. He would sooner fight than eat, and far sooner fight than submit to anyone poking his nose into his business. When I went to see him about where he might have been Tuesday mornin' I nearly ended up in a fight myself. Told me he wasn't in the habit of explainin' himself and wasn't about to start now, but not in such nice words."

"Do you think he did it?"

"Right now he is the most likely looking suspect but somehow I don't think so. He might have beaten him to death or stomped his lights out on the beer parlor floor, but I don't think he's your man for all that fancy knot tyin' and stuff."

"But if he is too proud to...."

"Well... somewhere, somebody, will have seen him. I checked with the mine. He worked the graveyard shift all right, got off about seven thirty, a bit early, but the day shift guys usually come in a bit early. No one likes graveyard. But where he was in the early morning of Tuesday is what matters, and he won't say."

"Poor man, and Mrs. McNeil expecting in a few weeks."

"What was that?"

"Mrs. McNeil, she is expecting their fourth child in a few weeks."

Without another word Two Bob went into his office and closed the door. He was just picking up the phone when he thought better of it. He opened the door again so he could keep Laura in view, her and the extension phone, which was on her desk.

"Hello, Operator, would you get me 237, please."

Two Bob knew that the town's central phone operator, Hortense Gabrielle, listened in on most conversations if she thought they might be even the least bit interesting. Everyone, in fact, knew this but no one had ever known her to divulge a word of what she heard. It was put down to the price of having a conscientious phone operator, one who sometimes could intervene in emergencies simply because she did know most of what was going on and where most everyone could be found at any given time. That Two Bob was asking for the number of Big Marie who ran the largest, and, far and away the fanciest of the houses of ill repute on North Avenue would be sure to catch her attention. The one-word conversation that followed left Hortense little the wiser.

"Hello?"

"Pray."

"Ok, bye."

Shortly after winning his first election, Two Bob had become aware that certain prominent persons in the town were extracting a goodly share of the take from the prostitutes on North Avenue. None of this money was ending up in the town coffers, and there was no questioning the fact that the industrious ladies on the hill conducted one of the biggest business enterprises in town next to the mine itself. Two Bob knew that Big Marie sometimes went to church, never on Sunday when her presence might cause raised eyebrows, but usually in the morning, midweek.

Since he couldn't be seen going to her place of business and as she was most reluctant to be seen at his (located next door to the RCMP office as it was), Two Bob had just followed her into the church one day and sat down beside her. It was at that meeting and a few more like it that a system of unofficial town business taxes was worked out. Anonymous gifts to the Boy Scouts, to the Ladies' Temperance League, to the Salvation Army and many more. All these groups were extremely grateful to their mysterious benefactor, but no one had any idea who it could be. Two Bob, for his part, had stopped the unofficial extortion with a few delicate hints to the parties involved. Every one except those three or four gentlemen were happy with this arrangement which, while not directly benefiting the municipal budget, went a long way toward making the machinery of the town hum along in fine style.

Twenty minutes after hanging up the phone, Two Bob entered the dimly-lit church and sat down next to a well-dressed lady who could have just stepped out of a meeting of the Ladies' Book and Literary Study Group.

"How are you, Marie?"

"Just fine, Robert, at least I was till you called. Who needs a donation now?"

"Nobody, but I need some help."

"I only dispense one kind of help, Robert, and you have been turning that down ever since I've known you."

"Gotta keep up appearances long as I'm mayor and all, Marie, but this is a different kind of help."

"You aren't getting any closer to stating your case, Robert, in fact you're babbling a bit as you sometimes do..."

"Well, the fact is... you know that murder... they found him on Tuesday mornin', ah, hangin' you know?"

"I heard, a fancy hanging and a useful murder, by any standard. Gets my vote whoever it was. If you're about to ask me if I know who did it, don't ask, but anyway I don't know."

"It's not that."

"For Heaven's sake, Robert, get at it. There are those who might believe I pray now and then but not many who might believe I want to spend the entire morning in here."

"You know Angus McNeil?"

"Don't tell me he's involved in this."

"Well, just at this moment he is one of the prime suspects. He threatened this Wilbur guy the night before, got off graveyard early and can't or won't account for his whereabouts on Tuesday mornin' which is when the Doc thinks the deed was done."

"You know I never talk about my customers, Robert. I am surprised you would ask me."

"Well you know Angus. He's so damned stiff necked, the old peckerwood would sooner hang than admit he's been up to your place. Ain't nobody who don't believe a man whose wife is out of commission has got to get his ashes hauled once in a while. I would lay a good-sized bet that's where he was Tuesday mornin'... up at your place, I mean, although like I said, that stubborn redheaded porridge gobbler won't say a word."

"Well, Robert, I still can't tell you where he was or where he wasn't. Its not only a matter of professional ethics, but my business would go to zilch in a day if my customers thought their pillow talk was going to go around town. No, I can't help you, but you and I have always been good friends, and there isn't a girl up there who doesn't appreciate how smooth things run in this town."

Big Marie drummed her fingers on the back of the pew ahead for a bit and then said, "Robert, I have never known you for a gambling man but if, like you just said, you are willing to bet Angus McNeil was at my place and not out murdering someone, then I would go and get as many takers for that bet as you can find."

"Well, Marie, I can't thank you 'cause, like you say, you couldn't help me none for professional reasons. But I do wish you a good day, Marie, and if you ever need me, call."

Coming out of the church into the bright morning sun, it occurred to Two Bob that he had promised himself a haircut this very day and he set off down the block for Barney's Barbershop.

Barney's shop was a narrow building squeezed in between the Stag Billiards and Hoskin's Fine Furniture. Two Bob had often wondered how such a small lot came to be set out on Main Street where all the business lots were about the same size. Once he had looked Barney's location up on the town's master plan map but, where Barney's shop was, the plan called for a lane running through to Church Street. This seemed to be one of those occasions when no political gain was to be had for solving a mystery and Two Bob had wisely rolled the plan back up and returned it to the town engineer's office.

Out in front of his shop Barney had a barber pole, a spiral of red and white stripes on a cylinder inside a glass casing. There was a spring wound motor in the bottom of the mounting and, morning and noon, Barney would take his big brass key and wind up the spring so that the cylinder revolved slowly around, giving the spirals a climbing effect. Barney was very proud of his sign, which was about a foot longer than that of our other barber's.

"Mornin' Barney."

"Mornin' Mr. Mayor."

"Got time to shorten this mop up a bit this mornin'? "

"Well, it's either that or you'll be dingin' me for a contribution toward buyin' you a violin, hee hee...be through here with this fine young man in just a sec'."

Barney dusted invisible hair off his young customer's jacket and let the chair sink down to its normal level with a loud hydraulic whoosh. Gravely, the boy offered payment and Barney, just as gravely, made change and thanked his young customer for the proffered nickel tip which he put in the Prince Albert tin on the shelf behind his chair. Barney and Two Bob watched as the boy walked out into the morning sun, his ears, unaccustomed to being uncovered, shining like white banners on each side of his head.

"That's Pearson's boy, Edwin."

"Gonna be a good lad. I see he's a big tipper like his old man."

"Well, a nickel might not seem like a big tip, but it's a big chunk of change for him and it would be no kindness to turn it down. Boys that age need all the confidence they can scrape up."

Two Bob settled into the chair. Barney loosened Two Bob's

tie, undid his collar and tucked a long piece of paper around his neck before placing a clean cloth over his shoulders.

"Just need a trim I think, Barney, Gettin' a bit shabby."

"Just over the ears like always?"

Barney always asked how you wanted your hair cut, but didn't always feel obliged to follow your directions if he had a better idea as to what sort of hair cut would suit you.

"Just back it all up about three weeks, Barney."

"I hear the new Constable's gone off down the lake lookin' for Tyndal Pockenbury."

"Needs him to help with his investigation, I guess." Two Bob replied in his best diplomatic voice. But the subtlety was lost on Barney. Normally he wouldn't have been so direct, a full haircut could take a bit of time but with only a trim to do he needed to get right down to business.

"Thinks he strung that shyster up, is what I heard."

"Well, he didn't say anything to me before he left, so I guess..."

"Ain't many as think it could'a been old Tyndal there, not his style."

"Well, nobody said he was a suspect right out, Barney. Might be others more likely from what I hear. This fellow didn't seem to have too many friends."

"But lots of folks who hated his guts... clip... clip... it was him sold the main street guys all that worthless East Lake Winnipeg Railway stock... clip... clip."

"Seems a small thing to murder a man about."

"Old George had to take his wife's... clip... clip... washing machine money when Otto The Bank called for settlement."

"Well, but still, you would think somebody had to a been hurt a lot deeper than that to actually go out and kill someone... and when you think of how he did it..." Two Bob couldn't repress a shudder.

"Had to be pretty strong...clip...clip...or else know something about ropes and pulleys and stuff... clip...clip... That was no small guy... clip... could'na been easy to dangle him from that pipe like that, unless he was a whole lot more co-operative than you might expect him to have been. Little extra off the back here for the summer?"...clip... clip.

"Yeh, I guess, you're the barber... but what gets me is why the guy never called out and, from what the fire chief tells me, there wasn't even any sign of a struggle."

"Could'a been knocked out somehow, smack on the side of the nog... clip... clip... Mickey Finn."

"No sign of that from what I understand, but the Doc sent some samples to Winnipeg. Should have heard by now, in fact, guess I oughta phone him."

"Well, I doubt he's gonna tell you much before the new copper gets back. Doc's down to The Pas and don't come back till tomorrow."

"Lordy lord, it's important we get to the bottom of this thing, Barney, and quick."

"Like before the new guy makes an ass of hisself hauling in old Tyndal there... clip... clip."

"Barney, there ain't much goes on in this town you don't seem to know about."

"Nope, and I know Angus ain't your man either...clip...clip...was up at Big Marie's all mornin'.'"

"He tell you that?"

"Nope. Ole Barstead seen him there when he was collectin' with the honey wagon."

"Ole was in here for a haircut?"

"Nope, he stinks too bad. Couldn't have him in the chair here, smell wouldn't never come out, but I go to his place now and then before the shop opens."

"You cut his hair at his shack up on the hill there?"

"Hey, Two Bob, he works for you, remember, and he's a part of the community here... clip... clip...we just sort of worked it out that way."

"Well, I had kind of ruled out Angus anyway."

"Who's your main suspect now, Two Bob?"

"Well to tell you the truth, Barney, there ain't any real good suspects. We seem to be ruling out almost everyone anyone's come up with. You got any ideas like?"

"Well, it could'a been a complete stranger, Two Bob, somebody just got on the train the next mornin' and took off, like...maybe somebody who was stayin' in the hotel,...clip...clip somebody who knew him from someplace else, more'n likely."

"Should go up and talk to the night clerk at the hotel. I guess. He might'a seen someone acting strange. McQuockle is talkin' to Staples Dibson about who might'a left town that mornin'."

"Speakin' of strange, you ain't never... clip... clip... gonna guess who I had in this chair Monday mornin'."

"If I ain't never gonna guess, Barney, you might just as well get to tellin' me."

"Well, you know old Irwin Winfield, I s'pose. Guy they call Good Rock."

"Sure, who don't know old Good Rock, didn't know his real name was Irwin Winfield though, but what'd he want with a haircut? Old fart's got a beard down to his belly button."

"Not any more, he ain't. Came in here and got hisself a full haircut and shaved off the whole damn beard. Gave me a dollar extra for all the cuttin', which I damn well earned, too. I don't think he ever washed that tangle since it grew."

"Good Rock shaved off his beard?"

"Yep, and got a haircut to boot. Actually don't look too bad skinned like that, kind of pasty and pale, but not too bad."

"He say what he was doin' it for?"

"Nope, you know he never talks, just grunted and pointed and put that leather bag with his big ore sample right on the ledge there where he could keep an eye on it."

"Well, there's no way that little runt could have hoisted that guy up into the air like that, but I wonder what the hell he's up to now."

"Nutty as a fruit cake, Two Bob. You don't need to look for reasons for a guy like that doin' somethin'. He just goes ahead and does it, like the time that ol' Missus McNab painted the whole front of her house red, even the window glass."

"Yeah, I guess so... easy on the Bay Rum Barney, I don't want to smell too good."

Barney continued sloshing on the Bay Rum as if he hadn't heard a thing.

"You ain't told me who your best suspect is yet, Barney."

"Nope I ain't, Two Bob, and that's because I got the same problem as you. I finger somebody local and I lose a customer and likely all his friends and relatives."

"Said that very thing to McQuockle who pointed out it might be worse if the wrong guy gets his neck stretched."

"Well, you might want to talk to Elmer Balcan at the hotel. He's a big guy and he lives right there, on the third floor."

"Well, bein' big and livin' in the hotel don't really say much, Barney."

"I heard he bought so many shares of the East Lake

Winnipeg Railway that he had to sell that boarding house he was building on Callinan Lane to settle with the bank."

"Is 'at so now? Well, maybe I'll just go down and have a talk to him."

"I'd do that careful, Two Bob, so I would. He's got a short fuse, that one."

"Thanks, Barney. Don't fancy the idea much myself but bein' the mayor got its responsibilities too, I guess."

"There you go, Two Bob, last you a while if you come in for a neck trim in a week or so."

The little chimes on the barber shop door jangled behind him as Two Bob stepped out onto the sidewalk. Two Bob was proud of that sidewalk. The mine had donated truckloads of finely crushed rock and a small roller to tamp it down. Not like your city sidewalks, all cement with little lines cut in them, but a whole lot better than the mud of Main Street. Two Bob was looking forward to the day when he could work things out to have the whole street paved. With approval, he noted the neat store windows he passed as he headed for the Corona Hotel. Frank Schindlemacher's wife had been an established artist before following him up north. Now she practised her magic on the window of his haberdashery. There was always some sort of artistic arrangement in it. Today, a couple dozen neckties were draped over some willow branches that had been peeled and painted white. A little papier-mache squirrel had an end of one of the ties in his mouth and seemed bent on hauling it underneath a display of Dak shoes. The necktie display itself didn't do much for Two Bob, but he did approve of any attempt to give his town a little class. Two Bob tipped his hat to the Widow Collins, Curly Martin's sister. She and Mabel Norton were admiring a display of summer frocks in the window of the Ladies' Style Shop.

The lobby of the hotel was dark and smelled of cleaning compounds and smoke. A sad and dejected looking moose poked his head through the wall opposite the entrance and, next to him, a dusty glass case contained what was purported to be the ear of a horse that had been in the Boer War. Along one side of the lobby ran a long counter with a pile of newspapers on one end of it and an old brass push bell for summoning the clerk. All the woodwork was dark with layers and layers of varnished-over dirt.

Two Bob tapped the bell with one finger and waited for

Foster Plummindale to come out of the back room.

"Mornin', Foster."

"Mornin' Two Bob. You still lookin' into the business on the second floor? If you want into the room, the constable said nobody wasn't supposed to go in there."

Going into the room wasn't really Two Bob's primary purpose in coming down to the hotel. What he wanted was to talk to Elmer Balcan but a mayor has to keep up appearances, so he waited a bit, staring stiffly at the desk clerk who caved in at about the split second Two Bob figured he would.

"Guess, properly speakin', a mayor ain't just anybody anyway, but don't, for God's sake, touch nothin'. That new constable would jail his own mother if she messed with the evidence."

"Well, Foster, I didn't really come to see the room. Been in most of the rooms in your fine hotel here at one time or another and they're mostly all the same as I remember. What I really came down about was to see if Elmer Balcan might have noticed anything unusual that mornin', seein' as how he lives here permanent and all."

"You think Elmer murdered that shyster?"

"No need to speak ill of the dead, Foster, and I never said Elmer was a suspect. I just want to talk to him. See if he can help out a bit maybe."

"Well, you can wake him up if you want to. I sure ain't brave enough. He's on graveyard so he woulda been in the hotel about the time the murder took place, I guess. Say, Two Bob, you got any idea how I'm gonna go about gettin' paid for that room now?"

"Well, I s'pose there'll be some sort of settlement of the estate if he's got one, but I wouldn't hold my breath, Foster."

"I don't suppose the Town feels any responsibility? I got a business to run here."

"Well, you could try that on George Burton down at the town hall but, like I said, I would go right on breathin' while I waited. What room is Elmer in?"

"Room 14 on the third floor, second one on the right from the top of the stairs. I'd kind of test him out a bit after you wake him up. He might be okay, but guys on graveyard don't much like gettin' woke up. They have a tough enough time gettin' any decent sleep as it is."

"Well, you got as much of a stake in getting this thing solved as the rest of us, Foster, but anyway, if he throws me down the stairs, try and catch me as I land."

"Hee hee, Two Bob, I try to catch you and I'll end up drove into the floor like a tent peg... Hee hee."

Two Bob was more sensitive about his ever expanding girth than he liked to admit and gave Foster his best cold stare as he started up the stairs.

Room 14 wasn't hard to find and knocking didn't seem necessary as the door was propped open with an old mucking boot in a hopeful attempt to let a little air circulate.

Two Bob tried not to breathe too deep as he stuck his head into the room. It didn't seem as though a lot of air had been changed in that room since the place was built, in spite of the mucking boot, and what was there had been used pretty bad. Elmer Balcan was sitting with his elbows on a scarred wooden table, his head in his hands. There was a quart sealer of murky-looking potato champagne in front of him. Well, not a whole quart, about half of it was gone and, from the looks of things the rest wasn't going to last all that long either.

"Elmer, it's Two Bob. I was wonderin' if you might have time to talk for a bit?"

"If i's about 'at murder, I don' know damn al 'bout it and I don' wanna know neither. Good riddansh to bad rubbers you ask me, if that won't get me hung for sayin' so."

"Well, if you got a minute or two to spare...."

There is an expression in the North that describes a man who has drunk more than he really needs to but hasn't found anyone to pick a fight with yet. It fit Elmer like fresh washed longjohns. He looked as "owly-eyed" as ever any one could have. Two Bob decided against sitting right at the table and took a handy chair nearer the door.

"Nobody's accusin' you of anything, Elmer, but it did occur to me that living right here in the hotel and all, and you comin' off shift early in the mornin' when the thing was supposed to have happened, that you might have seen or heard somthin' that could help."

"Heard your new Conshtable's got it all figured out awready.Hee hee" Home brew of the variety that Elmer was swilling down tends to make a man's face go all limp and drooly so that the smile that he tried for at this sally was pretty horrible to behold. Two Bob took the occasion of Elmer's refilling his glass to hitch his chair an inch or two closer to the door.

"Well, I wouldn't go so far as to say that, Elmer, no I wouldn't go that far. I think maybe he's likely got his own reasons for wanting old Tyndal's help and advice with his investigation. There's lots to this police business us ordinary folk don't understand."

"Think more'n likely he's gone off half-cocked an' y're out to save 's ass, Two Bob."

"Ah, well, anyway Elmer, you didn't by any chance see or hear anything out of the ordinary on Tuesday mornin' did you?"

"Two Bob, you wannna tell me why y're messin' roun' with thish when y'got a perfectly good Conshtable can go catch whoever dangled 'is rat 'thout you ever havin' to dirty y'r own mitts ?"

Two Bob sighed, thought a bit and sat up a little straighter. "Well, Elmer, we ain't never been all that close, never had no reason to be, but I see you as a citizen of this community like everyone else, community responsibilities and all that. And well, damn it, it does look like there's just an outside chance our new Constable could go and get the wrong guy hung the way he's goin'.... and I don't ever want to hear that from nobody else neither, Elmer."

Elmer focused his runny eyes on Two Bob as best he could and leaned forward, an act which caused Two Bob to involuntarily jig his chair another inch closer to the door.

"Two Bulb, I been watchin' yuh...even voted fer yuh las' time...seen how you took the heat off'n the girls on the hill, I seen 'at and I seen how you got the mine to put up the fill for the new ball diamond oh yeh, I seen all 'at. You ain't half bad for a garlic snapper an I s'pose you got some consid'ble worries, sumpin like this, and breakin' in a new cop and all..."

"Well it.."

"An' I trus' you Two Bodge."

Two Bob moved his legs slowly under him ready to make a break for it. He had seen a lot of drunks and Elmer had just reached that fine stage where he would either burst into maudlin tears or fly into a murderous rage; the odds on either one were about the same. Two Bob sat tight.

Elmer lowered his head and Two Bob was surprised to see how thin his hair was on the top. "Came off shift early mornin', Tuesday. Got Mclean to come in early on day shif', an' I tell you this Two Balls, an' its just you an' me see, but I was plannin' to go up to that room and beat the livin' shit out of that four flusher."

Two Bob wisely sat silent.

"I know where Myrna keeps her master key for the rooms, but there's 'is pasty faced old fart on a stairs. Soooo I jus goes down to Wong's, gets a coffee and then comes back maybe twen'y minutes, maybe half a hour. I got the key see an' I wen' up. Two Bobs ,you can't even think how much I was lookin' forward to draggin' 'at son m a bitch out a bed and kickin' his sorry ass all over 'at room."

Two Bob thought it might be safe to nod.

"There was one a 'em 'Disturbin' signs on a door, but I jus' stuck the key in and turned the knob. Two Bosh, I ain't never gonna get over see'in at face, all blowed, an 'is tongue hanging out like that, and him dancing on one foot." Elmer paused and took a swig right from the jar. "If I hadn' a gone for coffee, he might be shtill 'live, time I got back there, though, well, it didn't take no sawbones to make out he's long gone."

This time Two Bob couldn't think of any appropriate or safe response so he just sat still.

"I jus' backs out of that room and shuts the door. I put Myrna's key back an' comes up here an I ain't had a moment since when 'at purple face ain't been starin' at me and askin' me why I din't come straight up instead of goin' to Wong's fer coffee."

Elmer took a deep gulp from the jar and sat staring at the floor, at something only he could see.

Two Bob took the opportunity to move to the doorway.

"Elmer, you been a lot of help, and I don't know as I would blame myself if I was you. Doc Williston said that the knot around his neck was so dug in he couldn't hardly get it loose hisself. I expect he was dead long before you got there, so it ain't likely you could have done much. But, did you get much of a look at that pasty-faced old guy you mentioned?"

"At first I thought maybe... but nah, just a old pasty-faced guy. Had some kind of a club bag in his hand, so he was likely headin' for the mornin' train. Don't recall ever seein' him around the hotel but that don't mean much. There's been a lot of comin' and goin' lately."

"Well, thanks, Elmer." Two Bob had most of himself out the door now and felt a bit better about the future, especially his own. "You been a big help and I'll try to keep you up on what ever else we turn up if you want. It's sumthin' just narrowin' down the time and all."

"All I want is not to see that ugly purple face every time I shut my eyes." Two Bob closed the door as far as the boot allowed and wasted no time getting back down to the lobby.

"Foster, you have an old guy, sort of pasty-faced, check out of the hotel on Tuesday mornin'?"

"Nope, nobody at all checked out on Tuesday, except maybe ol' Pilchard, hee hee."

Two Bob was glad to get out into the fresh air of the street. When he got back to the town hall he was just in time to meet Baldy McMellon and Phineas McQuorquedale coming out of the vault, with a very flustered Laura Langmuir hovering close by, not sure at all about this unusual proceeding. "Afternoon Baldy, why don't you and McQuockle come into my office here, where we can talk private like."

Two Bob settled down behind his big desk. Maybe the one thing that kept him on in the job of mayor was that big desk. The good feeling of rolling his big green leather-upholstered chair up behind it seemed to make up for all the trials and tribulations of the job, although today he wasn't so sure.

" You find Staples? McQuockle, I mean, about the train?"

" I did, Robert. He reports that a gentleman he calls Good Rock, who I assume is the same one you mentioned this morning, left on the morning train, almost the only one who got on, in fact. He informed Mr. Dibson that he was tired of the north and planned to go down to South America to prospect for gold."

McQuorquedale looked down his long nose at a house fly that had made a landing on the edge of Two Bob's desk. "Said he had heard there was a big, I think he used the word 'placer', find down there and, in any case, he was tired of the cold."

"From what Barney tells me, he wouldn't have been easy to recognise, what with getting his beard shaved off and all."

"Mr. Dibson did, in fact, mention just that. He said that when he first saw this pasty faced old guy getting onto the train he didn't at first recognise him and said, I think I have this right... 'Good Rock, is that you ?' and Mr. Good Rock laughed and said, 'It's me alright Staples, got my good rock right with me' and he pulled it out of his pocket and showed it to him."

"You mean out of that leather bag he carries it in I guess. That chunk of high grade would never fit in a pocket."

"No, Mr. Staples was quite clear about that, he did say 'pocket' and even remarked that Mr. Good Rock's sample must have somehow become a good deal smaller if he could fit it in his pocket."

Two Bob watched the fly for a while, certain that there was something important in Phineas McQuorquedale's report, something that should have stuck out like a sore thumb. He just couldn't get on it though and decided to let it go for a bit.

"You two have been looking at the knots, I guess?"

"Yes, there were eight of them altogether, nine if you count the one on the end of the rope. There were three pieces of rope actually: one that tied his left hand to the pipe above his head, one that tied his right hand to that same pipe and then went on down to tie his right ankle to the bottom of the steam radiator." McQuorquedale studied his long bony fingers as he spoke, almost as if reading from a list he found on the ends of them. "And one piece that passed around the victim's throat and was tied to his left ankle. I should mention for clarity that it was the end of that rope that was trailed out across the room toward the door that had a round sort of decorative knot at the end of it."

"Can you make anything of all this, Baldy?"

"Well, I can identify the knots for you and, let me tell you, some of them are not very common. As to what it all means though..."

"Why don't you just start and we'll maybe make some sense of it as you go along; these knots all have names, I guess."

"Yes, and each one has a specific purpose. Perhaps the one useful thing I can tell you is that the choice of knots doesn't make any sense. Except for the slip knot, one good hitch could have done the whole job."

"Well, anyways..."

"Yes, well, the two that fastened the rope to the pipe overhead are called 'bends'. One of them is the 'Fisherman's Bend', common enough. The other one, though, is called the 'Top Sail Sheet Bend', not nearly so well known. The one that fastened the rope from his right ankle to the bottom of the steam radiator is called a 'Stunsail Halyard Bend'. It's one of the ones that appears in the tests for Scouting's Advanced Knotting Badge."

"There's a kind of a nautical sound to all these. You think that means anything Baldy? Our guy could be a sailor maybe?"

"I don't think so. The knot that was holding his left wrist is called a 'Kreutzklem' or 'Hedden' and is normally used to clamp onto a mountain climber's rope. The one that was on his right wrist is called a 'Rolling Hitch' and is used a lot by loggers for attaching logs to a drag rope. The one that was tied onto his right ankle is called a 'Bowline on a Bite', a slip knot that is easily untied once the tension is off it."

"I guess poor old Pilchard never got a chance to find that out."

"The knot tying his left ankle to the slip knot around his neck," Baldy plowed on as though determined not to lose even one chance to display his knowledge, "that one now, is a fancy one. That one is called a 'Sliding Sheet Bend'. Tricky to tie, it is used on tent guys and for tightening ropes where you need unbreakable holding strength. Incidentally, one of its properties is that it can be undone with a simple yank on the free end of the rope."

"The one around his neck? Was it something special too?"

"Well, it used to be used a lot but it's not well known now. It's called the 'Carter's Knot', it makes a noose that closes fairly easily, but it is very difficult to open when it is pulled tight as Doctor Williston discovered."

"You say that whadya call it, that 'Slider Sheet,' could'a been undone with a little yank on the short end of the rope?"

"Yes, but in this case the end wasn't so short. That was the long bit of rope that was stretched out along the floor toward the door."

"You said nine knots."

"Yes, well, the end of that piece of rope was done into a decorative ball called a 'Turk's Head'. It wasn't really part of the system of knots that was suspending the victim, but it could be considered part of a pretty impressive display of knot tying."

"We were thinking of meeting here again just after supper, Baldy, me, McQuockle here, and anybody else that seems to know something useful. Might help if we all compare notes about what we found and see if we get any bright ideas."

"About seven? Can do, although I might be a bit late. As you know, Erwin Winfield has decided to go to South America to get in on the gold rush there. Didn't even know he was gone until Loud Raight called me today. Erwin left his little shack up on the hill for the use of the Boy Scouts, free and clear. Don't know why Loud was restrained from telling me about it until today. I just got the key now and I 'm going to stop in and have a look at the place, likely need a good cleaning."

"You knew him then? Good Rock?"

"No, I knew of him though. He was a Scout Leader in Pickle Lake some time ago."

"So you don't make anything of those knots at all, eh, Baldy?"

"No, unless it was meant as a 'tangle'."

"Tangle?"

"Yes, in Scouting, one might often leave a sign on the ground, telling those coming behind where you have gone, what time, how many and so on. To make sure the sign was noticed, a 'tangle' might be set up...something to catch the eye like a small tree hung upside down or leafy branches on a pine, something that says 'there is a message here if you look'."

"A tangle. Whadya think of that, McQuockle?"

"I am becoming more confused by the minute but this whole bizarre scene does seem to be trying to tell us something."

"Yes, well, there is one thing really botherin' me still and that is why he never sang out. If that noose didn't tighten up until he couldn't hold that leg up anymore and let it drop and so strangled hisself, then he shoulda had lots of time to raise a racket and get some help."

"There must be an answer to that."

"Do you still have him in the cooler over at the Lucky Leaf Meat Market?"

"Yes, we can't bury him until the next of kin is notified

100

and even then we have to wait until Doc Williston gets back on the train so he can perform the autopsy."

"What if there was something wrong with his voice box, McQuockle? What if there was something stuck in his neck or something...would you be able to see that if you went and took a careful look?"

Phineas McQuorquedale sighed. It had been a long day and it looked to get even longer. In order to get into the cooler at the Lucky Leaf Meat Market, he would have to find one of the Dawson boys, provide them with some reasonable excuse and then get the key. "We have come this far, it doesn't seem that we can get in any deeper. Although if Doctor Williston ever were to learn that I had interfered with a corpse on which he was expected to do a forensic autopsy..." Phineas shivered at the thought, his long, grey self looking even stringier and greyer than usual.

"Ain't never gonna hear it from me, McQuockle, but it seems worth a look."

"Yes, yes it does. I will come back around seven when the others are here and tell you what, if anything, I have found."

Two Bob waited until he heard the outside door close and called Laura Langmuir into the office. "Laura would you be kind enough to get me connected up on the long distance phone to the Mining Recorder's Office in Pickle Lake. It's kind of urgent, you can tell them."

Not long after that, Two Bob was introducing himself to the Mining Recorder at Pickle Lake, and explaining something of the situation to him. If he inadvertently gave that good man the idea that he was doing something official as part of the investigation, Two Bob would certainly have denied the intention.

"So you knew this Erwin Winfield?"

"Yes, although most folks called him 'Good Rock'. He made a huge strike here about six years ago, richest damned ore you ever saw, free gold in pure white quartz. Samples looked like jewels."

"What became of the property?"

"Well, that's a long story. A syndicate was formed to develop the claims and somehow or another the Toronto financiers ended up owning the property and old Erwin was out in the cold."

"Well that ain't that uncommon."

"In Irwin's case it was worse. One of the mining promoters involved somehow convinced him that, if he could raise twenty thousand for his share of the first offer, he could buy his way back in and then turn around and sell some of his escrow stock to pay back the twenty thousand."

"Sounds like your gonna tell me more about this."

"Likely shouldn't, but I don't know of anyone who don't know all about it. He was arrested for embezzling the twenty thousand from the school district. Guess he thought he could put it back before anyone noticed. He got fired. Even the Boy Scouts, where he had been a Scout Master for years, thought they should kick him out."

"Must a tore him pretty bad, all that, and losing such a property to boot."

"Well, the Scouts thing really hurt. He had devoted most of his life to Scouting. But it only got worse. His wife left him and took the kids back down east."

"Was his wife by any chance a dancer or dance teacher, would you know?"

"That's a pretty strange question but I guess you investigators got your leads to follow. That might be a dead end though. She never did teach dancing far as I know, although she did teach some figure skating at the rink here."

"I guess I just got one more question: What was the name of that mining property he lost to the promoters?"

Two Bob nodded his head as he wrote the answer down on a slip of paper. He folded the paper carefully, put it in his pocket and headed down the street to the Golden Gate for his supper. He didn't particularly like eating at the Golden Gate but it was about the same as the only other choice, the Maple Leaf. Both were better than his own cooking. On his way to the cafe he met Svein Halverson puffing along the street still in his fish-house overalls.

"Two Bob, I was just comin' down to the town hall to see you. Got a message for you from the Constable."

"From the Constable?"

"Yep, had a bit of engine trouble. Them Scott Attwater outboards can be cantankerous now and then. They got it runnin' but they won't get in now until mornin'. They were going to overnight at Bigelow's cabin. The big lake was blowin' up pretty good when I came in."

"Then we won't see the Constable until about ten o'clock tomorrow?"

"Not unless he thumbs a ride with Arrow Air, you won't."

It seemed to Svein that Bob Bobdinsky wasn't as disappointed at this news, as he perhaps should have been.

Two Bob finished his meal, paid his bill and headed back for the town hall. At that time of year in the North, the sun stays up for a long, long time. Although the nature of the day changes somehow so that you know it isn't morning or midday, the light stays the same, as though the world's timer had somehow gone awry. By the time Two Bob got back to the town hall, Phineas McQuorquedale and Baldy McMellon were sitting on the railing of the front steps. With a little pang of guilt, Two Bob realized he had forgotten to make arrangements for Laura to let them in.

"Good evening, Robert."

"Evenin' McQuockle, Baldy. Sorry the door was locked, total forgot to tell Laura to leave a key for you. Too much on my mind, I guess."

"Nothing to worry about, Two Bob, beautiful evening even if the breeze is getting up a bit."

"Starting to roll on the big lake. Svein Halverson just told me that Ivar and the Constable have decided it's too late to make the crossing and will stay at Bigelow's over night."

"That should put them back on the dock here about ten I expect."

"About that Baldy. Shall we go up?"

The town hall always smelled of the oil used to treat the fir floors, that and the polish that the janitor applied religiously to all the railings and tables in the council chambers. The late afternoon sun had an odd, worn quality to it, coming in the windows at a low angle, tiny dust motes dancing in the sharp-edged beams.

The three men made themselves comfortable around the Mayor's desk.

Two Bob read from a note Laura had left under the bronze paperweight: "Says here that the Fire Chief can't come. They're havin' trouble with muskeg fires out along the pipeline again."

Two Bob looked at Phineas and Baldy, both sitting on the edge of their chairs. He was already to spring his news about Irwin Winfield, but the two of them looked so anxious to talk that he decided to wait.

"Baldy did you have a look at the shack that...?"

Before Two Bob could even finish Baldy McMellon took a small package out of his pocket. "Found this right in the middle of the kitchen table. It's addressed to you."

It was wrapped in brown waxy looking paper, like the kind you get at the butchers. The heavy little parcel was bound with a bit of store string tied in an elaborate bow. On the long side of the wrapping was scrawled in lead pencil, "For Mayor R. Bobdinsky."

Two Bob unwrapped the parcel to disclose a worn leather bag about eight inches long. There was something hard and heavy inside the bag and when Two Bob tipped it up a tiny two-barrelled Derringer pistol slid out onto the table with a thump. The Derringer was a very small nickel-plated gun about three inches long with a handle curved to fit in the palm of the hand. The gun had two barrels, one above the other and fired only two shots, but at the range a derringer was usually called into play, about five feet or so, the terrible damage that two .45 calibre slugs could do did not take a whole of imagining.

"That," said Phineas," might explain how the deceased was persuaded to cooperate in his own demise."

"And this, if I ain't mistaken, is the bag old Good Rock carried his sample around in all those years, but I wonder why he left it behind?"

"Maybe he doesn't have the sample any more." Phineas seemed to be leading up to something.

"Nope, he still has it. Remember, Staples Dibson said he took it out of his pocket and...Good lord! I just realized what's been botherin' me all this time! I should have twigged right away that that sample must have somehow got a lot smaller for him to be able to get it into his pocket. It barely fit in this bag before."

"I may be able to explain that." Phineas took an envelope from his pocket and, using a pair of tweezers he removed from a small leather case, carefully picked a jagged bit of rock about three quarters of an inch across from the envelope and placed it on the desk blotter beside the gun.

"That, I believe, will prove to be a piece of Mr. Good Rock's sample, one of several pieces I might add. I left the others *in situ,* to be found by the proper authorities."

"Many pieces McQuockle?"

"Yes, many pieces. It answers your question about the cry for help, Robert, because all these jagged bits of ore were forcefully rammed down the throat of the deceased. He couldn't have done anything more than gurgle if he could breathe much at all."

"Baldy what did you say the name of the knot was, the one at the end of the rope?"

"A Turks Head Bob."

Two Bob took a folded paper from his desk drawer, slowly unfolded it, smoothed it with the side of his hand and laid it on the desk in front of them. It was the note he had made while talking to the Mining Recorder in Pickle Lake, the name of Good Rock's stolen claim.

The three men looked at each other and then at the paper that lay on the desk.

Baldy looked almost ready to cry. "What a terrible, terrible thing for a good man."

Two Bob picked up the empty sample bag, feeling it's worn smoothness. "I guess he was trying to make sure the wrong man wasn't nailed with all these signs he left us."

"I suppose," Phineas McQuorquedale was using his 'intoning' voice in deference to the seriousness of the occasion, "I suppose that the usual thing in the absence of the Constable would be to alert the RCMP office at Regina to put out an all points bulletin."

"We don't have all points bulletins in this country." Baldy's correction was gentle. Phineas was Chicago born and bred and so could be forgiven and anyway both Baldy and Two Bob knew what he meant.

"Whoa, now, boys, let's just look all this over for a bit. All we got here is a bunch of things that sure do seem to point to Irwin Winfield but this really is a matter for the Constable. One thing I learned, and learned good, in my time runnin' this town is that you want to let each man do his job and not stick your foot in somebody else's toe rubbers."

"Robert, if we wait until the Constable gets back, looks at the evidence, contacts Regina, and Regina gets it out on the wire, then Mr. Good Rock could be on any one of a dozen tramp steamers heading for South America. You'll never find him"

"Exactly " said Two Bob.

And that is how the famous "Turk's Head" murder was solved. Our new Constable was called into Regina to receive a citation of merit which he later had framed and nailed up on the wall of his office alongside the letter of appreciation from the Mayor of the town.

Onion Evans

OUR TOWN WAS MADE UP OF PEOPLE FROM MANY CORNERS OF THE WORLD. Some recruited from the Slavic mining communities of Eastern Europe, some drivn by drought and early frosts from the English and German settlements on the Canadian Prairies, some hiding out, some starting over, and some just plain lost.

Most every one got down to the business of blasting and shovelling a living from the sulphide rocks in the tunnels and shafts of the mine, forgetting about the "old country," at least most of the time. They were too busy settling into their new land to think overmuch of the homes they had left behind. There were those, however, who couldn't get the "old country" out of their minds and the longer they stayed on this side of the ocean, the more beautiful the old country became to them. They forgot about the slave-driving land-lords, the marauding armies, the pogroms and the endless ethnic wars. Every waking moment was spent pining for the old country and planning their eventual return. We had Ukrainians more Ukrainian than their relatives still in Kiev, we had Germans who would have made a Prussian sabre master cringe, Norwegians whose accents got thicker by the year, but perhaps the worst case of all was Onion Evans.

From his name you would think that he was direct off the boat from the old country but Onion hadn't come from Wales at all, he was born Eynion Carridoc Evans in the town of Bangor Saskatchewan. And his father hadn't come from Wales either; Morgan Llwellyn Evans was born in Patagonia, Argentina, in the town of Port Magwyn.

In the 1860's, the English were taking harsh measures

to try and erase the Welsh language and culture in Wales. Most stayed to live as best they could, but some left to seek freedom in a new land. Onion's grandfather had landed with the first of the Welsh settlers who fled their native Wales and the English persecution to try and establish a new Wales on the banks of the Chaput River. They built up a fair Welsh world there in the Patagonian wilderness, irrigating formerly unproductive land, building Welsh schools, Welsh churches and a Welsh way of life in that strange river valley at the bottom of the world.

It had been the dream of the migrants to found a colony where the Welsh language and values could flourish. Sadly it was not to be. A series of savage floods destroyed their fledgling community, ripped the little thatched houses from their foundations and hurled them into the river, and buried the hard won fields and irrigation ditches under a tangle of trees and roots and river gravel. Some hung on, even under the increasing persecution of the Spanish, but a number, Eynion's father and mother among them, had left the little colony and returned to Wales where they took ship within days for Canada to try again. They established a new Welsh colony in the area of Saltcoats and Bangor on the plains of Saskatchewan. For a time they flourished. The church was strong, the language was in everyday use and their annual Eisteddfods attracted international acclaim. Children growing up in the dust-scoured heat and ice-toothed blizzards of the Prairie learned to love Wales, to love her language, to love the love of song and to long for the "Old Country." And Eynion Evans was one of those.

But the Great War emptied many a homestead in the community and then late frosts came two years in a row killing the winter wheat. The depression and the drought that followed took their toll. The Welsh community faded slowly away, its bits and pieces fitting themselves into other communities here and there and Onion Evans into ours.

He was a short, stocky man, as most of the Welshmen tend to be, with a round, ruddy face and ginger hair that stuck out in a wild fringe from under his hat. He had bushy eyebrows that made him look like he was hiding under a porch, and the big round liquid eyes that are also a mark of his race, unsettling to many, as he seemed always to be staring at something only he could see. People had been known to check their buttons and scuff for lint, muttering to themselves that he looked like an owl and perhaps had something of the warlock in him.

Some said the name "Onion" Evans had come from the sound of his own name; nobody could pronounce the Welsh of it properly and "Onion" came nearest to it. But it was Big Barney who had the last word on it. According to him, the name came from the fact that, no matter what question needed an answer, Onion would have one and most of the time, a right one, too. Did the old Corlis engine defy everyone's efforts to time it properly? Onion had once worked on them somewhere or other and knew what to do. When the big road grader slipped into the muskeg it was Onion, claiming he had once worked with the riggers in a shipyard, who set up the gin pole that got it out.

Since leaving the dried-out farm in Saskatchewan, he had tried many trades and followed many occupations, each one failing him at some point. But like a man jumping from one sinking log to another on a river drive, he somehow kept ahead of the fates. From one job to another he went, and learned along the way. Big Barney, the barber, claimed it was he, himself, who had named him saying, "That boy is like an onion. Every damn layer you peel away, you find another one underneath." It may have been true that he said that, but there were others that said he had been known as Onion Evans and nothing else since long before.

In the aftermath of the Great War, the builders of the huge complex that was our mine and mill and smelter had been forced to scour this country and a few others for machinery. Not much of what they found was new, and there were such a variety of makes and designs that no man could claim to be familiar with very much of it. Onion worked on the repair crew. It was his job to work out what was to be done with troubled mechanical things, such as the huge induction engine that was trying to shake itself to pieces or, a soot blower that wouldn't do what its builders had designed it to do. It was Onion's habit, faced with an ailing machine, to drag his small tool box up near to it, but not so near that it was impossible to take the whole thing in at a look, dig out his "roll your owns" and just sit there. At first, the foremen, a breed always troubled by the sight of anyone not moving, would mutter and complain, but they soon learned that the time spent by Onion in reaching an understanding with the machine was time well spent.

Onion would say, with great patience, to those who questioned his approach to the medicine of machines that somewhere, sometime, someone had lain awake at night dreaming of this machine, watching all its various parts and pieces moving back and forth, up and down, and never once getting in the way of each other. Before you could fix a machine, you had to know what was wrong with it and, before you could know what was wrong, you had to know what would be right and, to know that, you had to learn the dream of the one who made it first.

Onion didn't have many friends in our town. Not because he didn't want any...his good nature and willingness to pitch into whatever needed doing in the community could have won him many. He seemed content with a few cronies, all of them found among the Welsh underground workers the mine had recruited from the murderous coal pits that scarred the sacred green valleys of that perfection of countries. More Welsh than the Welsh fresh off the boat, Onion sang with them, drank with them, held his own as a teller of tales in the best Welsh tradition, and longed with them for the green valleys he himself had never seen. He even had a lady friend in Wales in a sort of a way for he had been exchanging letters with the sister of Hywl Rhyss for over two years now. What had started as a lark when Hywl had mentioned that his sister had never received a letter by post, had turned into a close correspondence between Eynion Evans and Bronwyn Rhyss. One that had, by the time of this story, determined Onion Evans to make a trip home, home to Wales.

Onion was not a tight man with his money. In the Corona, which was his favourite haunt, he bought round for round with the best of them. On his regular trips up to Big Marie's, " to have his ashes hauled" as he put it, none of the girls ever complained of his generosity.

Not being tight did not mean not being careful. Each payday, he would cash his cheque at the bank and make the rounds of those who had extended him credit since the last payday, each one carefully paid off. Onion, like most folks in our town, lived on credit, he charged his groceries, he charged for his tins of tobacco and anything else. On payday, (never questioning the account), he went round and paid, and the cycle started all over again. Many would joke that even if they never managed to save anything, it was their plan to die one payday behind in their debts. But Onion was managing to save. Every payday, once his bills were paid, and he had set aside a suitable amount for a visit to Big Marie's and enough for his payday bottle of rye, he would put what was left in the bank. And that little pile was growing, slowly, but growing nonetheless, because Onion had a goal. He planned, not only to go back to Wales, but to stay there, find a job and, if Bronwyn Rhyss would have him, marry and settle down. He hadn't quite got to the details of all this in his correspondence with Bronwyn yet, but, from the tone of her letters, he felt it was a likely plan. Her latest letter was in the pocket of his overalls as he made his way down the big hill and out to his little house on The Point.

Our town had a lake right smack in the middle of it, its west shore tight against the bottom of the big hill. Onion's house was on a long point that jutted out into the lake from the south shore. At one time, in the early days of the town, the lake had been a favourite place to picnic and swim. But the runoff from the mine's tailings pond came into the north end of the lake, and now the town's new sewage treatment plant was dumping partially processed sewage into the south end. No one swam there any more, or even wanted to find out if there were any fish. Out in front of Onion's little house, out in the bay, a flock of gulls would spend most of the summer seemingly anchored in one particular place, almost in the middle of the bay.

One day Hywl and Onion had been arguing about exactly how far it was out to that spot. Onion, claiming he had once been a helper to the surveyor for the highway department, promptly showed Hywl how to calculate the exact distance using a measured base on the shore and an old protractor. It wasn't as far as either of them had thought. Onion had even borrowed a neighbour's rowboat and gone out to see what it was that attracted the birds to that particular spot.

It wasn't birds, however, that were the centre of Onion's attention that evening as he sipped his rye at the kitchen table and reread Bronwyn's letter for the fourth or fifth time. There was, she wrote, a farm that was to be sold in the valley next to the one she lived in, in a valley that was only a short way from the one that Onion's grandfather had left all those years before. It was a relative of the Rhyss family doing the selling, and he had promised to hold the property until Bronwyn had a chance to find out whether Onion was interested. Oh and he was interested all right. Land in those valleys only rarely left the family. The chance to actually own a bit of a farm, in Wales, and so close to the roots of his own family was an opportunity such as Onion had never dreamed of. As the god's arrange such things, the amount asked was almost equal to the total that Onion had in his savings. There was no question that he would send the money and even send a telegram to tell her it was on the way. There was one problem however, and it was a big one. Or it seemed big to Onion, at any rate. If he sent the whole amount of his savings to buy the land, it would take two years, and likely more, before he could accumulate enough money to actually make the trip over, and with enough left to make Bronwyn a decent offer of marriage. For that was his plan. They had never actually used the word "marriage" in their letters but she knew and he knew what the land buying was all about.

As was his habit when faced with a problem, Onion began to think on it, turning the problem around and around in his head, examining all the factors and possibilities, thinking of what was needed, and what might be needed to obtain what was needed. Mentally, he tried one scheme after another to come up with the fare to the old country, and a bit of pocket money to carry around, but every scheme seemed to hit some flaw or other. He stared and stared at the happy birds motionless on the surface of the water out in the bay, and he was late to bed.

Three Piece Thompson, who owned one of the town's busier furniture stores, was a small man, a small bald-headed man, with small feet and small hands and a tiny button of a nose. Every thing about him was small except his voice and his dedication to the community. If somebody's house was damaged in one of the all too numerous chimney fires that plagued our wood burning community, Three Piece was first on the scene, finding out what was needed and then finding someone who would fill the need. When the tin slide that the kids used in the winter park developed a dangerous tear, it was Three Piece who found the money for the tinsmith. He loved this strange isolated community perched on its smoke-blighted rocks, and never tired of doing his bit on committees and volunteer work groups.

He had arrived late for his morning coffee at Wong's, not complaining, mind you, as it had been a cash customer for a new kitchen stove that had delayed him. Instead of the usual gang, he found only Hughie the Movie left, lingering over his second cup in one of the booths. Hughie could linger all he wanted to since he didn't have much to do until evening when the theatre opened, except on train days when he had to pick up the tin boxes of film and Saturdays when there was a matinee.

Hughie, like Three Piece, was at his happiest when he could throw his considerable energies into some laudable community effort. His reasons, though, were different than Thompson's. For Hughie it was a chance to make himself useful, to overcome the terrible anxiety that always blackened his hours, that feeling that no one really cared if he was around or not. He was a bear to work, volunteering for nearly everything. The only problem was that nearly everything he put his hand to somehow went awry.

Most agreed that even his greatest disasters had not been entirely his fault. Still, as many said, when Hughie picked up the reins, the horses would bolt. It didn't take a lot of prying on Three Piece Thompson's part to get Hughie to open up about what was bothering him. He had volunteered, as usual, for almost every committee of the Rotary Club and had finally been put in charge of the one project it was thought no one could mess up. He was to look after the ball diamond that the Rotary Club had raised the money for two years before.

What could go wrong with a ball diamond? Nothing, you would have thought. But about a week before, just as the lake was freezing over and the snow starting to fly, a Caterpillar tractor left idling on the new road had somehow slipped into gear, trundled it's ponderous way through the ditch and across the ball diamond, totally flattening the bleachers. It would be up to Hughie to come up with a way to raise sufficient money to have new bleachers ready when the first "play ball" was called out in the spring.

"You could hold a raffle, Hughie, raffle something off. Maybe I could come up with something, a radio maybe, eight tubes, a big one, folks go for the tubes, Hughie."

113

"Never raise enough from a raffle and, besides, that last time, when two people won first prize, wasn't my fault if the ticket's got printed wrong."

"Well, these things happen Hughie, but how about a talent show? You got the theatre and there's always people to perform, 'specially for a good cause and..."

"We nearly burned the theatre down with the last one and the theatre company says never again and..."

Well, as I have observed before, an unemployed god is a dangerous thing. With no wars or pestilence or earthquakes to entertain themselves with, a god gets to just sitting around bored. First thing you know he, or she, as the case may be, is hanging over the edge of a cloud looking down at the earth for a bit of mischief to get into. And so...

The head that popped over the top of the neighbouring booth to the one that Hughie and Three Piece were sitting in wore an odd round hat and there was an untamed thatch of ginger hair sticking out all around it. Underneath two eyebrows that projected out from a broad forehead like the roof of a badly shingled front porch, two of the biggest most penetrating eyes Hughie had ever seen seemed to be staring right into his soul. "I don't know if you might recall my name Mr. Three Piece, I bought it off you about two years back, the Toronto couch yes."

"Well of course Mr. ah..." Here Three Piece did the "storekeepers mumble." There were maybe three thousand employees at the mine, with some considerable turn over. Anyone who had ever bought anything and went on to actually pay for it, automatically assumed that his name would be indelibly engraved on the memory of the store keeper he had dealt with. The storekeepers, in self-defence, had developed a way of mumbling names that sounded as though they really remembered. All of them had trained their clerks to come to the rescue when needed.

"Well, and it was a long time back wasn't it now?" Onion said, recognising the mumble for what it was. "My name is Eynion Evans, I work with the Millwrights, got a little place down on the point there, couldn't help overhearing." Onion turned his saucer eyes on Three Piece just to let him know it was his overloud voice that was at fault, not eavesdropping on his, Onion's, part.

"Lived one winter in Timmins, didn't I, had much the same

114

problem, yes, fund raising that is, and we ran a dandy project that raised more money than you can imagine. No trouble at all, not even anything to buy except maybe a big sheet of cardboard and from somebody get a bit of rope and an old car."

"Well, Mr. ah, Onion..."

"Evans."

"Yes, Evans, there is a committee, see and..."

"No trouble at all, just tell me when the committee is meeting and if I am not on shift well then, I'll be there, won't I? And it couldn't hurt a bit to listen could it?"

And it would be remembered later on that it was Hughie who said "No, no harm in listening, I guess."

The meeting turned out to be on Thursday evening and that worked out fine for Onion. A bit nervous, but determined to do things well, he put on his best clothes and presented himself at the door of the reading room in the Jubilee Hall promptly at seven. The committee was already there. That is, Hughie the Movie and Three Piece Thompson were there along with Max Eliross who ran one of the local haberdasheries. He was this year's club chairman and, as such, ex-officio member of all the committees.

"Gentlemen, good evening, and a fine evening it is, a bit of a chill but nice, is it?"

"Come in, Mr. Onion, we have just been telling Mr. Eliross, here, that you have an idea for a fund raising project ...perhaps..."

"Why, yes, and I do then, don't I, and wasn't it a very fine project too and made a good deal of it, money, yes, a good deal."

"Perhaps you could..."

"Yes, of course, and I wasn't part of running it or anything so there may be things I don't know, but you gentlemen are all men of trade and I am sure all you need is just the bones of it then, yes?"

It took Eynion but a few moments to outline the basic project: put an old car out on the ice of the lake, and sell tickets on when it would drop through in the spring. It was the refinements of the proposal, however, that really caught the attention of the committee.

"And so each person is allowed only one ticket, you see, and only one person may have one of the half-hour spaces unless he divides it privately with another. People are greedy and will pull all kinds of tricks to get more tickets if they think others are doing it too. Their wives, their grandmothers, their dead uncles will all have tickets in their names." Eynion paused for breath, but not too long as he didn't want to lose the floor while he had things going so well. " And as the winter goes by and the weather goes this way and that, the time thought to be the prime ticket will change. There will be experts, all kinds of experts, won't there? Each one with a new idea, and with each new opinion on when the ice will go out, well, there will be a rush to be sure that no one else gets the best ticket."

"Are you sure you wouldn't like to be on the committee Mr. Onion? You aren't a member of the Rotary Club, of course, but you could serve as...."

"No, no, Your Honours, it wouldn't do, but I do like to do my bit. I'm a ball player myself you see, on the Smelter team, I am, short stop, isn't it? No, it wouldn't do, me a working man and all, but I do have a long rope you can use to retrieve the old car in the spring, since it won't do to litter the lake bottom. And there is a lovely big tree right in front of my little place on the point to tie one end of it to."

"Well, it sure sounds like a good idea to me. How about you guys, what do you think?"

"If it worked in Timmins, it ought to work here, seems to me."

"There is one thing gentlemen, if you would be so kind"

"And what's that?"

"This is a very big small town and it will be known, my part in it, it will be known. And to keep everything on the up and up, I will buy the very last ticket on the list, eleven thirty to twelve noon on the first of July, the final day. That way no one can say I didn't buy a ticket and support the cause and no one can say I bought a prime ticket as an insider like."

"Sounds fair enough to me, and I think you're doing a very fine thing. Not necessary, but, still appearances are everything, right? Hughie?"

"There's just one more thing, Mr. Evans." Mr. Eliross was buying into the project but still wasn't clear on the details. "How do you determine the exact moment this old car sinks through the ice?"

"Well, you don't, you see, and that's the beauty of it, for

the winner is the one who holds the time when it was last still visible. And when it gets near the time you can be sure that there will be no shortage of judges among the ticket holders. But, of course, the committee must have the last word."

"I still don't see the difference between when it sinks and when it was last visible"

"Well, you might not at first, and there are many who wouldn't, but if it is still visible it isn't sunk isn't it? But if you say when did it sink, well, there might be disputes and no one wants that now do they? No."

"What if someone wanted to change tickets? To a different time?"

"It was thought of, wasn't it, and the rule was that a man can sell his ticket to someone else and thus free up his name to be put on some other time period. But the best part is that the new owner of the ticket must pay the committee the price of a ticket to get it put in his name and so many tickets will be sold over and over again."

And so the committee opted for the proposal. A huge sheet of plywood was painted white and divided up into squares, one for each half-hour period of the ninety-two days from April the first, to July the first, four thousand four hundred and sixteen choices. Of course not all of them were expected to sell. The ice usually went out around the third week in May in our area so the tickets in April and June were not likely to be too sought after. Even the sale of the more likely times would easily take care of the repairs to the bleachers and, under Eynion's suggested rules, many of them would sell two or three times as they changed hands.

That night Eynion went to bed early but he tossed and turned and couldn't get to sleep, going over the whole thing again and again in his mind. Twice he got up and looked again at the figures he had scribbled on the back of his water bill when he was showing Hywl how to calculate how far it was to where the birds congregated out on the bay. At last he dozed off, only to wake with a loud yell: "The tree! My god, the tree! It is thick, isn't it? The rope goes around it yes, and then there are the knots by God. What has become of my mind!" Without a moment's hesitation Onion grabbed a bit of string, rushed out to the tree and wrapped the string around the trunk to measure its girth. A neighbour coming home from afternoon shift a bit early saw him out in the back yard with his arms wrapped around a tree and the back door of his longjohns none too well fastened, but it was the day after payday and stranger sights were not that uncommon.

Onion made it back to bed and was just dozing off, his mind slowly turning the whole project this way and that, when suddenly he was up again. "The catenary curve! My god, the catenary curve! Ten feet if it's an inch!" He rushed to the kitchen table to redo his calculations and giving up all notion of sleep, put the kettle on for tea.

First thing in the morning Onion was at the door of the Eaton's Mail Order. When the lights came on, he had his well-thumbed catalogue in his hand and enough cash to avoid the COD charges. "Rush Delivery," he said, or more nearly shouted. "Rush Delivery, item number a-772cd01 rope, three quarter inch hemp, three hundred and twenty one feet, not a foot more not a foot less, and item number t-5543 on page thirty two, a book, *Slight of Hand Made Easy*" and all of it Rush Delivery, so when?"

A bit taken aback by all this, but used to dealing with the needs of a whole community that lived through Eaton's Catalogue, (with a few social misfits opting for the Simpson's Catalogue), the agent checked his list and assured Onion that his order would arrive on Thursday's train.

Sitting at the table in Eynions tiny kitchen that evening sharing a "rye and ginger" with his old friend, it seemed to Hywl that Eynion was in an odd mood.

"You don't seem to be altogether here this evening, my lad."

"No, Hywl Rhyss, nor would you be yourself if you were about to take a step from which there was no turning."

"What can be as serious as all that now? What are you up to, Eynion? Speak of it now."

"Well, you know, Hywl Rhyss, that me and your sister Bronwyn have been exchanging letters by the post for some time now."

"She mentions it now and then and I am not in disfavour of it."

"I haven't asked her to marry me as it seems a man must be standing before the woman where she can get a good look at him before he does that. I do have the understanding, by the correspondence, do you see, that, if she does not find me too ugly, that she would not say 'no' out of hand, like."

"I think she might say 'yes' and do as well as ever she might. You are not a handsome man Eynion, in the ordinary way of thinking. But you are a fine looking Welshman, not too tall and with a general look about you that she would not find against, I don't think."

"Hywl, it is in my mind that, since we well might be brothers-in-law soon enough, there are a few things I would like to discuss with you."

"Well, if you must, then out with it Eynion Evans. Speak as you wish."

"Well, then if, in the course of doing some bit of business, a man knew of something no one else knew and profited by that, would you think ill of him, or would she, do you suppose?"

"I don't think it likely, every bit of business has something of that in it. You sell a horse that has bad teeth, it is up to the buyer to make him smile, yes."

"But what, for example, would you make of a man who might sell a mining claim he knew to be as dry as the paps of the witches of Endor and let a buyer think he might be having something of value?"

"I think the general rule is that the buyer is to take care for himself, barring, of course, salting a claim with gold dust from somewhere else and the like."

"So the rule might be, would you think, that all is a fair bit of business if nothing is introduced into the deal that wasn't there before for the buyer to find out for himself."

"I would think that would put it pretty well, I do."

"Would you have a bit more of the whiskey, Hywl, as we might one day be related by marriage, if all goes well."

" I would that, and here's to you and to Bronwyn, too, and that little farm you sent the money for."

The prize was to be half the value of the tickets sold. Because, as Eynion had pointed out to the committee, as the tickets sold, the prize would get bigger and more people would get excited about not missing out and they would buy more tickets, and the prize would get even bigger and so on and so on. As promised Eynion bought the last and most hopeless ticket, July first 11:30 to 12:00 noon. And following his example each of the committee members bought and paid for equally unlikely tickets on the last day of June to assure everyone that the event would be fair and above board in every way. Hughie assured himself that nothing could possibly go wrong this time.

At first sales were slow. After all, no one knew what the prize would be and tickets were fifty cents each, a big price in those days. But there were a number who felt that it was a good cause anyway and plunked down their four bits for the privilege of writing their name in one of the squares. Originally, it had been planned to hang the board in one of the beer parlors but whichever one was suggested brought cries of outrage from the other three. When the women pointed out that they weren't allowed in the beer parlors, but enjoyed a ball game like every one else, the "man from the mine" had someone from the company carpenter shop hang the big sheet with the names and time slots on it on the wall of the Jubilee Hall. Names started to accumulate and the half-hours around the twenty fourth of May, when the ice usually went out, started to fill. And as they did more and more people began to feel they should at least get a decent chance of winning before the good tickets were all gone.

Sureshot Martinsky, who had eleven kids and one on the way, bought thirteen tickets. One in each of the half-hours of late afternoon on the 20th, 21st and 22nd of May. There was a big argument when he wanted to buy one in the name of the kid that his wife was in the process of producing. After due deliberation the committee ruled against him on the grounds that he couldn't buy a ticket in the name of someone who hadn't been named yet and he couldn't name it till he saw what it was. Sureshot wanted to lodge a protest but no one paid any attention. Then someone thought to consult the Farmers' Almanac and, when it turned out there was a prediction of an early spring, there was a rush on tickets for the earlier part of May.

The old car had been hauled out onto the ice in front of Onion's place. He had been kind enough to lend the committee the use of his new rope so the wreck could be retrieved after it fell through the ice in the spring. He did raise a few eyebrows, though, when he insisted, as the owner of the rope, that he be the one to tie the rope to the old car and to the tree in front of his house. It did seem that he was being unusually particular about getting the car out on the ice directly in front of the tree. Onion insisted also that the whole length of the rope be used, and he seemed strangely concerned that the old car be pulled far enough out from shore that the rope would be suspended above the ice in a long graceful curve between car and tree. Onion's explanation for all this was that it wouldn't do if the rope got frozen into the ice and somehow affected the results. Having the old car directly in front of his house he claimed would prevent any complaints from his neighbours, although no one had heard the neighbours making any comments along those lines. All this fussing over details seemed a bit queer to some but Onion had a bit of a reputation as a queer one, as had lots of others in our town and the community's way of dealing with such queer ones was just to pretend they weren't.

And so the old car sat out on the ice, precisely on a line projected straight out from the near edge of Onion's kitchen window frame and south side of the old tree, tethered to the very end of Onion's new three hundred and twenty-one foot rope.

The bay where the old car was sitting, waiting for its final plunge, was the same bay into which the town's new sewage disposal plant dumped its effluent. Around the outlet of the pipe the warm water was starting to affect the ice. The town engineer had "**BEWARE OF THIN ICE**" signs put up, and this promptly started a stampede for tickets earlier in the winter. Tickets for mid April, which had been going begging, now became a hot item, with spirited trading taking place in the beer parlors and kitchens around the town. The committee hung a big sign made in the shape of a thermometer on the corner of the Post Office. Every day the red line crept higher and higher as the tickets sold. Every time it went up a little, and the potential size of the grand prize increased, more tickets sold.

Oddly, Onion Evans, who had started all this, was seldom seen around town. One or two people made enquiries of his friends, but the most anyone knew was that he had become obsessed with learning magic tricks and slight of hand from a book he had purchased from the catalogue. This wasn't at all out of line with his usual behaviour and no one thought much more about it.

Some of the muckers coming off shift were heard joking that a stick or two of dynamite would make the date of the sinking a bit more certain. The new town constable had to remind everyone, pointedly, about town bylaws against setting off dynamite within the town limits without a permit and proper notification in the papers.

The *Daily Staple* copied the thermometer idea and featured a big thermometer on the front page every day. Heated arguments started breaking out, and church bingo revenues started to drop off as housewives diverted their bits of surplus cash into tickets that gave them a shot at a prize that now was getting to be a very respectable sum of money indeed.

Barge Pole Smith, whose odd nickname was not discussed in polite circles, made a special trip out to Pelican Narrows to find an old man named Merasty. The old man was not only reputed to be a genuine Shaman, but his family had once lived and trapped in the area where our town was now growing. The old man sat on the big hill overlooking the lake for some time while Barge and a couple of friends paced up and down waiting to hear what he would have to say. After long study, Mr. Merasty announced that in his opinion, the geese going north in the spring would still be able to see that car. This started a whole new run on tickets later in the season and two fights in the Corona.

The thermometer kept on climbing. Father Dollardeaux, perhaps concerned about the drop in bingo revenues, preached a strong sermon against greed and gambling. The Reverend Saint John Philbert harassed the Anglicans one Sunday for almost half an hour on the topic of lusting after undeserved riches and neglecting duties to the community and the church. The fact, however, that no one could buy more than a few tickets no matter how innovatively they defined family, meant that no one could really hazard any serious money on what came to be called "The Great Car Sinking Derby."

The size of the prize continued to grow and was starting to attract attention even outside the town. The committee began to debate tough questions like whether someone who lived in Cranberry Portage most of the summer could be classified as a resident and entitled to buy a ticket.

Just after the first mine payday in May, Onion Evans turned

up at the office of Otto the Bank, dressed in what passed for his "Sunday Best," his hair and even his eyebrows combed into semi submission.

"Well, Mr. Evans, and what can our bank do for you this fine day?"

"As you know sir, I am a single man, not married, and not getting any younger that one could notice, no, and in need of a wife, I think, yes. The town has a school now, and schools need children, and I am thinking that it is time to settle down like."

"Well, to be married is a good thing, children, a home, and all that, stability and a regular life with a little put by for the future..."

"Well, yes, but up to now there has been a bit of a problem for me in that there were no Welsh women to be had anywhere near to here, no, not any, and that is a thing that is very important, you see, for I would not wish too...ah..."

"Well, yes, of course, perfectly understandable, but I don't..."

"It is the sister of Hywl Rhyss, isn't it. We have been corresponding by post for some time and Hywl himself has no strong objection and it needs only that I go and ask her in person, like, as it is not something a man would do by the post is it? Yes."

"Well, that sounds wonderful, but why are you..."

"She lives in the old country still, in Wales you see, and it is no small thing to make a trip to Wales which is almost as far away as England, and then to marry and then bring us both back and to settle in and all..."

"Ah...I see and you will need money for this of course."

"About two thousand dollars." Onion almost shouted this last statement as though this major sum had been blocking his throat and now burst out on its own.

"That is a large sum, Mr. Evans, Onion, Eynion, yes and I suppose you would have security for such a loan?"

"My house on the lake, on the point there, is all paid for free and clear and worth twice or three times that and its value going up every day, isn't it, since the smelter smoke doesn't come so blue there as it does in other places."

"That may be, but as I recall the new sewer system dumps into the lake not too far away."

"And there's no bother either because of the marvellous

engineering that has gone into the new treatment system and that only to improve as time goes on." Onion tried not to sound too doubtful about this last bit although on warm days of late the lake had begun to take on a strange odour sometimes.

"Well, the loan you are requesting would carry interest at, ah, six percent and be payable on demand, although, of course, you could make monthly payments. You would be required to lodge the title to your house with us until such time as...."

"Ah, well, there is a problem, isn't it, because in Wales, you know, the Welsh, that is, us as it were, we have a thing, a thing about any stranger, not that you should be offended, but against anyone not family laying fingers on the titles to our lands. It was the English you see. Once they had their hands on a bit of paper, well, it was some Welshman for the colonies and the land gone, isn't it, no, I can't see..."

"Well, without the title to the house as security the bank would certainly be..."

"Oh well, it's not that, you see, not the having of it,no, it's just the touching of it, the paper you know. The actual laying of foreign fingers on a Welsh title isn't it? I have thought though, of a nice thing, if your honour will allow. We can put the title in an envelope, and that way no one touches it see, but you still have it see, and all is well, isn't it. Yes."

With that rush of information Onion whipped an envelope out of the inner pocket of his old suit jacket, folded the title once and once again and slipped it into the envelope. All this happening so fast that Otto the Bank hardly had time to comment before Onion gave the envelope a good juicy lick and sealed it shut. Then, without a pause, he whipped a fountain pen out of his shirt pocket and signed his name across the envelope seal. At that point Otto was again about to say something but Onion wasn't finished. Out of yet another pocket he produced a stick of red sealing wax and his old bullet lighter. With one flick of a practised thumb he produced a long steady flame and melted a chunk of the wax over the opening of the envelope partly covering his signature, then, to top things off, bent his knuckle down over the still soft wax and pressed his Masonic ring into it as a seal.

"There now and it's done, isn't it, sealed in and no one

touching it yes, but you have it and no better security for such a loan, I think."

Onion held the envelope out toward Otto but it was evident from his trembling hands that, in spite of his apparent confidence that Otto was going to accept this unusual arrangement, he was still anxious. So anxious in fact that he dropped the envelope and had to stoop quickly behind the desk to retrieve it and hand it to Otto. In spite of Onion's strange behaviour, the loan of two thousand dollars was approved. A few days later, Onion's friends, down to see him off on the train, shook hands with him, every one, and wished him the best of luck on his long journey home and the finding of a wife.

April was unusually warm and those with tickets for late May or June were soon trying to make deals to unload them. As often happens in the North however, a howling blizzard drove its stinging needles of snow across the town and the lake on the back of a blast of frozen Arctic air and the lake was locked in more ice that it had had all winter. The whole town was having a wonderful time wheeling and dealing and the ball park committee could hardly believe their own figures as they tallied up the money that was rolling in. Except for a very few that had managed a family load of tickets, no one had more than a dollar or so invested. Although from the amount of time devoted to researching weather patterns, studying the flights of birds and consulting anyone willing to offer an opinion, you would have thought that thousands had been wagered.

Hughie the Movie basked in the open approval of the members at the Rotary Club luncheons as the potential profit soared. He could picture himself presenting the President with the sizeable cheque the committee could even now anticipate. He felt he had good reason to believe that all past fiascos would be forgotten.

The drifts from the late April blizzard were still on the ground in the third week of May when the weather took a decided turn for the better. Soft warm spring winds came up from the South scented with the smells of black earth and new leaves. The remnants of last year's wood piles emerged from the grimy snow and the frozen slops tossed to freeze in the alleys during the winter began to turn into rivulets of greasy grey water that made small Niagaras over orange peels and other odds and ends still frozen down. The ice on the lake turned black and one evening, just before the beer parlor waiters began calling "time" someone stuck his head into the door of the Corona yelling that the ice had started to candle and was breaking up along the shore. This started a stampede for the big hill overlooking the lake. It was the only time anyone could remember that the beer parlor had ever closed for lack of patrons. The crowd made a festive night of it, watching the old car shuddering on the groaning ice. Once, indeed, it gave a sudden lurch and seemed as if it would actually go through and a great cheer went up, but by morning it was still there.

Two days later, on the 28th of May, it actually went through the ice and the holders of the tickets who saw it suddenly drop didn't even wait to see it out of sight before they rushed off to Three Piece Thompson's store to claim the prize. Great arguments broke out; the committee, hastily called, stuck to their guns. The rules said "The half hour time block in which it was last in view" and, even though it had fallen through the ice, it seemed to be hung up on something and hadn't sunk completely out of sight.

Well, it hadn't sunk completely later in the week when there wasn't a speck of ice left in the lake and a week after that the old car was still there, awash up to the running boards, but still "in view." It became pretty plain that the car had landed on a reef that was just under the water. Just that kind of thing that could happen to one of Hughie the Movie's projects. Some laughed, some grumbled, Hughie didn't frequent the Corona much and the committee counted its considerable profits and waited for the official end of the project to declare a winner.

Otto the Bank filled his fountain pen from the bottle of blue-black "Quink" on his desk and arranged it alongside the bronze letter opener that the Board of Trade had presented him as the outgoing president a year or two earlier. Otto was proud of his big mahogany desk and the spotless green blotter in its leather holder. Ready for the day, he looked up to find his secretary ushering Phillip Rondeaux into his office. Phillip had come to our town from somewhere south of Winnipeg. He was a native born Canadian, but his French accent was thick enough to require careful listening.

"Ah, Mr. Rondeaux, and what can our bank do for you

this fine morning?"

"I heve come," said Phillip " to take the loan to pay off my new house."

"I see, and how big a loan do you have in mind, Mr. Rondeaux?" Otto twiddled his letter opener and turned it so that the dedication from the Board of Trade was uppermost.

"Me I heve purchase this house on four tousan dollar, hef I pay down from money when I did sell the farm. Hef I pay by month but me, I think, hey! Better pay all and have loan here at the bank. Pay from my paycheque every pay-day."

"I see, and does the balance you owe on the house bear interest?"

"Seven percents, but the bank he don't ask so much, so you see...."

"Yes, well, we would need the title deeds and the legal description and so on as security, do you have them with you?"

"Yes in here, I have them all." Phillip handed over a title deed and a couple of pages of papers with the town's letterhead on them.

"Hmm, yes, all seems to be in order, but...." Something looked a bit familiar to Otto, a bit too familiar. "Just who did you buy this house from Mr. Rondeaux?"

"Onion Evans, I buy it when he goes back to the old country. Don't know why but he says, don't tell nobody till after first of July, and today is..."

"I don't understand where you got these papers from but they can't be the real title, I have that in my safe at this very moment."

Phillip retrieved his papers from the blotter and held them close to his chest as though suspecting some banker's trick was about to deprive him of his house and his savings. "No sir, this title is all one hundred percent real. I went to town hall when I bought the house and he says okay. Taxes and everything, all up to date."

Otto got up from his desk and went into the vault. After a bit of rummaging around he returned with Onion's envelope, still sealed with the red wax bearing the impression of Onion's own Masonic ring.

Slapping the letter down on the desk he slashed it open with his brass letter opener and both men stared at what fell out. On the desk lay a single sheet of folded paper, and a ticket bearing the official stamp of the "Car on the Ice" fund raising committee. The ticket was for the half-hour period from 11:30 to 12:00 noon on July 1st, the last possible selection. Since the old car was only too visible, still perched out in the bay on the underwater reef, there was no disputing that it was the winning ticket.

Otto picked up the sheet of paper and unfolded it. It was a letter from Eynion Evans to himself:

"Dear Sir;

This letter will be your authority to cash my winning ticket on my behalf and use the proceeds to pay off my bank loan and any interest that has accumulated. I expect there will be a considerable surplus and this I would like you to give to Mr. Hughie the Movie toward his fund for the ball park as I expect he will be in need of some good news to announce at the Rotary Club Meeting.

In anticipation of your kind agreement and service,

I remain
Yr hmble svt,
Eynion C. Evans esq. "

Some time later a couple of the gods happened to look down over the edge of a cloud at a beautiful Welsh valley, green with the bones of a thousand years, and they saw new smoke rising up toward them from an old chimney and they were pleased.

The Night Of The Angel

MAYOR ROBERT BOBDINSKY HAD BEEN IN OFFICE FOR TWO TERMS, A LONG TIME. Some people had even begun to think of him as "Mayor" like some Englishmen think of "King," like you just go on and on till you die or get run over or something. Two Bob, though, didn't think of things that way, especially not now with an election in the offing. He was particularly aware that all democracies find the best man they can find, put him in office for a couple of terms and then turf him out in favor of someone whose only proven quality is that his quality hasn't been proven. Gunther Volkstein, Deputy Mayor and Two Bob's perennial opponent, was putting his all into this election. He had always had a certain following, but now he seemed to be picking up support from a segment of the community that had not been much of a factor in the politics of the town before.

Our town had started life as a rough, tough, mining camp. True, there had always been a gem-like kernel of married women and growing families, but up to this time no one had ever thought of the town as anything but a mining camp with all the needs of a mining camp. The beer parlors kept all the hours legally allowed them and the houses kept by the likes of Big Marie up on North Avenue tended to the other main service requirements of a mining camp.

Two Bob had always been well attuned to these needs, but almost under his nose things had begun to change. More and more the little shacks perched here and there on the rocks had become homes and contained families. Every year the school board was having to come up with a half dozen more classrooms.

There was a new feeling in the air. It was a little like "spring breakup." You couldn't really see the snow melting or the ice getting thin, but you knew things were on the move. You might not be able to find a leaf on a tree, but something in the air told you things were changing.

Two Bob had never studied politics, or social change, or any of the other disciplines that made up the tool kit of a politician. But the throngs of kids who jostled him on the street during the noon break from school, the stream of notices of marriages, births and birthdays in the *Daily Staple*, all whispered into his political ear: "Look out Two Bob, nothing is going to be like yesterday." Almost before anyone realized it, our town had gone from a mining camp with some families in it to a family town with some unattached miners in it. A whole new approach was going to be required and Two Bob was keenly aware that Gunther Volkstein had grabbed the ball, so to speak, and was already running with it. Gunther had made several speeches lately about "cleaning up the town" and how it needed to be made a proper place to raise families and so on. He didn't have to spell out that he had the industrious ladies up on the hill in mind.

The services of these ladies in a mining camp were seen in Two Bob's practical mind as being in a class with the city snowplows, the water delivery and the electric lights. From time to time issues would come up that required a meeting between the mayor and a representative of the ladies. It was, of course, impossible to meet at their own place of work and even less acceptable for a delegation of them to present themselves at the town office.

Two Bob and Big Marie, the acknowledged leading lady, had worked out that if they both ducked into the dimly lit Catholic Church of a morning when other people were generally not at prayers, they could get a few things settled in private. The setting up of an arrangement whereby generous but anonymous donations to certain needy charities and other community endeavors would take the place of a business tax, (which would have been difficult to explain on the town's tax roles), brought the town's second biggest industry into line with city policies. On one or two subsequent occasions, meetings had been required and these were usually triggered by a one-word invitation to "Pray" delivered by phone. On receiving this particular morning's invitation, Two Bob looked at his watch and realized he would have to make directly for the church. Actually he enjoyed these very occasional meetings with Big Marie. In any other society she might have been a university president or the head of a successful company. As it was, her chosen line of work prevented her from moving in the town's first circles, but nothing could hide her intelligence and class. Two Bob entered the dimly lit church and took a seat next to an attractive middle aged lady wearing a very expensive cloth coat of the very latest fashion and sporting a very modish fox collar.

"You're starting to show your age like the rest of us, Robert. You should learn to take it a bit easier." Two Bob was having a bit of trouble getting his breath back after the two flights of stairs up to the church.

"Marie, I may be showing my age, but I must say that you are certainly not."

"I'll take that as a compliment even if Miss Prestoupoulious might not give you a passing grade for English sentence structure. Since I called this meeting I should get down to the business at hand. Do you suppose that old lady cleaning up at the back of the church can hear us?"

"Well, she might report our meeting to Father McFinn and I might hear about it the next time the two of us go fishing, but no one else will."

"A big change from Father Dollardeaux."

"Well, Father McFinn does have a bit better understanding of the needs of a town like this."

"It's those needs we need to talk about, Robert." Uncertain just what Big Marie was getting at, Two Bob sat quiet. "You have no doubt noticed how many children there are in school now and how many married ladies at church of a Sunday, not to mention a good many men who didn't used to be found there."

"I guess nobody could argue with that."

"Well, this is not my first mining camp, Robert. It may be my last as I am thinking of retirement and both my auditor and my banker, not to mention my tax accountant, are giving me advice along those lines."

"You have a..."

"Of course, Robert. No one runs a business the size of mine without them, a necessary evil you might say. But we are getting away from the reason this meeting was called and that old lady is starting to stare."

"Well go ahead, I came to listen."

"You are worried about Gunther Volkstein or you should be. He is dumber than a sack of hammers, but cagey smart, if you know what I mean."

"Gunther always has his eye to the main chance."

"Well, in this case he has spotted the change in the nature of the town...a change by the way, Robert, that every mining camp goes through. It's like growing up. They start off as a rough, tough camp and change into a town. It happens every time. Well, Gunther is already getting on the "close the houses" band wagon and it's a tune that is a good deal more popular than it might have been even a couple of years ago."

"You suggesting I start singing a duet with Gunther?"

"I wouldn't care to sit through that kind of a concert, Robert, but you have always been good to us, so I am going to hand you a little bomb you can set off under Gunther. Something that will help pull your dog team out ahead of him so far he won't even know where the goal post is."

Two Bob pondered this metaphor salad for a moment before replying. "And what kind of bomb are you talking about Marie?"

"On the fifteenth of June, Robert, you are going to order all the houses to close and I can tell you that they all will close the moment you issue that order."

"I would never do that to you ladies, Marie. You're as much a part of this town as anybody."

"Well, it's not all sacrifice, Robert. As I said, every mining camp goes through a period early on when we ladies can provide a service and provide it at a handsome profit. This town has gone past its prime in terms of business and there are other, newer camps like that new Yellow Giant Mine and maybe, if my broker is right, even that Gold Boot play up in the Yukon. No, Robert, we are closing up, and moving on. If you order us to close our doors on the fifteenth of June and we do it that very day, then Gunther will have to run hard just to get elected dog catcher."

"I don't suppose there might be something you would like me to do in return for all this?" Two Bob had a feeling all this was coming a bit too easy.

"Well, of course, Robert, that's the way the world goes."

"And what might this *'quid porker'* be Marie?" Two Bob wasn't all that well educated, but he did like to get off a good Latin phrase now and then.

The old lady at the back of the church kept her sweeping to a discrete distance. Somewhere in the church a door slammed. Up by the altar a half dozen slender candles flickered in a box of sand. Some of the candles were nearly completely burned down, but a few still stood tall. Two Bob remembered whispers that Father Dollardeaux used to nip the tall ones as soon as their purchasers left the church and put them back in the box for resale. Father McFinn was of the firm opinion that each soul should be allowed its chance to burn down in its own way and at its own speed.

Two Bob thought about all these things even as he listened with growing interest to Big Marie. She told him of the girls on the hill that had gotten married to miners in the town over the last few months. She listed the girls who had decided that they had a good little nest egg built up and would go back home to hunt down childhood sweethearts and the ones who had already left for more lively mining camps and the prospect of good earnings. By the fifteenth of June, it seemed, most of the houses would in fact no longer be doing business, although nothing would be announced. There remained, however, three of Big Marie's favorite girls. These three were among the most industrious and savvy of all the girls on the hill, and could have gone anywhere and done very well for themselves. They had, however, the three of them, decided to marry and settle down. Each one had selected a prospective husband but, as Marie pointed out with a sigh, not one of these men had shown any interest in becoming husbands.

The solution seemed simple enough: the three men in question had been getting drunk with their favorite ladies and waking up broke so often they were used to it. It seemed only a small step to get them drunk and have them wake up married. Two Bob watched the candles burning down and listened to Marie as she related her futile efforts to persuade any one of the growing number of priests, parsons, preachers and reverends in the town to conduct the marriage service under such conditions. Finally, she had used her connections to track down the Right Reverend Phillouby Phillcrater, a tent revival preacher well known to both the law and the prophets. For a not inconsiderable fee, he had agreed to bring his tent revival meeting to town and if Marie could provide the brides and grooms, he would marry them on the spot, regardless of condition. The only problem, as Marie had discovered when she contacted the town hall for permission to hold the tent meeting in the town's only park, was that Gunther Volkstein, in his run for the family vote, had already licensed the Royal Whitstone Shows to use the park on the only available day that the Reverend Phillouby Phillcrater could find in his busy schedule.

"Well, you know, Marie, it would be pretty hard now to get the circus to change its date."

"Robert, that park is small, but I checked with some old carneys I know and the layout that Whitstone is using would still leave a small part of the park at the back end near the swamp unused. All I am asking for is the use of that little bit of ground."

"Would that be enough space for that big revival tent?"

"Almost, a little bit of the back end will actually be just in the edge of the swamp but the Revered Phillcrater always puts up a bit of a stage and altar at that end, so that would keep him up out of the wet."

"And you say all this is connected to the business of announcing the closing of the houses on the fifteenth?"

"On that very day, Robert."

"Well, Marie, I don't see the harm in it and those three boys you mentioned would be a lot less trouble to the town and to our constable in the married state, but who is marrying who?"

Well, it turned out that Scissor Grip Bushelski, one of Marie's oldest and hardest working ladies, had been planning for some time to marry and retire from the trade. Her choice of man for the job was Two Lunch John Magorski from the smelter slag train gang. Two Lunch was a big amiable man much given to telling very bad jokes and playing the Tzimbala with his buddies in the woodshed behind Zielski's place. His nickname had come from his habit of carrying two lunch kits to work. One could never hold the amount of garlic sausage, sauerkraut, black bread and raw onion necessary to keep his huge frame stoked for the hot work of loading and dumping the huge slag kettles in the smelter. Ever since he had come to town he had been Scissor Grip's exclusive customer on pay nights, stumbling back to work the next day hungover, broke and happy.

Hairy Mary had her eye on Electric Johnson from the construction department. They, too, spent payday evenings together, and had been known to attend the odd movie in each other's company, patronage the movie theater manager was not truly delighted to have. The lady making up the third couple was Soft Boiled Halverson, a sturdily constructed blonde from the Interlake. Her nickname had not come from any unseemly softness of heart but from the fact that she was rumored to keep an egg timer on the bedside table and would set it to "soft boiled" on busy nights. A lady with the blood of fishermen in her veins, her choice of husband was Tullibee Thorbjornson, a commercial fisherman from north of town who sometimes tried running his own outfit, but mostly fished on contract. Tullibee was one of the most successful of this hardy breed with a good business head and a feeling for the market. His only weakness being his habit of coming to town, collecting all the fish company checks from his mail and partying till it was gone, most of the time spent with Soft Boiled Halverson.

Two Bob stood up, sighed and said, "I'll get you the permit for that bit of ground, as good as done, Marie. How you are going to convince those three hard cases they want to get married and settle down is something I don't even want to know. Are you sure those bunkos are any kind of a catch even for those three? They been pissin' their paychecks up against the wall ever since I've known them, can't either one of 'em have a pot to..."

"Well, easy Robert, this is a church. But don't worry, for a long time now they have been getting drunk as usual and waking up a total blank as usual, but instead of watching them spend those checks the girls have been investing the money with a bit of help from me. Financially anyway, those boys are in better shape than they know."

On the fourteenth of June, Elmer Balcan and Ole Thorstienson were drinking beer in the Corona. Elmer had just ordered what might have been their eighth, or maybe eighteenth, round of draft and the conversation had gotten around to who, of the two of them, was the best man on the twelve pound sledgehammer. Ole had served a number of years on the track gang, and cited the thousands of railroad spikes he had driven with one blow and never a miss. Elmer countered Ole's claims to hammering fame with an equal or greater number of years underground busting up over-sized chunks of rock that wouldn't go through the grizzly screens. Just as the argument was really heating up, Big Barney leaned over from the next table and offered the opinion that neither of them could pound candles into a birthday cake compared to his own famed performance pounding stakes for army tents. Wherever Big Barney had gathered his experience on the big hammer, it wasn't likely to have been in the army. Some might have guessed the chain gang, but that didn't really matter to Barney. What did matter was the fact that a good argument was to be had and, even better, the argument had excellent possibilities to develop into a fight. Fast Eddie Barr was on duty that night, however, as canny a beer waiter as ever was, with a nose for trouble that a Colonial sergeant major would have traded a stripe for. Fast Eddie hurried over as soon as he saw Big Barney leaning over from his own table to one where he had no business putting his battle battered nose.

" Now then, gents, what's your pleasure?"

"Well, Barney here claims he can drive a twelve pound sledge better than any man in the room and Ole claims he can drive a twelve pound sledge better than me, and I claim Barney and Ole are full of loon shit and so...."

Elmer was just pushing his chair back from the table, getting into the best position he could for the inevitable dust up. Fast Eddie Barr, however, had had too much of his bar room furniture busted up in similar disagreements. "Look guys, there's that circus coming to town tomorrow and they got that "watchyamacallit," that thing where you pound with a hammer and a little thing flies up a slide and rings a gong. Why don't you, all three of you, go down and see who is the best man on the hammer peaceable like. In the meantime, how about a round on the house?"

Early the next morning the Winnipeg train huffed into the station with five more cars than it usually had. Shivering in the early dawn, children, who had been known to defy a threat to call the Mounties if they didn't get out of bed, were drawn up along the main siding in such throngs that the station agent was obliged to go out more than once and shoo them back onto the platform. The first boxcar stank wonderfully and from barred gratings set into its sides, an assortment of fangs, whiskers, and claws promised as much excitement as any child could contemplate. There were two flat cars covered with wonderful "Mechano-like" constructions, looking a bit like the Eiffel tower had been partly dismantled, painted a wild variety of colors and sent off up north. Strapped to the top of this pile of girders, cables and pipes were all sorts of wonders: wooden horses, wooden camels, and painted chariots for the roundabout. The enclosed benches for the ferris wheel were on top of the second car whose main cargo consisted of huge piles of brown canvass, stacks of painted wall panels and a wonderful assortment of poles, ropes and iron pegs.

Two standard "sleeping" cars made up the rest of the extra length of the train. Wide-eyed children and not so disinterested adults gaped at the assortment of humanity descending onto the platform. A tiny little couple in formal dress who didn't stand more than about three feet high negotiated the high steps, followed by a huge man whose pants were held up with a leather belt about six inches wide. Two absolutely beautiful ladies, with more bosom showing than was customary for the time, followed. Directing the movements of all these and a couple of dozen of the seediest looking roustabouts any one could imagine, was a man in a brown suit with yellow checks. A huge, floral-printed necktie vied for attention with an equally eye-straining vest. The entire outfit seemed to be pinned together with huge diamonds that flashed and glittered in the early morning sun. No child there had ever beheld such splendor.

By noon the whole trainload had been transported down to the town park and by mid afternoon the Big Top was up as well as a whole street of smaller tents and booths. The banging, hammering and good natured shouting never seemed to stop as every single soul connected with the circus went about their appointed tasks and a few, deliriously excited and very self-conscious local boys hired for the day ran here and there on various errands.

About three thirty, Two Bob dropped by to see how things were coming along. What he was really concerned about was whether Gunther would have figured out some way to mess up the arrangements for the Gospel Revival Tent. He was relieved to see that structure neatly erected on the edge of the swamp directly behind the Big Top and a busy group of people carrying in folding chairs and benches. Two Bob was about to continue on when a soft voice to his right addressed him: "Good afternoon, Mr. Mayor, I didn't know you were a fan of the circus."

Two Bob turned to find himself looking into the biggest, darkest and perhaps the most beautiful eyes he had ever seen. Miss Prestoupoulious never ceased to affect him this way and he never could seem to get used to it. It turned out that Miss Prestoupoulious had brought her class to the park to watch the circus going up, at least partly on the pretext that they would learn something about a catapult used in one of the circus acts, a device which was constructed along the same lines as the ancient Roman catapults that the class had studied as part of their course in Roman History. It didn't require mentioning that it was a glorious day, the circus was in town, and it was so near the end of the official school year that it was almost impossible to get the class to settle down to anything like school work.

At Miss Prestoupoulious' request, Two Bob went over to greet the class where they clustered around "The Great Gabrielli," listening intently as he explained how the great catapult worked. Across an axle raised on two tall upright beams lay a long slender structure of criss-cross ironwork and taut cables that would, in the days of the Romans, have been a wooden beam about thirty feet long. The axle wasn't at the balance point of the beam, but rather at a point about eight feet from the one end. From the short end of the beam a huge, canvas-lined basket was suspended by strong chains. A padded seat with a high back and armrests was fastened to the long end of the beam. Two workers were piling sandbags on the seat, and two others were busy filling the canvas-lined basket with water. Two Bob couldn't see it, but there seemed to be some sort of latch or trigger mechanism holding the chair end down. The beam was straining visibly as the big tank filled.

"Now then, class, lets show Mr. Gabrielli that we have been paying attention. What is the name of this wonderful machine?"

"A CATAPULT!"

Mr. Gabrielli smiled.

"Ah, but what kind of a catapult?" Miss Prestoupoulious was not going to let them off so easily.

"I know, I know." Two Bob knew that voice. It was Sophia Mykelnetlicoff, who had once appeared on the local radio station with him to read an essay she had done on the suggestion of renaming the town. Miss Prestoupoulious had confided in Two Bob that her marks had picked up considerably since that experience. She had even expressed a wish to become a mayor when she grew up as opposed to the usual nurse or schoolteacher career path selected by most of the other girls. "It's a trebuchet."

Mr. Gabrielli looked confused

"That's true, it is a type of trebuchet Sophia, but what makes it so?"

"It is a catapult operated by a counterweight instead of twisted ropes"

Mr. Gabrielli smiled

"And what great advantage did the Romans have with the invention of the trebuchet? Class?" This time it was Tony Maloney, one day to be head of his own engineering firm. "Because by changing the amount of weight on the counterweight you can throw things very accurately."

Mr. Gabrielli gave the class his best Mediterranean smile.

"Correct, very good, but what else do you need to know to throw things accurately? "

"You need to know the exact weight of the thing that you are throwing."

"And since this machine is going to throw Mr. Gabrielli did any of you notice what the workmen were doing as we came up? He was sitting on that scale over there while the workmen were doing what?"

There was a chorus of voices and many hands waving in the air, "They were weighing him against the bags of sand." "A lot of sand," a piping voice in the background added.

Mr. Gabrielli frowned and pulled in his stomach a bit.

"Now then, who can see the wonderful improvement Mr. Gabrielli has made over the Roman version? Bruce?"

"In the Roman version the counterweight was a big basket of rocks. It took many slaves to pull the long end down in order to raise the counterweight basket up and it was very hard to get the right, the exact weight, using rocks. Mr. Gabrielli has a canvas tank filled with water. After firing,

139

you can empty it, pull the long end down with one man, lock it, and then refill the tank to the exact level you need, the exact weight."

"Very good, very good indeed. And what would happen if you got too much, or too little water in the tank?"

"Well, any increase in the weight and he would fly too far, or if a decrease, not far enough."

Mr. Gabrielli shivered.

His act consisted of being launched from the catapult by a very accurately measured amount of water in the counterweight and hurled over the intervening tents and down the length of the Big Top. Splendid in his gold lamé jumpsuit, outstretched golden wings trailing flame, he would soar over the heads of the people in the stands, shrieking his patented cry "Gabrielli! Gabrielli!" and landing safely in a net at the far end of the tent. The catapult was tested each time against sand bags that were carefully filled to match his exact weight. Gabrielli was only too aware that a leak in the tank, or a workman careless about putting in exactly the right amount of water, could result in him flying wide of the safety of the net.

"Wonderful class, now you can all thank Mr. Gabrielli for his kindness in letting us see how a real catapult works. It is near three thirty, which is pretty close to four o'clock, so you can all go home!"

The first show in the Big Top had already started when Elmer and Ole showed up at the sledge hammer machine to settle which of them was the better man with a hammer. They hadn't invited Barney and he didn't come. Dusk was just falling. There was a good crowd at the Big Top and a satisfactory one at the tent revival meeting. The crowd around the concessions was still light and Elmer and Ole were able to get a turn at the machine almost as soon as they arrived.

The sledgehammer machine consisted of a short heavy balanced beam set almost on the ground. At one end of the beam there was a hammering point made of old car tire rubber; the other end was set at the bottom of a fifteen foot tall slab of plank with a metal track built into it. When the rubber target at the end of the balance beam was struck with sufficient force, the other end of the beam flew up to hit a metal slider, which was propelled up the track and rang a gong at the top of the plank. The whole thing looked pretty easy, especially for the hard rock miners in the crowd. The shill who was selling the tickets would urge them to step up and demonstrate what real men they were, offering a stuffed doll for the lady friend of anyone who could ring the gong three times in a row. From time to time he would take the hammer and, with a seemingly effortless swing, send the slider flying up the track to show how easy it was.

Elmer Balcan bought the first batch of tickets, six for a dollar. Handing all six to the circus shill running the game he took the hammer, swinging it back and forth a few times as though testing the weight. Then, after spitting on his hands to improve his grip, he proceeded to pound the gong machine with such powerful overhead swings that the bell could be heard ringing all over the lot. The crowd cheered and Elmer stepped back and took a small bow. Holding the hammer at arm's length as though it weighed nothing at all, he pointed it at the shill: "I think I just won two of them dolls. Give 'em to those lovely ladies over there." He handed the hammer to Ole Thorstienson who had his strip of six tickets ready and waiting.

Elmer was pretty confident that the bet was already won. He had reason to feel that way. Earlier in the day it had occurred to him that nothing about the carnival was ever just exactly what it seemed to be, so he had set off to find Bingo Mickey who had once worked in the big shows, The Royal American and the Conklin Brothers. Bingo even knew Gypsy Rose Lee and her sister, Lili St. Cyr. Sure enough, Bingo was only too happy to explain the secret of the sledge-hammer machine or "High Striker" as he called it. To start with, the short balance beam with the hammering point on it was heavy and inertia absorbed a significant part of the blow. The thick rubber striking point also served to dampen the force of the hammer. The real secret, however, was a small hidden brake under the beam. If that brake engaged, as it almost always did, the most powerful blow would only serve to lift the striker a few feet. But then how could the shill make the gong ring with such ease?

"Easy," Mickey laughed, "You swing the hammer, then, just as it is about to crash onto the pad, you pull it toward you. The slight movement of the beam produced by the angled blow causes it to miss the brake and 'bong' goes the bell." Elmer was so certain that the bet was already won he could taste the free beer. He would have been a little less certain if he had seen Ole a little later that same afternoon making his own visit to Bingo Mickey's store where Bingo had been only to happy to entertain him in his turn with the secrets of the High Striker.

Ole rang the gong with such style that a worried look furrowed what brow Elmer had, but the worried look on the face of the High Striker operator was even more pronounced. On a bad day, bad for him that is, he might give away three or four dolls. These two had just taken four dolls in as many minutes and it looked like they planned to keep right on. Ole gave his dolls to two ladies in the crowd on the side opposite the two Elmer had chosen, thus creating in a moment two opposing teams of supporters who took to cheering their respective champions. When the desperate High Striker operator began to offer other men in the crowd a cut rate on tickets they gallantly refused and called for the contest between Elmer and Ole to continue. BONG! BONG! all over the lot the carneys' heads came up. The bingo dealers absently made change and listened, the lion tamer paused in the middle of cuffing the boy who cleaned out the cages and listened, the Ring Master heard, even over the braying of the calliope he heard, and paused just one brief moment in his spiel.

A circus may look like a moving riot, but there is an order to it, a predictability. On any given night, a certain number of people will play bingo. On any given night, a percentage will opt for trying to toss pennies into glass saucers only to watch them bounce right out again. There will be a number, not varying by much, who will pay to get into the tent to see if the Dog Lady really is hairy all over. Of those, a reliable percentage will pay to get into the second part of the tent to see if she really is hairy in those areas not shown in the first tent. And, of those, a smaller but dedicated percentage that will pay to get into the third section only to find themselves hustled back out into the crowd with a blurry photo pressed into their hands. Although the circus appears to be a riot of confusion, to the members of the troupe it is a steady, predictable, reliable sort of confusion. Tonight, though, there was something wrong. BONG! BONG..BONG!

"Hey! Give the other folks a chance. You there in the green shirt, a free ticket, try your luck, win a doll for the lovely lady there, how about it?" But no one moved. Ole pressed another dollar into the ticket man's hand and took a length of tickets from the roll. "Hey wait a minute there, wait a minute! Hey, this game is closing down, closed you hear? Okay folks, that's all, the game is over, the.."

He never finished his sentence. Ole was already swinging the hammer, BONG! BONG! Elmer lifted the protesting carney up by a fistful of the front of his shirt as effortlessly as if he was a bag of chips, and set him up on the top of the big travelling case the High Striker was packed in for moving. "You just sit up there now and don't distract anyone. You're gettin' your money, so just keep quiet."

There is an old tradition in the circus that when trouble comes to one it comes to all. Let one member find himself with a situation going out of control and it is the business of all. The rallying cry of that old tradition, the call to arms that would bring every member of the troupe to his aid was the unlikely cry of "HEY RUBE!" Out-weighed and out-muscled by the two obstreperous giants wielding the mallet, the High Striker operator still had the one strength he had really been hired for: a powerful set of lungs. He put them to good use now.

"HEY RUBE! HEY RUBE!"

The age-old cry of a carney in trouble rang out over the lot. The circus strong man dropped what he had been doing and picked up the huge wooden mallet he used for driving tent pegs. Several of the roustabouts armed themselves with those same tent pegs. Those tent pegs were made from the rear axles of Essex and Chevy cars (prized for their length and the bevel gear attached to the end which made a fine tie down for a tent peg), a formidable weapon indeed. The ball game man picked up a bat and threw a couple more to the men jumping over the counter of the penny pitch. From every corner of the circus grounds a menacing crowd converged on the High Striker. Not the least fearsome was the Big Cat Lady, popping the dust in front of her with a fifteen foot whip.

It was, in fact, that popping sound that caught Elmer's attention as he waited his turn on the hammer. "Hey Ole! Look down there!" He pointed to the menacing crowd advancing between the booths. "I like a good set-to as well as the next man, but the odds don't look too good here. I think we maybe should be somewhere else as quick as we can manage it." It didn't take Ole, survivor of an uncounted number of barroom brawls, more than a second or two to come to a similar conclusion and follow Elmer as he dove under the wall of the nearest tent.

In the Revival tent out behind the Big Top, things were not going too well. Scissor Grip, Hairy Mary, and Soft Boiled had used their practiced expertise to get their men into that particular state of drunkenness in which every idea seems like a pretty good one. Roaring with laughter, the thought of a mock wedding at a tent revival seemed to them the best idea they had heard in a long time. Not trying too hard to focus their eyes and concentrating on the delicate art of not falling down, they stood before the preacher, arm in arm with their respective ladies.

It had been a bit of a trick to fit the big old canvas tent onto the little bit of ground the circus wasn't using, but the faithful had managed it. At the back of the tent, which actually projected a little way out over the edge of the swamp, they had erected a small platform. It was on this platform that the Reverend Phillouby Phillcrater stood facing the three swaying couples he had contracted to marry. Directly behind him stood a cloth covered table with two golden crosses on it. There were those who thought that gold crosses looked suspiciously Anglican, but the Reverend was proud of them and liked to think they added a bit of Christian dignity. He had won them fair and square in a poker game with a church deacon and felt they gave the stage a nice religious touch.

All should have been going like clockwork, but the Reverend Phillouby Phillcrater, falling in love with the sound of his own voice, had forgotten for a moment the immediate task at hand. He had done a verbal sideways pirouette into a long sermon on the evils of something or other. A sermon whose every sentence was embellished with numbers of chapters, numbers of verses and numbers of gospels until not a few began to feel that he sounded a bit more like the bingo caller in the church basement than the preacher upstairs. Once he had the chapter and verse bit in his teeth, there was nothing that could bring the Reverend back to the real world. Nothing, that, is until Scissor Grip kicked him sharply in the shins. "Shut up, you old fart, and get to marryin'. Can't you see these apes are starting to lose it? Get goin' with it before I crack your..." What Scissor Grip planned to crack wasn't put into words, but the preacher hadn't lived on the edge as long as he had without developing some nimbleness of mind. Without a break he swung into the marriage ceremony. It was too late.

Tullibee Thorbjornson turned to leer at the crowd as though to invite them to join in the fun. "Hoo Hoo, did you hear what he said? Marryin', he said, hee hee, listen to that he..."

Soft Boiled got his attention by driving her heel into his foot. "Shut up you Icelandic salami and drink this or you won't hear the rest of it." Tullibee took the large flask she produced from a purse the size of a small suitcase and dutifully took a couple of snorts of the 100 proof potato champagne Soft Boiled had brought for just such an emergency.

In spite of the liquor, Electric Johnson's eyes were definitely beginning to focus and Two Lunch had started humming a Ukrainian lullaby in concert with the rumblings of his vast belly, a very bad sign. The situation was rapidly going out of control. The Reverend Phillcrater tried desperately to get things back on track. Along with the standard marital admonishments he included a few old testament threats of the kind that involved fire and brimstone and avenging angels, mentioning the Angel Gabriel by name as being particularly noted for showering flame and torment on reluctant husbands.

With the armed horde of carneys that the 'Hey Rube' had called out bearing down on them, Elmer and Ole had rolled under the edge of the nearest tent hoping to gain a moment of respite from the murderous mob. But they had the bad fortune to sit up in the middle of the tent where Jo Jo the Dog Lady was having the last bits of fur gummed to strategic bits of her anatomy. That lady's scream of outrage brought whip, crowbar, mallet, and baseball bats into the tent on the run. Out the other side of the tent our two heroes rolled, ending up directly under the huge catapult that stood ready to launch the Great Gabrielli into the air and down the length of the Big Top. Mrs. Gabrielli had just given her husband the traditional glass of brandy he took before each flight. Half he drank, and half Mrs. Gabrielli poured with great ceremony into the water tank as though to emphasize the importance of retaining the exact proportion of weights. That same huge water filled tank, its white bulk swinging against the night sky above them, looked like a desperate haven to Elmer and Ole. It was only the work of a moment for the two of them to clamber up the frame and leap in. At the very moment that Gabrielli gave the signal for his launch into the air; at the very moment that his assistants had ignited the oil-soaked trailing edges that would make his wings appear to be aflame; at the very moment the Reverend was invoking the strict and precise admonishments of the Lord concerning holy matrimony and the potential outrage of the Avenging Angel Gabriel; at that very moment, the addition of those two huge men to the counterweight changed Gabrielli's carefully balanced calculations by a good six hundred pounds, if you counted the beer.

Gabrielli began the flight of his life.

Not at first realizing that anything was wrong, he stretched out his arms to get the full effect of his blazing wings, brilliant in his gold lame suit, he began his trade mark chant of "Gabrielli! Gabrielli!" Looking down at the world passing beneath him, the people in front of the Big Top seemed curiously small, in fact the Big Top itself seemed curiously small as he passed right over it, high in the air. People craned their necks to wonder at the flaming comet that flashed through the night sky, arcing over the Big Top and descending beyond it.

The Reverend Phillouby Phillcrater could sense it, he was definitely losing the three men. The sight of Electric Johnson's focused eyes was even worse than the horrible rolling effect he had displayed coming in and Two Lunches' humming was starting to take on considerable volume. The good preacher was in the midst of redoubling his threats about how the Angel Gabriel would deal with reluctant grooms when the roof of the old tent was blasted into flaming fragments with a terrible earth shattering Boom! A figure, all gold from head to foot, soared the length of the now flaming tent on fire-trailing wings. It roared over the heads of the couples on the platform, scorched the top of the Reverend's head, picked up the two gold crosses from the alter in a reflex action (probably dating back to a youth spent on the mean streets of Naples), blasted the rear wall of the tent into another mass of flaming shreds and roared out into the darkness over the swamp trailing sparks and a strong smell of fuel oil.

On the platform in front of the altar the three grooms stood frozen, like deer caught in a jacklight. Completely oblivious to the crowd behind them who were rushing for the exits as the old tent rained fragments of burning canvas down around them, they stood transfixed.

The Reverend Phillcrater, not one to neglect the long life and happiness of his mother's only son, had just reached the end of the platform on the way to making his own escape from the flaming tent when Scissor Grip caught him by the ecclesiastical coat tails.

"Hold on there, you chapter chantin' bible thumper, you got to finish the marryin' or you ain't gonna get paid and that will be the least of the troubles you can look forward to."

Imminent death by fire and avenging angels was one thing, but the thought of the fury of those three women, not to mention Big Marie, and keeping in mind the hefty fee he had been promised, the Reverend skidded to a halt and turned to face the matrimonial couples. In the loudest and best preaching voice he could manage, and he could manage a pretty impressive bellow, he gave it his ecclesiastical all.

"I now pronounce the whole goddam bunch a youse man and wife. Run for your lives!"

And so married they were. In fact, the Reverend's clerical blast had been so strong that not a few couples still trying to exit the first couple of rows felt themselves sufficiently married to move in together that very night.

The congregation found The Great Gabrielli sizzling softly on the far edge of the swamp in a patch of bull rushes. His gold suit gleamed wetly in the light from the burning tent, his hair was wreathed in green swamp grass and he held a golden crucifix in each hand. The fire on his wings had died out but that bothered no one. The good people swept him up and, singing several hymns at once, headed for the nearest church. Gabrielli was well on his way to becoming a real religious happening. Our town could have been rich, like Lourdes, or Santiago Compostello, but Mrs. Gabrielli snatched him from the crowd and marched him off to get cleaned up for the second show.

Electric Johnson woke up the next morning beside his new wife, Hairy Mary, (now just plain Mary Johnson), and found himself the proud owner of a respectable bank account, a thriving boarding house on Church Street and a well established bootlegging business.

Tullibee Thorbjornson opened his eyes to find he had given up drinking for good, owned a lovely welded steel fishing boat with two licences on Lake Winnipeg and an ice house in Gimli. His new wife, Helga, pleased him even more when she murmured in his ear that she no longer even owned an egg timer.

John Magorski was jolted awake when the train pulled out of the station in the morning. He was tucked into the lower berth of the sleeper car with his new wife Annie Magorski, nee Bushelski. Beside him was a bag containing a huge chunk of kubasa, several mild onions and a gallon of "Danforth's Three Aces" port wine." His tzimballa swung safely in the net overhead. They were on their way to the little farm Annie had purchased with the money John thought he had spent. It was just south of Birch River, a bit of land already broken, a good sized poplar stand for firewood and a sweet well. The house was log, coated with a mixture of cow manure and straw, which had been painted a bright blue with laundry bluing. Inside was a huge oven made with mud and rocks that had a sleeping place on top of it for cold winter nights. The house was small, but Annie and John knew very well how to make a good life in such a place.

Elmer and Ole turned up later that "Night of the Angel," as it came to be called. They walked into the Corona soaking wet and thirsty. No one ever heard them arguing about sledgehammers after that night.

Oh yes, and Two Bob got elected Mayor again.

Hole Eared Horse

WE HAD A LOT OF CHARACTERS IN OUR TOWN, SOMETHING ABOUT THE ISOLATION AND THE COMPLETE LACK OF ESTABLISHMENT SEEMED TO ATTRACT THEM. One of the most colourful was an old soldier named McLennan who claimed to have fought in the Boer War in Africa. It was never difficult to get Hole Eared Horse McLennan to talk about how he got his medal in the Boer War. Mind you, it was understood that the listener would stand a round of beer or two. McLennan thought it such a good joke on the high and mighty English that he never got tired of telling it. No one ever got tired of listening either since the story changed a bit each time it was told. If this says a lot for McLennan's talent for literary embroidery, it should also make us think about the stuff we get as history these days.

The military exploit for which McLennan won, or at least was awarded, his medal took place near a dusty South African desert way station called Blau Findong, or maybe it was Blop Fontain. (McLennan's ear for Afrikaans lacked a little something). The exact location isn't important since the Infantry Company to which our Brucie McLennan was attached seldom knew with any great precision just where it was in any case.

Brucie and his fellows passed the greater part of the day of the medal-winning battle, as well as the day before that, pinned down behind a low rocky ridge. Each man huddled behind his own bit of shelter with the exception of those few dedicated souls who were keeping the outfit's floating crap game alive behind one of the larger boulders. The men had good reason to be content to stay exactly where they were.

Facing them across a low grassy swale, a ridge similar to their own sheltered a troop of Boer soldiers who were entertaining themselves by taking sporting pot shots at anything that moved on the English side.

Every foot soldier since Hannibal's time, and likely since before that, has accepted as a basic truth that no officer can bear to see an infantryman safe, happy or comfortable. No one was surprised, then, when orders came down the line, whispered from boulder to boulder and from the shelter of hastily built turf walls to shallow rifle pits. They were to make preparations for a charge, stand up like real soldiers and attack the Boer positions some one hundred yards away on the other side of the shallow depression that separated them.

No one but the officers thought this was a particularly good idea. It was too hot, and much too far to sprint in the cumbersome kit that was regular issue in those days. That the Boers seemed to be shooting at any one who dared poke his head up only added to the unavailing objections raised by the troops as they prepared for the charge.

Sometimes the gods take it into their heads to have a bit of fun and this scorching hot African day was apparently one of those times. The Afrikaaners, bored to death with shooting the English soldiers one at a time, had convinced themselves that the truly manly thing to do would be to leave their nearly impregnable position and charge the Imperial troops. The charge would naturally be made on horseback since the Boers, sensible Nouveau Africans that they were, never went anywhere under the hot tropic sun on foot.

The Imperial troops had only just leapt from cover and started their charge when, to their utter astonishment, they were met not by the expected hail of bullets, but by a full fledged charge of Boer cavalry brandishing some very nasty looking sabres and shrieking uncomplimentary things in Dutch.

Before one of the commanders on either side could come to the conclusion that his opposite number had done something truly stupid, the battle was joined. "Joined" is really not the best word to describe what happened next. "Sifted," perhaps, or "Passed Through" or some other descriptive word equally foreign to standard military parlance might provide a better picture of what took place. You see, what the Boers had thought to be English troops were not English at all. They were Colonials, Canadians to be precise, with a typically Canadian aversion to leaving their bones in any corner of any foreign field, let alone one so far from the northwest quarter of the old homestead on the South Saskatchewan as this bit of sun-scorched African plain.

Instead of standing up to get their heads lopped off in pucka military fashion, the Canadians dove for the long African grass and lay flat, letting the sabers swish harmlessly overhead as the charge passed them by. The moment the charge had passed, they picked themselves up and ran on to occupy the recently abandoned Boer position, that being the only reasonably safe place in sight.

The Boers, expecting a blast of rifle fire from the rear as soon as the Imperial troops got themselves together, spurred their horses madly on across the little valley and threw themselves into the positions just vacated by Brucie and his fellows, or rather vacated by everyone except Brucie.

In every battle there are one or two or sometimes dozens who, for one reason or another, don't manage to charge with everyone else. Cowardice might hold some back and confusion might send some astray, but in Brucie's case, it was a loose and demanding lower bowel that was the cause of the delay. Squatting behind a barely adequate African shrub, our hero found himself in the midst of what had now become the Boer lines in the exchange of positions. Frantically hauling at his army issue suspenders, bare ass hanging out in the wind, our hero flung himself aboard a momentarily unoccupied Boer horse. Effectively substituting language designed to unstick a froze down prairie stoneboat for the horse's native Afrikaans, Brucie got his captured steed into motion. Clinging to the unfamiliar saddle with one hand and clutching his loaded rifle in the other, he pounded out across the valley in a desperate bid to rejoin his fellows.

There is an old saying that "the gods are never satisfied with less than an eight ender." It must be true because at the very moment that Brucie McLennan began his frenzied dash across the little valley, a lone Boer horseman, (perhaps delayed by the same intestinal mite that had contributed to Brucie's desperate situation), came charging out from behind the former Boer position where the Imperial troops were now reforming. Desperately he spurred his horse forward in a despairing bid to gain the shelter of the former British position, now occupied by his fellow Afrikaaners.

One moment Brucie and the Boer were terrified fugitives frantically seeking the safety of their respective positions, the next moment found them, not one whit less terrified, facing each other in a headlong charge toward single combat between the lines.

The Boer, good Boer that he was, rose to the occasion. In the best tradition he shrieked his most fearsome Dutch obscenities and waved his sabre in the most menacing style he could muster as his runaway charger thundered over the veldt toward McLennan.

Brucie, also a traditionalist, but of the Canadian variety, opted for survival. Trying his best to remember every tale he had ever heard of the prowess of the Red Indian horsemen of his adopted homeland, he hung himself over the side of the horse and clung to the saddle with one hand, hoping to avoid the Boer and his menacing sabre. The Blackfoot strategy might have worked, in fact, should have worked if there is any truth to Indian lore, but Brucie wasn't an Indian. He wasn't a Canadian either, except by the grace of his C.P.R. land grant. Brucie was first and foremost a Scot. Even when dangling by a leg and an arm from the saddle of a careening cavalry horse, Brucie was mindful of the effect that a loss of any of his issued equipment might have on his paybook. And so he hung on to his rifle with a hand that could certainly have been better employed hanging on to the horse.

In some versions of the story the gun was deliberately fired at the oncoming horseman. In other versions, it went off by accident. The effect was the same in any case for the bullet; before flying harmlessly off into the African dust, passed cleanly through the left ear of Brucie's kidnapped charger.

Now that horse, it must be admitted, was having a particularly bad day. He had been put to the charge against an enemy that disappeared into the grass. He had been left unattended in the horse lines, kidnapped by an obscenity-shrieking half-dressed foreigner and, as a final indignity, forced into an unseemly gallop with a rider who not only couldn't sit a saddle well, but even insisted on hanging upside down over the side. To be shot through the ear, from behind, by one's own rider, was absolutely the last straw.

Determined to suffer no more, that horse produced a sky-grabbing, belly-twisting sunfishing buck that would have earned him a lifetime pension and a place in the Hall of Fame at the Calgary Stampede in better times. Our hero, catapulted into the air like some bizarre Victorian guided missile, had only seconds to admire the yellow African veldt passing below him before he crashed, Topee-helmeted head first, into the midriff of the oncoming Boer soldier.

For a very long moment the field of battle was silent. Both sides gazing with awe at the results of Brucie's majestic launch, bold flight and awful impact. Both combatants sat motionless in the dust, separated from each other by a space of two or three feet.

The Boer, the wind knocked completely out of him, still had his sabre clutched firmly in his right hand, determined to decapitate our man the very moment his straining lungs could entice even one breath of air into his battered body. McLennan supposing he had somehow been blinded in the crash, sat with his sun helmet jammed over his eyes and swung his rifle back and forth with great menace, but had no idea where his adversary was.

At this point our story could have taken a very different turn if the Boers had recovered from their shock and seized the initiative. But it was the Canadians, remembering that Brucie had most of their pay stuffed into his purse as a result of the previous night's crap game, who moved first. Their charge to the rescue not only swept up Brucie and the Boer, but carried them clean across the little valley where they ended up retaking the position from which they had departed not twenty minutes before.

The Boer War was one of the first conflicts to be covered by what later came to be called "War Correspondents." Generals and Majors, used to reporting only to God or the Battalion HQ, were learning the hard way that a war correspondent not provided with printable material would either dig up some of his own or, not infrequently, make something up. In either case, that something was nearly always damaging to the reputations and careers of the unfortunate officers involved.

The officer commanding Brucie's troop was only too conscious of the mischief-making powers of this new breed of scribbling camp follower. Back in the same command post from which he had launched his charge less than an hour ago, he watched the Boers disappearing over a hill a mile or two away. He contemplated with dread the permanent damage to his military career that would result from a well-embroidered account of the charge and counter charge that had ended so ridiculously with the retaking of the same position he had held such a short time before.

The situation called for a diversionary manoeuvre, and that good officer, watching Brucie's fellow soldiers struggling to release his head from his crushed sun helmet, suddenly knew just what that diversion would be. In dispatches that evening, Brucie's exploits were described in the most glowing terms that the formal language of dispatch writing would permit: "great resourcefulness!"..."bravery under fire!"..."single handed capture of a prisoner!." It was a slow day for the correspondents and they gobbled the bait. Brucie McLennan's heroic tale was about the only thing going and they made the most of it.

In London the story made the headlines at a time when the reports from the front had been uniformly dismal and public morale was at an all time low. Faced with an increasingly restive House of Commons, the War Lords and the Ministers were also in need of a diversionary tactic. They decided that Brucie McLennan, the brave Canadian, was just the kind of hero needed to rekindle the fighting spirit of the Empire. Brucie was awarded a medal and brought to England to receive it from the King.

Some inspired officer, with an understanding of public relations that was very advanced for his time, even thought to send the punctured Boer horse to England on the same boat.

And so it was that "Hole Eared Horse" McLennan, proudly waving to the cheering crowds, rode the length of Pall Mall through the Palace gates and into history.

"Into history" at least as far as the beer parlor in the Corona Hotel was concerned anyway. It was there that "Hole Eared Horse" McLennan parlayed his adventure into several decades of free beer, and it is there that his medal hangs on the wall to this day, sealed in a glass case along with a shrivelled hairy object that Foster Plummindale swears is the original and famous perforated ear, removed after it was no longer required by its original owner.

Oscar

THE **DAILY STAPLE** CARRIED THE NEWS ON THURSDAY, BUT JUST ABOUT EVERYONE IN TOWN KNEW ALL ABOUT IT ON THE SATURDAY BEFORE. This was normal for news in our town (as it is, I guess, in most other small towns). In such communities there are two standard kinds of news: "what everybody knows" and "what has been officially announced."

The fact that "what everybody knows" varied from person to person and from moment to moment during the day didn't diminish its quality as news because, over time, just about everything that could possibly be true, and a whole lot that wasn't, was included in that category. So when the " officially announced" news was finally published, the details had all been covered at some time or another, by someone or another, and everyone promptly forgot that they had even considered anything other than what the paper said.

Even after the announcement in the paper, there were still points that were vague enough that there remained room for good discussions in the kitchens and the beer parlors, where most discussions took place.

Mayor Two Bob convened a special meeting of the town council and the president of the Chamber of Commerce called the executive into a special session. The Ladies of the Royal Purple were meeting anyway, so all that was needed for them was a change of agenda, which Mrs. Doddlinton handled with her usual aplomb.

There was a meeting of The North of 54 Ladies Literary Club on the Sunday afternoon following the announcement. These ladies didn't consider themselves to have a politcal role in the community; they contented themselves with offering their services to the Vicar of the Anglican Church.

In the back room of Wong's Cafe the real pushers and shovers of the town met on Monday morning. The "man from the mine" was there, and the mayor and two or three members of the Rotary Club and all the lawyers the town had. Most of the leading businessmen were also there, especially those that were active in town affairs, being presidents or past presidents of the Chamber, or the curling club or the like. It didn't take them long to get the facts sorted out from the rumours and to decide what would have to be done. To quote the mayor, "If we're gonna get a visit from the Governor General, whatever the hell the reason might be, we don't want him to get the idea this is some shit-assed mining camp. We got to put on a good show."

"The man from the mine" murmured that, of course, the mine would be happy to contribute what it could in the way of men and resources, which is pretty much what everyone expected him to say, but it was only polite to wait until he said it, officially like.

The first thing that had to be done was to set up a committee. This was not as much of a problem as it might have been in other places since our town pretty much ran on committees. It didn't take too much time to settle on a small group consisting of Mayor Two Bob, the "man from the mine," and Loud Raight, one of the town's senior lawyers who was listed as an advisor, but whom everyone knew represented the Liberal Party. The Chamber and the Rotary Club each contributed a member, and, out of courtesy or a sense of self-preservation, Mrs. Teddy-Keedy, the President of the Daughters of the Empire was invited to join.

The first meeting of the committee was held two days later. If this seems like unseemly haste it must be understood that the diversion of the Governor General's cross-country tour to include our town was a last minute change in plans. This meant the town had only a matter of a couple of weeks and a bit to make all the arrangements necessary to receive the first Governor General to visit the place, in fact, the first Governor General anyone had ever seen, even including "the man from the mine."

Accommodation was, of course, no problem since, in those days, important people travelled in private railroad cars, usually with their own dining car attached as well as other cars for any necessary staff and equipment.

Arrangements for a tour of the mine and the town's new water treatment plant were quickly agreed upon. Loud Raight as the liberal lawyer had his suggestion of a speech to a combined luncheon of the Chamber of Commerce and the Rotary Club accepted as inevitable and unavoidable. A suggestion that the Knights of Columbus should be officially represented was the equally inevitable contribution of the town's leading Catholic who was not in anyway surprised when the idea was quietly dropped. The last evening would be an appearance, with speeches, at the local community hall which would give the general population of the town a chance to see the nearest thing to royalty most of them would ever see, unless there was another war. The evening at the community hall would wind up with a short talent show. Mrs. Teddy-Keedy, as she was expected to, volunteered the Daughters of the Empire for this part of the festivities and "the man from the mine," as he was expected to, again murmured that the mine would be pleased to assist in whatever way it could.

The Daughters of the Empire met every Thursday afternoon in the basement of the Anglican Church. Not all of them were Anglicans, of course, but the Anglican Church basement was free and none of the Daughters were unmindful of the careful ways of their ancestors. Actually, the Daughters were not all daughters in the pure sense. Over the years, it had become a club that included all the ladies who considered themselves, (and had their opinion acknowledged by others), to be among the leading ladies of the town. Many of them had no remote connection to the families that had chickened out of the business of rebellion against King George the Third.

The club had, of necessity in a town where everyone came from somewhere else, opened itself up a bit in taking in members who were not descendants of the Empire Loyalists, or even of the Empire for that matter. Those who could boast a true lineal descent, however, still claimed a certain priority of rights over those whose origins were merely British and these in turn enjoyed a rightful feeling of superiority over those whose place of birth, accents, or polysyllabic surnames, branded them as "foreign."

The president that year (and most other years) was Mrs. Teddy-Keedy. She was considered to be ideal as president. She was English, recent enough to have an accent like the Queen used when she spoke on the radio at Christmas. She looked English, in that her front teeth proceeded her down the street as she gallumped along in her stout English shoes, and she was willing to put in the time required by the position which was perhaps the main reason for her string of elections by acclamation.

When the request of the Town Council was put to the members, it was a foregone conclusion that Mrs. Teddy-Keedy would be put in charge. Mrs. Mosberg was kind enough to emphasize in her proposal of Mrs. Teddy-Keedy that she had perhaps the best and most recent experience of all of them in the sort of thing one did to entertain royalty. Not a year ago she had actually been in London when the Queen had driven by in her carriage accompanied by the Horse Guards. Mrs. Teddy-Keedy accepted her appointment with just the right mixture of modesty and confidence and immediately proceeded to name the members of a committee to aid her. The members so chosen sighed and accepted in the full knowledge that membership on the committee did not mean that Mrs. Teddy-Keedy intended them to play any significant role. At the first meeting they would be handed a complete plan for the evening which Mrs. Teddy-Keedy would give them a moment or two to read through before calling for a vote of acceptance, time that Mrs. Teddy-Keedy would use to point out how ridiculous and socially suicidal any opposing proposals would be. A day or two later that meeting was held and Mrs. Teddy-Keedy outlined the predictable program to the committee members. She had received the predictable approval from the meeting when something unexpected was added. Mrs. Teddy-Keedy began to describe to the assembly her plan to make the evening such a memorable occasion that it would impress upon the Governor General, in no uncertain terms, that this was a town that was not only right up to the mark in loyalty and devotion to the empire, but had a fine sense of the dramatic and artistic as well. All this would be accomplished, Mrs. Teddy-Keedy explained, by the singing of the national anthem.

There never would have been any trouble if Mrs. Teddy-Keedy had left well enough alone and just done the standard thing. The gods are ever at their eternal mischief though, and somehow Mrs Teddy-Keedy persuaded herself that the evening could rise above the mere routine if she put her own personal mark on it. The national anthem was, of course, to be sung in any case. The smashing innovation that Mrs. Teddy-Keedy planned to introduce was that, instead of the usual announcement that every one would rise to sing, and the usual few guiding oompahs from the Elks Band to establish the key, the whole thing would be given an air of joyful spontaneity by having one person in the audience rise and begin singing the national anthem all alone. That individual would rise to sing with no accompaniment as though inspired by the presence of their honoured guest, at which point everyone would spontaneously and joyfully join in.

The idea did have a certain attraction to it. Everyone was agreed that it had the potential to present the visiting Governor General with the evidence that ours was not just any old town, and was certainly not a "shit-assed mining camp," although the ladies wouldn't have used that exact term.

Starting the singing on just the right note without benefit of piano or tuning fork would be an absolute necessity. No one worried for a moment about that. Everyone assumed without question that Miriam Rosenbaum of the breathtakingly clear soprano voice and absolutely flawless sense of pitch would be the one to set us all on the correct musical path.

A little later in the week, however, as Gvendur Siggisdottir-Questerling sat in her cozy parlor above the jewellery store entertaining some of her friends, she was shocked to her core as a tearful Mrs. Vertcouver told of the embarrassment and humiliation of Miriam Rosenbaum. Mrs. Rosenbaum had been told by Mrs. Teddy-Keedy that because it was, after all, the Governor General, the King's own personal representative, it would be better if someone identifiably English led the community in the spontaneous singing of the national anthem. That someone would be Mrs. Teddy-Keedy herself.

Gvendur Siggisdottir had come to Canada by choice, looking for adventure and the fine free life that she had read one could find here. No one in her family had been surprised when she announced her intention to immigrate to Canada for Gvendur Siggisdottir was truly the daughter of her father,

Siggi Snorrison. There was no one who really relished the idea of trying to thwart her when she announced whatever latest rebellion or defiance she felt a need to.

Siggi Snorrison had been disappointed when his only child announced that, following university, she would marry the diminutive, painfully shy Questerling boy instead of the fine silk-bearded fisherman that Siggi had singled out for her, but he secretly admired her independent spirit.

Oscar Questerling had finally finished his training as a watchmaker-jeweller, and had then been married to Gvendur exactly as she had planned. Siggi only sighed when she handed him a calculation of the amount that should comprise her dowry, along with the announcement that it would be used to set her Oscar up in the jewellery business in the New World.

Accustomed to being Siggi Snorrison's daughter, Gvendur had been a little taken aback to discover that all the wealth and high social position of her ship-owning father back in Norway had not qualified her for a leading position among the women of the town. We were still living in the days when only the English were not immigrants. Gvendur did not even try to disguise her flute-music Norwegian accent, nor did she try to break into the group of women who made up Mrs. Teddy-Keedy's circle of sycophants. Using her confident charm she built up a circle of friends of her own, seeking out women in the community whom she admired, with little or no reference to what the establishment thought their status should be. Although Gvendur seldom entertained, those who had been lucky enough to find themselves on her list spoke in awe-struck tones of heavy silver, of china that was nearly transparent, of fine linen and glittering crystal. Gvendur was no stranger to wealth, and no stranger to power for that matter, but her life with her dreamy little watchmaker was all she wanted or needed.

You shouldn't get the idea though that Gvendur was withdrawn from the community. She took her part in community events, was active in the Lutheran church and produced marvels of sweet pastry for the bake sales that were always being held in aid of something or other. No, she didn't reject the community, she just wasn't dependent on it for anything. There was one issue however, about which everyone agreed it was best not to cross Gvendur. Not caring herself about whether or not she was accepted into the inner circles of female power in the community, she was dangerously sensitive to any slight to other immigrant women who found themselves relegated to second-class status by the Teddy-Keedy's of the world.

Abel Simmelman could vouch for this. He had still been a bit pale and shaken when he arrived for the Rotary Luncheon in Wong's back room after his encounter with Gvendur. Like all good businessmen of Middle European experience, a certain obsequiousness toward the upper classes was ingrained in his approach to customers, and this was contrasted with an air both surly and condescending when addressing customers who where not considered part of the privileged class. Abel had been unfortunate enough to be somewhat abrupt in his speech as he turned to serve a babushka-wearing Ukrainian baba waiting at his counter. Unfortunate, that is, in that he did it in the presence of Gvendur Siggisdottir.

Some said that the blood of Harold Bluetooth, and even of Eric Forkbeard, ran in the veins of Siggi Snorrison and thereby of his daughter. No one witnessing the rising flush of righteous outrage that lit the snowy cheeks of Gvendur Siggisdottir, as she listened to the report of Mrs. Rosenbaum's humiliation, could have doubted this lineage for a minute and might even have thrown in a bit of Cnute. There was no one, she announced, who was better suited to open the singing of the anthem than Miriam Rosenbaum and no one who would dare to even...

Terrified by the budding berserker she seemed to have unleashed, and by the ancient blood lust flashing in the eyes of her Norwegian friend, Mrs. Vertcouver hastened to add that she, too, had planned to object, but that the matter was now settled. Mrs. Rosenbaum, hurt and shamed, had taken the train to Winnipeg to visit her aunt.

But Gvendur was not about to let Mrs. Teddy-Keedy have such an easy triumph. And so it was, that she presented herself, unannounced, at that final Daughters of the Empire committee meeting, the meeting at which Mrs. Teddy-Keedie was to go over the final details of her plan for the entertainment. This review was of course a formality since everyone in town already knew every item of the plan. The Boy Scouts would build a living pyramid by having rows of boys kneel on each other's backs to demonstrate the manliness and fitness of our youth. The local singing club would stage excerpts from Gilbert and Sullivan's "The Mikado" to demonstrate how well the culture of the mother country was valued in this far-off corner of the world. ("The Pirates of Penzance" had been considered but rejected as it was rumoured that the Governor General's family had naval ties and might interpret the choice as a bit of lese majesty.) The Girl Guides and the CGIT would combine to present a medley of choral selections stressing loyalty and love of empire and the Booker twins would do an exhibition of Indian club exercises as a subtle reminder that we knew how big the empire actually was. There was more, but it was all pretty standard stuff. Except for the bit about the national anthem.

As it happened, Conduit Pankowitz was up on a ladder changing some light bulbs in the meeting hall when Gvendur made her entrance. "It was" said Conduit, "like watching a dreadnought sailing down the ranks of the fleet." Conduit had been in the British Navy in the Great Disagreement and knew what size of simile he needed. "You know how some mucker looking for a brawl might heave into the beer parlor, shirt open, hairy chest, sleeves rolled up to show his muscles, looking mean, stompin' around in his big boots? Well, Mrs. Questerling did it, only woman style, you know? A shiny silk dress that told you right off she didn't need no help to fill it out, rings that any woman in that room could only dream about, but she had one on each finger, or so it seemed. Around her neck, two of them foxes, hangin' on to each other's tail with solid gold teeth. Draped over the classiest set of boobs in town was a necklace that must have cost about what, maybe, the Elks' hall cost."

The effect was immediate, for Conduit had it all right. Gvendur, savvy in the ways of the rough fishing docks of Norway and the deadly swordplay of the corporate board rooms of her father, knew what warfare was. She knew that victory went almost always to the one who played from strength from the start and, in the world of women, Gvendur knew what needed doing.

There was a long silence as she made her entrance. Mrs Teddy-Keedy knew she was beaten from the start but, being English, she made one good try to regain control of the meeting. "Mrs. Questerling, how nice, but this is a meeting of the select committee only, as you know..."

"Ya," Gvendur's English seemed to have become even more heavily flavoured by Norwegian than usual. "Ya, I know" Gvendur moved up the aisle between the folding chairs, only a little way because she knew enough not to give Mrs. Teddy-Keedy the benefit of the height of the stage, but enough to give the impression that she was among the members as she spoke. "Ya, and it's too bad about Mrs. Rosenbaum."

"Well of course, she... I, ah... I think she's left anyway... ah, gone to Winnipeg I heard..."

"Ya, vell ve ladies, the not-so-English ladies, ve feel that it's too bad, so, ve, I, am going to take her place. I Gvendur Siggisdottir-Questerling will lead the singing. That vill make everyone happy I think?"

Gvendur turned her Atlantic prow bosom to the right, waited a moment for the flash of the real diamonds to sink in, and then to the left, leaning forward just a little to let the sheen of the matched pearls glow against the silk. It was no contest. Nobody takes on an owly mean mucker flexing his muscles and looking for trouble and, in a female way, Gvendur was flexing a very formidable set of muscles indeed. Receiving no protest, she turned and made her stately way down the aisle between the chairs and out the door, pausing, as Conduit Pankowitz would later swear, to wink at him as she went by.

The day of the visit dawned bright and clear. Oscar Questerling, carefully shaved and tidily dressed came into the bright kitchen above the jewellery store for his breakfast. It had been their custom since they first met, or at least since the first time they met early in the morning, to whisper a few words of endearment to each other as a way of starting the day off in the right direction. So Oscar was startled when Gvendur, bending low over his ear, whispered nothing at all. Rising in consternation, he looked at her for some clue as to what sin of commission or omission she could possibly suspect him of to break this homey habit of years.

It was not some dereliction on his part, however, that was causing the silence, but a stray germ that had attacked his beloved wife, a germ of the laryngitis variety. Gvendur was mute, not a sound issuing from her tortured throat. Desperately she indicated a slip of paper that rested on the table by his kippered herring.

"I cannot speak. The laryngitis has taken me. Tonight, the singing, I can't, you must, Oscar, you must."

With complete dismay, Oscar realised that she was indeed serious, serious when she wrote that she was so stricken that she could hardly make a sound, let alone sounds of any musical value, and serious also in her plea that he take up the falling sword. This was not as outlandish a suggestion as it might seem. Oscar had a fine tenor voice and used it to very good effect in the Lutheran choir. His sense of pitch, although not of the precision of Miriam Rosenbaum's, and not of the confident certainty of Gvendur herself, was still good enough to start a hall full of miners off on the right note.

Our community hall was a large wooden structure, with a hardwood floor that had lines painted on it for various games and a stage at one end for the presentation of plays or concerts. In short, it was an all-purpose hall that could accommodate a movie, a badminton tournament, or a slide presentation. It served for recitals, the annual music festival, meetings of various groups and even the marching practice of the local militia. This last was important as we had no armoury and, at forty below, no one could really expect the army to practice outside.

Just below the stage and a bit to one side of the painted basketball centre line, the "man from the mine" had the mine's carpenters build a raised platform for the official party. There they could be easily seen by the crowd occupying the folding metal chairs on the main floor, and would have an unobstructed view of the proceedings on stage.

The evening went very well. Like it or not, Mrs. Teddy-Keedy could organize. The very thought of having to endure her cold British stare of outrage should there be a slip up contributed greatly to making certain things stayed organized. The Scouts made a very impressive pyramid and managed to dismantle it just as Johnson Gibson and Marty Freeman on the bottom were starting to collapse. The Girl Guides and the CGIT sang a nice selection of songs, including Mrs. Teddy-Keedy's personal favourite "Hearts of Oak are Our Men."

The Booker twins did their Indian Club hurling act where the two of them, their bodies painted gold and wearing gold lamé breech clouts, would stand at opposite ends of the stage and hurl the clubs at each other. There was a bad moment when one of the twins, distracted by the presence of so much royalty, threw his club badly and gave his brother a nasty bonk on the forehead. Fortunately, the injured twin managed to recover and finish the presentation. His mother later reported that he had chased his brother around the back stage with one of those same clubs until collared by the fire chief, who was back there looking for infractions to do with the fire escape doors.

Strategically placed in the middle of the audience, Oscar was nearing the moment when he would stand and, it was hoped, with flawless precision, begin the national anthem to be joined by all the rest of the hall in a joyous and spontaneous outpouring of loyal song. But Oscar was, as he so often was, dreaming of tiny perfect gears, of springs so small one could hardly see them, of jewels and counterweights and escapements of elegant precision. It was not until someone sitting next to him gave him an urgent jab in the ribs that he began to take notice of what was going on on stage.

The signal for him to spontaneously rise and begin singing was to have been Mrs. Teddy-Keedy lifting both arms from her sides to about shoulder height and letting them drop. She had done this and, when Oscar had not responded, had done it again, and again and yet again. Desperately trying to get Oscar's attention, she repeated the flapping motion faster and faster, until most of the audience, including the long suffering Governor General was convinced that the "piece de resistance" of the program was to have been a demonstration of the first human-powered flight in history. Reluctantly relinquishing his dream, Oscar gazed with awe at Mrs Teddy-Keedy's apparent attempt to take off and flap her way around the hall, only belatedly remembering that this was to have been the signal for him to commence the national anthem.

Terrified at the thought of Gvendur's wrath if he failed to carry out his mission, Oscar leaped to his feet and began to sing, strong pure and certain notes delivered with a lyric passion that not many knew him capable of. There was a long silence, a silence that only drove Oscar to redouble his effort to inspire the assembly to rise up and sing. However, it was not that his singing was not up to expectations, far from it. The silence was because the national anthem he was singing was not the Canadian one, but the national anthem of his beloved Norway.

It was the Welsh who stood first. Far from home and in a

strange wild land, it was song that gave them strength. Although they had no way of knowing that Oscar had made a terrible error, his passion and spirit sang to their very hearts, and the boys from Penrhyn, and Llangollen and Betsy-coed tuned "Men of Harlech" to Oscar's pure notes and even somehow made the phrasing fit. Never to be outdone, the entire bakers dozen of the LaPointe family rose as one and the "Marseilles" in all its power and grandeur soared in beautiful counterpoint to the Hungarians who were singing something no one could understand. Behind them, voices trained to the vastness of the steppes rose in Ukrainian, unbelievable resonating basses gilded with the high voices of the women. One after the other the anthems of two dozen countries joined the chorus. It was even said afterward that the Saddleburgers, who were Germans at a time when it was still not too popular to be German, could be heard softly singing something that sounded like "Deutschland Über Alles."

Up on the stage the regal party rose as one. Never let it be said the English have no sense of occasion. On this particular one the Governor General, sounding to some ears a bit teary-eyed and choked up, contributed a good baritone "God Save the Queen."

Yes sir, no one could ever say our town was any "shit-assed mining camp."

A MUNICIPAL HORSE

IN THE WORLD OF HUMANS THERE ARE THOSE THAT FOLLOW THE ADVICE OF ST. AUGUSTINE. They content themselves with whatever hand life has dealt them and are not too much troubled by thoughts of improving things. There are, however, those who have a dream, those few who have a goal and what's more have a route mapped out to reach that goal.

In the world of horses Big Daniel was such a one. He had been born on a farm and started his career as an ordinary farm horse, but it didn't take long before his natural talent for the horse business began to attract attention. Every one knew Daniel was destined for big things. His first move up was to a position as dray horse in a small town, kind of the equivalent of a promising young ball player playing on a farm team. He wasn't in the minors long before he was offered, and accepted, the post of Municipal Horse in our town. Big Daniel had a dream and by his own calculations was well on his way to realizing it. From Farm Horse to Municipal Horse in a few short years, and there wasn't a one who wouldn't agree that Big Daniel was headed for the major leagues of horsedom.

You don't rise up in the world without having a good understanding of your public. Your fans and supporters are, after all, the ones who will underpin your career moves. Big Daniel's relationship with his fans was a model to other professionals. Dressed in his best harness, he was always at the head of the First of July Parade pulling the town float.

In winter, wearing his own Clydesdale Tartan horse blanket, he snorted child-pleasing clouds of steaming breath as he dragged the school sleigh ride out to IceHouse Lake and back. Big Daniel's ability to plow open snow packed winter roads was the stuff of legends. In the summer, sporting his prize straw hat with the holes cut out of the brim to accommodate his ears, he could be found on any day patiently applying his huge strength to one or other of the town's wagons or pieces of rolling equipment. At night, in his snug stall in the municipal barn, he would dream of the illustrious ancestors that had deeded him his impressive size and power.

Most people have a vision of the knights of old charging into battle on some slender-legged horse of the type found hurtling around today's race tracks, but Big Daniel knew that this was far from the truth. You have only to imagine Henry the Eighth, a man who hit the scales at around two hundred and eighty or so and wore a suit of armor that weighed almost as much. No, it wasn't the spindly-legged racehorse types that went to war; it was the likes of the ancestors of Big Daniel...Clydesdales, Percherons, Suffolk Punches and the giant Shire horse.

Those were the days when the great heavy horses knew true glory. Battles were won and lost when those behemoths thundered down the field carrying steel clad warriors swinging heavy maces and broadswords over their thick shields.

The horses, too, carried their own armor and the combined weight of horse and rider could scatter the most determined legions of foot soldiers. Once or twice, Big Daniel had gotten so deeply into his dreams of glory that he had actually lashed out a great hairy foot and sent the side of his stall scattering in splinters across the barn. Most of the times, though, well practically all of the time, he exhibited that most noble aspect of the truly powerful in that he was as gentle and thoughtful as could be. Rain or shine, through blizzards and the kind of stinging snow-cold only a northern town like ours can produce, he carried out his duties for the town with dignity and class and waited confidently for the break that would launch him into the big time.

Most everyone in our town had grown up with horses, understood and loved them, and were pretty well attuned to their likes and dislikes. It was a good town in which to be a horse, especially a horse showing the big league potential of Big Daniel. There was one person, though, that definitely wasn't a horse person, and that was the Town Engineer.

For Daniel this was something of a problem, since, as Municipal Horse, he reported directly to the Head Teamster who in turn reported to the Town Engineer. Big Daniel knew how the engineer felt about horses and there was no love lost between the two of them. The engineer, for his part, had a healthy respect for Daniel's warlike capabilities and would never have dared put himself in range of tooth or hoof.

The Town Engineer was a small man, invariably togged out in a Smokey the Bear type campaign hat, a short leather jacket cut along military lines and army style riding britches tucked into high topped leather boots that laced nearly to his knees.

He was intensely proud of his campaign hat and word was that he sometimes soaked the brim with sugar water and ironed it with a hot iron to make it stiff. He was a man who understood the world in terms of machines, of steam, diesel, beams, bearings, clamps and cables. He dreamed of the day when the town would graduate from horsepower to tractor power and would get a tractor written into the town budget every spring and fall, but so far with little success.

Most of the roads in our town were soft sandy gravel or finely crushed slag from the mine. In the winter, because there was no need to sand them they became long polished ruts of ice. Winter or summer they were ideal for horses but not for machines. This lack of consideration for machine powered vehicles was a constant source of irritation to the Town Engineer. He even had a small stretch of hard-top road constructed right in front of his office to demonstrate to people how nice the town would be paved over. Big Daniel, whenever he got the chance, would try to arrange his day so that he could leave a huge steaming pile of used hay right smack in the middle of the Town Engineer's sample road. The Town Engineer liked nothing better than to look out his office window and watch Big Daniel or some other horse trying unsuccessfully to get a purchase on his hardtop road with their iron shoes.

The town council meeting was in full drone and near the end of an over long agenda when the budget of the Works Department came up.

In one of those inexplicable oversights that happen now and then during the pursuit of the democratic process, the Town Engineer's request for a new tractor was approved without comment and the meeting adjourned. The next morning, going over the minutes, Mayor Two Bob sighed with resignation and asked the town clerk, George Burton, to place an ad in the Winnipeg Tribune calling for tenders for a tractor.

"What kind of a tractor?"

"Why a Caterpillar D2 of course. That's what the engineer's specs called for."

"We can't just specify one maker; we have to at least seem ready to look at other proposals."

"George, it don't seem to me to make a lot of difference since a D2 Cat is what we will end up with anyway but, if you need to, you can have the ad read 'D2 tractors' and leave out the Caterpillar part. That way it just gives an idea of how big a tractor we want."

"I'll get on the phone this morning."

Two Bob had some misgivings about George and the long distance phone. George was still having a lot of trouble with his new teeth and it took a bit of getting used to to understand him at times.

"Hello! Hello! Is this the Winnipeg Tribune in Winnipeg?"

George was of that generation, still new to long distance phones, that conceived of the contrivance as some sort of pipe that you shouted down, louder shouts being necessary for longer distances.

"Hello Hello! I want to plathe an ad."

"Yes sir. Just go ahead. I will write it down and give it to the advertising copy writer."

George gave the name of the town and the address and then the body of the ad, trying his best to get his new teeth to stay put as he talked. "Requesths thenders for D2 thractors." he shouted.

"I didn't quite get that sir."

"D2! D2!" George shouted, but with his teeth rapidly losing their grip it sounded more like 'Thee Thooo'."

"Got it, sir, thank you. Your ad will be in the Monday edition of the paper, an excellent placement for a business advertisement. We will bill the city at the end of the ad run."

The advertisement that appeared in the Monday edition of the Winnipeg Tribune gave the Town Council quite a shock. 'D2 Tractors' filtered through George Burton's new teeth had reached the advertising department as '32 Tractors'.

That the town had actually advertised to buy thirty two tractors got some of the councillors pretty riled up but Two Bob, realizing what must have happened, reassured them that a correction would appear in the next paper.

There was, however, another and completely unexpected result of the decision to buy a tractor that was demanding the attention of the councillors.

An uproar outside the Town Hall was rising to near riot level, urged on to greater and greater outrage by a strident female voice that sounded horribly familiar to Two Bob.

"What on earth is all that hubbub about?"

"It's about this!" Laura Langmuir, the Town Secretary held out a copy of the *Daily Staple*, holding it at the top corner by thumb and forefinger as though it was something a nice girl might not want to have in her hand. Staples Dibson, the owner, editor, publisher and reporter of the *Daily Staple* sometimes went a bit overboard with his headlines but this one had even Two Bob sputtering as he read:

'Town Goes Diesel
Big Daniel to the Glue Factory'

At that moment the Town Engineer burst into Two Bob's office, his usually ruddy face looking as if it might burst into flame. In one hand he held a copy of the Tribune, with the error in the Town's ad which changed D2 to 32 underlined savagely in the purple, indelible pencil he favored. In his other hand he held a sheaf of telegrams, all from different tractor companies, but all saying pretty much the same thing.

They were all shipping sample tractors up on the next train, complete with all the newest attachments, and assuring the Town Engineer that they could be relied on to fill his order for 32 tractors with no delays.

Business was pretty slow in the tractor line in those days. Every tractor company sales boss that had seen that ad on Monday had a flat car loaded with sample tractors and equipment on its way on the Tuesday morning train, each man convinced he had stolen a march on the opposition. Two Bob ordered the necessary corrections phoned in to the Tribune. Even though it was too late to call back the shipments of sample tractors, he had Laura call each manufacturer to apologize on behalf of the Town and went home early to see if there was a wee bit of Red Label left from the weekend.

In the morning things were no better. Two Bob had been right about the voice hectoring the crowd outside his office window. Mrs. Teddy-Keedy had sewn herself a red dress with the outline of a big black hammer stitched down the back. She was standing on the steps of the Town Hall waving a huge red banner with:

"Northern Luddites Against Heartless Machines"

painted on it in bold black letters. Two Bob could stand a lot of pressure but not without his morning coffee. This morning, though, it seemed prudent to pass up his usual stroll along Main Street and use the back alley to get to the drug store. Most days, Two Bob would join the local businessmen at Wong's Golden Gate Café for coffee but every now and then he liked to go down to the drug store where another group of the town's citizens met in the morning.

The undertaker, the doctor, the town constable, fine people all, but they knew instinctively that their presence would be a damper on the conversations at Wong's.

Moishe Fineberg was just pouring refills for Doc Williston, McQuorquedale the undertaker and the town constable when Two Bob walked in. What had been a lively conversation suddenly stopped on Two Bob's arrival and a very strained discussion of Moishe's new line of cinnamon buns and the likelihood of rain took its place.

Two Bob was sensitive to the fact that they were doing everything possible to give him a break from the debate over the town's decision to switch from horsepower to tractor power. It was Two Bob who finally plunged in.

"The crowd in front of the town hall is getting pretty testy. Thought I could hear Mrs. Teddy-Keedy out there."

"I saw her this morning." McQuorquedale the undertaker could look down his long nose at you when he said something and make it seem that each simple statement was code for something else.

"She has sewn herself up a red dress with a big hammer cut from black cloth on the back of it," Moishe put in.

"A big hammer, you say. Has she taken up Communism or something?" Even as Two Bob posed the question he knew it was most unlikely given Mrs. Teddy-Keedy's feelings about the Monarchy, and a mercantile nobility appointed by God.

"No, not Communism, she is carrying a big sign that says:

"NORTHERN LUDDITES
UNITE TO DESTROY THE GODLESS MACHINE"

"Luddites?" Two Bob was mystified. "We got three kinds of Catholics: Roman, Greek and Orthodox." He ticked them off on his fingers as he spoke. "We got Anglicans high and low; we got Lutherans, reformed and standard; we got Baptists, Southern Conference and Northern conference; we got Mennonites, dippers and dunkers; but we ain't got no Lignites, as I know of, and Mrs. Teddy-Keedy was born a card carrying Anglican."

McQuorquedale set his coffee cup down carefully, exactly half way between the edge of the counter and the sugar dispenser. Then, with the same care, he fitted all the long fingers of his two hands together, except for the index fingers which he placed along each side of his down-curved nose. When he did this you knew you were about to get more information on some topic than you ever thought existed or maybe more than you even wanted. Two Bob signaled to Moishe for more coffee.

"In England, in the early eighteen hundreds..."

Two Bob added an extra shot of sugar to his coffee, "McQuockle, what on earth...?"

McQuorquedale continued as though this impolite interruption had never happened. "...there was considerable unemployment and hardship when the introduction of machinery began to replace weaving done at home on hand looms. A movement arose led by a gentleman called Ned Ludd, hence the term Luddites, to smash up the machines and return to the older way of doing things. They used hammers to attack the power looms, breaking the frames and causing general destruction." McQuorquedale stirred his coffee, tipped the self-measuring sugar dispenser over it and carefully stirred again.

Like any good storyteller he knew when he had his audience firmly hooked and a theatrical pause was called for. " Since that time, those opposed to the replacement of living beings by machines have identified themselves with the Luddite movement and the hammer has been the symbol of that movement."

Two Bob was no slow learner, he took a long sip of his coffee and said resignedly, "Like tractors replacing horses. I see your point, McQuockle, but we can't have these Lignites..."

"Luddites."

"That's what I said. But I hope they aren't plannin' to take their hammers to the town's new tractor."

"It might very well come to that. Feelings are running pretty high, especially after the reference to Big Daniel and the glue factory in the *Daily Staple*."

Two Bob turned to the town constable, who was just finishing his coffee. "Maybe you could go out and tell that crowd in front of the Town Hall to go home or something. Sort of calm things down a bit?"

The constable didn't respond immediately and seemed particularly tense as he adjusted his Sam Brown belt with the big holstered revolver and settled his Mountie hat on his head with unusual care. "Mr. Mayor", the chill in his voice caught Two Bob's attention immediately, "Mr. Mayor, it is true that I serve as the town's constable but I am, as you know, a member of the Royal Canadian Mounted Police... Mounted Police, Mr. Mayor, ...mounted on horses."

The town constable paused a moment to let this sink in. "I see nothing unlawful in the citizens of this town protesting against horse mistreatment. In fact, Mr. Mayor, mistreatment of horses is itself against the law."

Two Bob was still trying to put his response together when the constable stomped out the door, letting it slam behind him, causing the little set of bells Moishe had attached to the door to ring violently.

Before any one could recover from this wholly uncharacteristic behavior on the part of their usually soft-spoken constable, the door chimes were set into another clanging frenzy with the entry of Angus Bell the owner of the Bell Hardware. His sudden entrance was made even more impressive by his considerable size and his habit of stomping his feet when he walked, as though every thing his size twelve boots leveled out restored a little order to the world.

Angus liked order, thrived on it. You had to have order in your very blood to run a hardware store.

The thousands of items that made up his stock in trade could turn into a hopeless jumble if you weren't the type of person whose central purpose in life was to have things in order. Nails were stored with nails, pots with pans, axes with saws, big nails, then middle-sized nails, then little nails, left to right, common nails, then box nails, then finishing nails... well, you get the picture. This morning, though, this morning as the group at Moishe's counter was to learn, this morning things had definitely strayed from the path of good order.

"Two Bob, you got to do something about that damned horse thing. There is going to be trouble, mark my words, more trouble than you can imagine. That damned Teddy-Keedy woman and those four flat cars of tractors that came in on the train this morning and Staples Dibson and his bloody glue and..."

"Wait, wait, hold on, Angus! It's true there has been some opposition to the town switching over to tractor power but..."

"Two Bob, I'm tellin' you there ain't been nothing like this kind of trouble since god was a dog, and..."

"Hold on, Angus. Sure Mrs. Teddy-Keedy has her Lignite sign up but she ain't got but one or two women from the Daughters of the Empire behind her and..."

"Two Bob, you gotta listen. It's getting' outa hand, I tell ya. Now the Women's Christian Temperance Union have joined up with her sayin' that the godless tractors will lead men to drink and the Anglican Ladies Altar Guild and the Lutheran Ladies Choir, not to mention the..."

"Well, hey, Angus, a bunch of ladies, most of 'em pretty old and..."

"There ain't been nothin' like this since god was a dog, I tell ya. They,re buyin' hammers, all kinds of hammers, and when I run out of hammers that Mrs. Questerling bought herself that big fire axe that I had in the window."

Two Bob was definitely paying attention now. The thought of Mrs. Questerling with a fire axe was enough to chill the blood of the most hardened mayor and Two Bob was only in his third term. Angus continued, "And Mrs. Wienermacher..."

"That little old lady that lives up on Hillcrest Street, the one that came here because she said it was as far away from anywhere as she could find on the map? That little old lady? She couldn't even lift a hammer, Angus."

"She bought a one pound ball peen hammer, an Eastwing with a long handle. My God, Two Bob, I still got the shivers! Thought to tease her a bit and said ' Hey, you're goin' to be some outclassed with a little hammer like that', and she looked at me like... Two Bob, I tell ya, I don't think there's been a pair of eyes like that set loose on the world since god was a dog. No color to 'em, grey and hard, like a new bar of number two cold rolled steel. She gave me a look, Two Bob, a look that froze me to the bone and said: 'Almost every summer some army or other rolled through our village in the old country and a girl had to learn where to hit to get the best results even with a small hammer'."

"Hard to get a picture of that into your mind," Two Bob mused. "That tiny little old soul with the frizzy hair that might have been red once and those spindly little legs, she..."

"There's gonna be big trouble, Two Bob. Mark my words. Ain't seen nothin' like this since god was a dog. Big trouble, all them women with hammers and Mrs. Questerling was swinging that axe in one hand like, like, well, you're the mayor, Two Bob, and I tell you right now the boys down at Wong's this morning were clear it was you has to get this mess in hand."

The tractors and all their attachments had been unloaded and were all parked in a row across the south end of Main Street on the Town Engineer's sample section of pavement. A heavy pall of blue smoke hung over the street from the tractor exhaust. The noise was deafening, and it wasn't just the roar of the tractors. A considerable crowd had gathered, shouting and waving signs and banners. Some of the signs bore the stenciled imprint of the Northern Luddites but there were also many hand lettered signs supporting Big Daniel and all other horses. The Town Engineer was trying to ignore the mob. On his sample section of pavement he was having each tractor salesman in turn demonstrate how easily their bulldozer blade could be mounted, how the controls of their dragline attachment worked and how much cable their winches could hold. Some of the men were getting interested in spite of themselves and edged a little closer to get a better look, but Mrs. Teddy-Keedy and her followers turned their ire on them and drove them back into line.

Two Bob had the windows of the Town Hall closed to cut down on the noise a little and went back to working on the speech he was to give that evening at the grand opening of the Town's newest beer parlor. A whole shipment of beer had come in on the same train that brought the tractors, beer that was to be given out free after the opening ceremonies. With the beer had come a very important-looking representative of the brewing company, all the way from Chicago. At the far end of Main Street, workmen were just putting the finishing touches on the new hotel.

You couldn't have a beer parlor in those days unless it was part of a hotel so our town, a town that got down a lot of beer and that already had three hotels, was about to get a fourth.

Suddenly a huge roar, loud even through the closed windows of the Town Hall came up from the crowd surrounding the tractors. The Earthworm Tractor salesman had been about to demonstrate the ripper hook attachments used by their tractors. A ripper hook, for those who haven't met one, is a very heavy steel hook that is mounted on the back of a tractor so that when the tractor pulls it through the ground it will rip that ground up like a crude plow. They are used mainly to destroy old roadbeds prior to laying new ones. The Earthworm salesman had just lowered his hook when an astonishing apparition darted out of the crowd.

Wearing a long purple dress that did nothing for the wild fringe of once-red hair circling her head, a tiny woman shrieking what might very well have been obscenities had anyone understood the language, dodged through the mob and leaped onto the Earthworm tractor. The Earthworm salesman, not aware, at first, of the cause of the swelling roar of the crowd, continued his discourse on the power of the ripper hook to destroy packed material like old roadbeds. Alerted by the Town Engineer, he tried to mount the tractor but was met with a barrage of blows from a ballpeen hammer, some so delicately aimed that the Earthworm Tractor Company's favourite salesman ended up rolling in pain in the dust of the street. Mrs. Wienermacher began yanking every lever she could find and swinging her hammer at everything that looked vulnerable.

The one lady boarding party inevitably yanked the lever that set the machine in motion. Off down the street she went, whanging away at any part of the tractor she could reach, awash in shouts of encouragement from the crowd, with the ripper hook leaving a trail of torn up street behind her.

The half frozen permafrost that lurked under most of

the roads in town was already starting to ooze to the surface through the gash in the roadbed when the change in the crowd noise alerted the other salesmen. They had been lounging around awaiting their turn to demonstrate to the Town Engineer how powerful and how destructive their own ripper attachments were and now watched with astonishment as the Earthworm, with its wildly shrieking purple clad driver, tore a long furrow down Main Street.

"Boys, it looks to me like that miserable little Earthworm rep has made a private deal with the Town Engineer to get a little city work done and make himself look good. Well damned if he's going to get away with it. Our ripper can make that puny little can opener of his look like a toy...Fire 'er up, Midge, and catch up to that little four-flusher."

In less time that it takes to tell about it, all four tractors were racing down Main Street, ripper hooks down, leaving a trail of ripped up street and a menacing upwelling ooze of half frozen muskeg in their wake. Leo Lapoint's barbershop sign was torn from the building by an errant machine that mounted the sidewalk. Angus Bell, who had run out into the street to see what all the uproar was about, only saved himself from becoming part of the roadbed by diving headlong back through the door of his hardware store.

The Town Engineer, almost lost from sight in the clouds of exhaust smoke, and certainly lost from any hope of influencing the course of events by sound stood on the one remaining fragment of his treasured hard top road jumping up and down, and perhaps shouting something.

The Earthworm, given its head start, was the first to finish. After ripping a furrow down the complete length of Main Street, it ended up churning its tracks in the gravel of the station platform, its hook caught firmly in the rails of the CNR team track.

Within moments, the other tractors crashed into the same rail embankment and sputtered into silence.

Behind them, under the heavy haze of blue exhaust smoke, the entire length of Main Street had been turned into a sea of oozing mud. For a few moments all was quiet, no chanting, no motors roaring. From the Town Engineer to the Second Vice President of the Anglican Altar Guild, every one stared dumbstruck at the scene before them. Main Street was a sea of mud from Pyrite Road to First Avenue. Mrs.

Wienermacher cackling wildly in her purple dress hastily scurried behind the box cars on the team track. No one knows what might have happened next in this mad spectacle because the silence was broken, not by any of the participants, but by the sudden urgent wailing of the town's fire siren.

Fire in the new hotel! A workman's torch had started a fire in the beer storage annex! A collective groan went up from the crowd, at least that part of the crowd who were not members of the Women's Christian Temperance Union. The fire already had a good hold in the insulation of the new walls and it looked certain that the kegs of beer, that were to have been given out free at the grand opening that same evening, were going to go up in hops flavored steam.

Our town had a volunteer fire department. Members who were close to the fire hall when the alarm sounded would race the truck to the fire. Other firemen would head directly to the fire guided by announcements on the local radio station. A cheer went up as the fire truck roared around the corner and a collective moan of despair followed as the great red truck, loaded with tons of water, hoses, axes and ladders sank to its axles in the roiling ooze that had been Main Street.

Hasty volunteers, beer drinkers mostly, waded into the muck around the fire engine and started to push. The firetruck's big tandem wheels spun helplessly throwing a huge plume of loon shit into the air but only managing to mire the truck even deeper. Some of the firemen began pulling hose off the truck and laying it along the street toward the hotel but it was obvious that it was never going to reach. Somehow that heavy truck was going to have to be moved down the street and it was then that the cry went up...first one voice and then many: "Big Daniel! Big Daniel! Get Big Daniel down here or the hotel's a gonner!"

Almost as if he had been standing in the wings waiting for his big moment, Big Daniel came around the corner from where he had been pulling up boulders from the schoolyard nearby. Dragging his teamster and about thirty feet of heavy logging chain behind him, Big Daniel moved out in front of the fire truck. By the time he was far enough out in front to give the logging chain a decent angle for pulling, it was evident that there was going to be trouble as he was already up to his knees in muck. He turned back to size up the situation. It seemed hopeless, but he was a professional through and through and determined to give it his best shot.

Everyone who could get a grip on the truck pushed, pulled and heaved while Big Daniel, head down and every muscle straining, hauled on the tow chain until it seemed to sing under the tension, but only succeeded in driving himself and the truck deeper into the muck.

The new hotel and the free beer seemed all but lost but just at that moment a loud clattering and clanging announced the arrival of Big Daniel's arch enemy, the Town Engineer. He might indeed have been a small man but it was evident that he was accustomed to command. Behind him, and following his urgent orders came Big Barny and Ole Thorstienson, each dragging a long sheet of roofing iron from the Monarch Lumber Company's yard at the far end of Main Street. Following his shouted instructions Big Barney dragged his piece of roofing iron to the left side of the truck, set one end on the running board as instructed and with one good jump bent it into a rough toboggan shape. Ole had already done the same thing with his piece and, goaded by the sharp barking voice of the Town Engineer, they rammed the two slabs of iron under the front wheels of the truck.

It had only taken the engineer one glance to figure out that without some sort of slide to lift the front wheels out of the muck, nothing was going to move. He didn't have the strength and beauty and crowd-pleasing abilities of Big Daniel, or the organizing skills of Mrs. Teddy-Keedy, but he knew his angles and inclined planes. Even Big Daniel, who didn't like to admit the Town Engineer had any redeeming features, was impressed.

The slides were in place under the front wheels. Two Bob had mounted the roof of the truck and was directing the eager crowd of volunteer pushers and pullers. Everyone was ready for one more try but it was going to take a superhuman effort to start the front end of the truck up onto the makeshift roofing iron slides.

Even Big Daniel's most ardent admirers were not too sure the big horse, mired almost to his belly in the mud, would be able to generate enough pull to start the truck moving. There were even a number of ladies down in the mud, including some members of the Womens Christian

Temperance Union...no fans of beer, free or otherwise, but very committed to civic duty and unquestioning fans of Big Daniel. Mayor Two Bob up on top of the truck warned everyone to put their utmost into it on the count of three and started to count. Big Daniel then did something that was to be talked about in the beer parlors and kitchens for many a day after. Surging forward through the mud until he had the chain as tight as it would go, he moved his back legs forward until his hind hooves were almost touching the front ones. Then, as if to show the Town Engineer that he wasn't the only one who understood angles, leverage and points of purchase, he suddenly raised his huge body into the air, balancing on his hind legs. The crowd gazed in awe then as Big Daniel, lifting his forelegs clear of the mud threw his full ton and a quarter of weight down, using his firmly planted back legs as a pivot. It was a demonstration of professional heavy horse technique the likes of which no one, even old hardened teamsters, had ever seen.

The front wheels of the truck slid up onto the sheets of roofing iron. The crowd roared. Two Bob counted the cadence, "ONE TWO HEAVE! ONE TWO HEAVE!" and slowly but surely the heavy truck tobogganed through the mire, yard by hard-won yard, until at last a cry of triumph announced that the fire hose was able to reach the truck. The hotel and the free beer were saved!

The crowd of admirers around Big Daniel was three deep; everyone wanting to touch his heaving sweat-soaked sides. By his head, the town teamster stood holding Big Daniel's beloved summer straw hat in his hand. It had fallen into the mud and been trampled into a ruined rag. Then an odd thing happened. The Town Engineer, covered with mud but still managing to look natty in his breeches, leather jacket and stiff campaign hat, walked right up to Big Daniel and stopped not a foot away from him. Now this was something he never did under ordinary circumstances knowing full well that Big Daniel might take the opportunity to either kick him into the middle of next week or bite an important chunk out him.

For a long moment they stood like that, nose to nose, eyeing each other in the mutual respect to which only two committed professionals are entitled. Without for a moment breaking his eye contact with Big Daniel, the Town Engineer took off his prize hat, pulled his folding knife out of his pocket, and right then and there cut two big holes in the brim and set the hat right on Big Daniel's head.

It took quite a long time for the cheering and yelling to die down. In fact the noise still hadn't died down much when the beer company representative, up from Chicago for the grand opening, waded through the mud and tugged at the Town Engineer's elbow. "That horse, that horse, that's the most magnificent horse I have ever seen. Who owns him? And how much would you sell him for?"

The Town Engineer, looking somewhat less pukka without his hat, turned to look at the crowd. Everyone was holding their breath waiting...

"As to who owns this horse, I don't think anybody can claim to own him. He does report to the town teamster and the town teamster reports to me so I guess you could say he is a member of my department, Public Works." Then, remembering the ball peen hammer hastened to add, "And I don't know about selling him either."

"Well, I want to say right here and now that that is the most magnificent horse I have ever seen. As you know our brewery prides itself on having the finest horses in the land pulling it's Oktoberfest beer wagon and I am offering this horse a place on that team."

Big Daniel lifted his proud head as a collective gasp rose from the crowd. Big Daniel was being offered a chance at the really, really big time. The NHL of horsedom, a spot on the Chicago Oktoberfest Beer Wagon! "Now sir, you say this horse is not for sale but money talks sir, money talks. Name your price and my company will meet it."

The Town Engineer, sunk as he was up over his knees in the mud and minus his trademark hat, hardly came up to Big Daniel's chin. When at last he spoke he raised his voice high enough that the whole crowd could hear....

" This horse is not for sale but, given the great contribution he has made to this town on this day, there is no one would deny him a chance at the majors. There are, however, a few conditions and I think that, as head of the public works department, I am qualified to act as his agent."

"I am listening."

"First he gets top post, right hand lead horse..." The crowd murmured at the audacity of the engineer's demands but he wasn't finished yet. "...a private stall, his own teamster, a double ration of oats every Sunday..." the beer company agent had paled a little but he was still nodding his head up and down, "...and a guaranteed lifetime membership at a Kentucky Blue Grass horse farm when he chooses to retire."

"You drive a hard bargain mister, but this horse is one of the most up and comingest horses I have ever seen. You got yourself a deal."

"Oh, and one more thing..." By now the Chicago beer man was beginning to think he would have nothing left but his paisley patterned shorts to go home in. "... one more thing, Big Daniel gets to wear his new hat whenever he wants to and wherever he wants to as his own personal trademark."

Well, the town ended up buying the Earthworm tractor, figuring that they were going to have to pay for all the dents Mrs. Wienermacher had put into it with her hammer anyway. The "man from the mine" arranged for enough crushed rock to fix the Main Street, and by the time the special horse car sent up from Chicago to pick up Big Daniel arrived at the CN station, things were pretty much back to normal.

On Tuesday there was a big parade down Main Street, Big Daniel in the lead, wearing his new hat. The Town Engineer walking on one side of him and the Chicago beer man on the other side, he passed through the cheering crowds come to see him off. It seemed odd to have the Women's Christian Temperance Union marching, all flags flying, in a parade for a beer wagon horse but Big Daniel's fans weren't about to spoil his triumph on a technicality. Big Daniel had achieved his goal, a spot in the big league of horsedom. And no one even thought to question whether he could handle the job. It would have been like asking if Bobby Clark could play hockey...

Krzwyks' First of July

THIS STORY COULD HAVE BEEN TITLED "MISS PRESTOUPOULIOUS' FIRST OF JULY," OR EVEN "HUGHIE THE MOVIE'S FIRST OF JULY," SINCE THEY BOTH PLAYED IMPORTANT PARTS IN IT. But Miss Prestoupoulious moved away to Winnipeg and never came back, and Hughie the Movie managed to escape and stay hidden for two weeks. So it is to Anton Krzwyks that this story must be dedicated, because it was Anton who came the closest to death of any of us on that fateful First of July.

Long ago everyone used to take a day off on the First of July and do patriotic things. These were pretty much the same patriotic things we do now on Canada Day, but since we didn't really think there was much doubt about which country we were being patriotic in, we called it the First of July.

Celebrating the First of July in our town traditionally called for three main events. The first was a big parade, which followed a route down Main Street, and then out to the beach at Hard-To-Find Lake. Following the parade, there would be a Sports Day with speeches which nobody listened to, a bathing beauty contest which everybody watched, music provided by the Elks band, soft ball and horseshoes. There were three-legged races and bag races for the kids, and lots and lots of food. The final and main event was a grand firework display timed to begin just after sunset.

The fireworks display was the major event of the First of July. Money to support it was donated by nearly every organization in town and each year a different group took responsibility for staging it. This year it was the turn of the

184

Rotary Club.

Hughie Benson who operated the Rexland Theatre was a long-time member of the Rotary Club. Hughie, better known as Hughie the Movie to keep him sorted out from other Hughies in town, liked to think of himself as a pillar of the community. To demonstrate this sterling quality to others he devoted a good deal of his time to community good works. This would have been acceptable enough, but Hughie had a penchant for planning and organizing that was not matched by his ability to do that. The result was that Hughie's involvement in a project, particularly if given scope to apply his runaway enthusiasm, was a sure guarantee of disaster.

The last Rotary Club meeting prior to the First of July droned on as usual until finally, after the routine committee reports, the President called for plans and volunteers for the fireworks.

Now it happened that the President made his call at a time when everyone was talking to everyone else and nobody was paying attention to the chair (not an unusual state of affairs at Rotary meetings). Under ordinary circumstances somebody like Frank Schindlemacher would have volunteered to look after the fireworks. He would have gotten up a little committee and called Winnipeg to order a nice presentation like "The Fountain of Vesuvius" or "Sky Fire," or something, and that would have been that. But the inattention of the members created a dangerous gap and Hughie the Movie stepped right in. Before anyone realised what was happening, he had the floor and was presenting his plan.

Hughie's plan for the fireworks was beautiful, simplicity in itself, topical and elegant. No matter how hard they tried, no one could really find any fault with it, except for the fact that it was Hughie the Movie's idea.

Hughie proposed that members of the club use fireworks to recreate one of the great sea battles that so occupied our attention in those wartime days. Just off the beach at Hard-To-Find Lake, where the First of July celebrations would take place, there was a low rocky island that stuck up out of the water like the back of whale. Hughie's description of how the rock could be armed with rockets, pinwheels, Roman candles and quantities of cannon crackers to simulate the guns of a huge battleship, got people paying attention in spite of themselves.

Several of the local pleasure boats were to be outfitted with a wooden platform over the front deck and each would be equipped with a supply of rockets and crackers so that in the dark they could swoop around the battleship-reef, blazing away like attacking destroyers. The whole effect would be the grand spectacle of a battle at sea. In spite of the misgivings generated by the fact that this was Hughie the Movie's plan, everyone began to get excited about the idea.

In fact, that very excitement was a good indication of the sort of thing that would happen to Hughie's plans. The more excited everyone got, the more determined they were not to miss out on the fun. Instead of the three or four rocket-armed boats that Hughie had envisioned, nearly everyone on the lake started fitting out their Peterborough Lakesides and Wallaston Freighters with firing platforms festooned with rockets, whizbangs and fire fountains. No one thought Hughie's planned allocation of fireworks was sufficient either, and many began to order extras from Winnipeg. The CN Express Agent was heard to complain that more explosives were passing through his wicket than were going to the front.

The First of July dawned bright and clear and hot. Just before noon the parade began to assemble on the Team Track at the CNR Station. The noise and confusion as the various floats and marching groups began to jostle for position was tremendous. Near the railroad crossing on Main Street the mine's Pipe Band, which would lead the parade, was tuning up. The process of tuning twenty sets of pipes at once can only be appreciated by those who think that even pipes that are in tune sound like a strangling stork. At the far end of the station yard, the members of the Local Temple of the Burning Sand who would bring up the rear, were creating a balancing auricular horror as they attempted to tune their oriental pipes and gongs and settle on what tune they were playing. In between, the floats constructed by the various ethnic groups and social clubs were assembling.

The Dutch community had constructed a complete windmill on a wagon. The French used plaster and lath to build a replica of the Eiffel Tower and had mounted it precariously on the Flague's Bakery delivery truck. The Swedes, Icelanders, Danes and Norwegians had combined to build a replica of a Viking boat complete with square sail, brightly painted shields along the bulwarks and real oars. The boat was manned by a crew dressed in a passable imitation of traditional Viking dress, right down to the horned helmets. Fortified by a good breakfast of pickled herring and aquavit, they waved the oars around with such dangerous enthusiasm that their float, mounted on a wagon from Polker's Ice House, took up more space than any other three floats combined.

The Ukrainians built a beautiful replica of an old country farm yard, a small-plastered house painted blue and a mudbrick outdoor oven in the yard. The whole scene was mounted on a wagon donated by the Beaver Lumber and had a delightfully beribboned group of girls dancing to tzimbala music. The music was provided by a very happy group of old men who seemed to get a bit happier with each trip they made to stick their heads into the outdoor oven.

There was a Hungarian Castle and a very large replica of the Queen Mary that the English community had built originally for the Jubilee and had resurrected for the First of July. Mounted on a heavy wagon from the mine, a large wire-mesh elk, covered in lead foil was the pride of the BPO Elks Lodge No. 22.

The Rotarians, who traditionally ran the Bathing Beauty Pageant, had constructed a huge symbolic gear wheel covered with lead foil and toilet paper flowers dyed yellow and purple. All the entrants in the beauty contest were seated on blue crepe paper waves. The whole thing was mounted on the back of Cotton Charlie's new five-ton truck. That new truck was an attraction in itself as it was wartime and it had taken Charlie nearly a year to wangle a permit to buy it.

Amid all the noise and uproar, no one could hear the Parade Marshal blowing his whistle for the start, a problem he finally resolved by having the pipe band set off on its own leaving every one else scrambling to get into line as best they might. The parade went off pretty well. The constable quickly quelled what could have developed into a major battle between the Vikings and the Hungarians, caused when someone, (it could even have been Anton Krzwyks), made a comment about the pointed shape and content in Imperial gallons of the armoured vest worn by the Viking Maid of the Mountain who was riding on the long boat.

The Eiffel tower got caught in the new phone line into Wong's Steam Laundry and two spectators on the sidewalk near G.& B. Bakery were knocked into the gutter by enthusiastically manned oars on the Viking ship. The Royal Canadian Legion float depicting a section of trench from the First World War, tipped over on the last turn but one before Hard-To-Find-Lake, producing a very realistic wartime tableau with the ditch filled with torn sandbags interspersed with a tangle of military equipment and groaning Legionnaires.

The parade arrived at the lake to much cheering from the assembled townsfolk. After a suitable address of welcome from the Master of Ceremonies, the floats were hauled off to the area where each group had its camp.

During the morning of the "First," those not involved in either watching or being in the parade would select a spot along the beach, build cooking fires and, in most cases, put up a tent. Every ethnic group had its own traditional area. The English liked to put up their tents in orderly rows down near the dock. The Ukrainians set up a huge circle further back near the trees with the French and the Hungarians between them and the change house. The Dutch made orderly rows like the English, but closer to the water. Whole families of Norwegians, Swedes, Icelanders and Danes all crowded around Hjalmerson's old log icehouse that was situated between Maundie's Lakeside Store and the dock.

During the afternoon the Elks Band would set up on the old bandstand on the hill behind the flagpole. Under the capable direction of Sigmunder Goodmunderson, the band would play a medley of patriotic airs, more medley than Sigmunder would have preferred most of the time, due to the custom of having several cases of beer stored away in the crawl space under the bandstand.

Kids swam, made cannon balls off the diving board or played softball, trying hard to avoid the "entertainment for children" that the Rotarians always organised. Nobody wanted to be seen making a fool of themselves in a sack race or a three-legged sprint. Slender women stood gingerly on the edge of the dock waiting to be pushed in. Not so slender women sweated in the shade and made critical comments. Men visited around, drinking if they weren't churchy or, if they were, helping with the Vestry Guild ball-throw booth.

Dishes got washed, kids waited the eternity of one hour after eating to get in one last swim. Up by the Ukrainian tents the tzimbala band tinkled in the soft air, and everyone waited for the setting sun to signal the start of the fireworks display.

Down near the dock, right alongside the spot where the English families pitched their tents, Pendlebury McNeish parked his little Austin van. Pendlebury, who was the chief (and most of the time, the only) announcer at the local radio station, was also its repair man and was considered to be something of an electronics wizard. Using what was pretty innovative circuitry for that time, Pendlebury had fitted his van with a collection of huge amplifiers, a microphone and a turntable, all powered by the motor of the van.

Pendlebury and his van were, in fact, part of Hughie's plan. Pendlebury was to provide a running account of the mock sea battle and produce realistic battle-type background sounds to augment the spectacle of the fireworks sea battle. For a vantage point from which to observe the action in the bay Pendlebury had constructed a high and somewhat shaky platform. It was supported on one side by the roof of the van and on the other by a single wooden prop. The prop was hinged to the platform at its upper end and its lower end rested on the ground.

Right beside Pendlebury's van, the Stebenses were erecting their tent with the help of the schoolteacher they were boarding. Miss Prestoupoulious was a French teacher. Not that she was French herself, she was Greek. In truth, she couldn't really speak French but, in those days, it didn't really matter if one could speak French when teaching it. French as a subject was largely a matter of memorizing enough verbs and exceptions to the rule so that you could pass the provincial exams.

Miss Prestoupoulious was as good a French teacher as any, in fact better than most. The previous summer she had shocked the entire town, not to mention the school board, by taking the summer vacation and actually going to France! She went to a place called Nice on the River, only you don't call it "Nice on the River," you call it "Neese on the Rivyerah." Anyway, that's where she went and she came home with a funny accent and an inflatable rubber horse. Even though she was stoutly defended by Mrs Stebens, that bastion of good British propriety, the coffee tables of the town fairly smoked with speculation about what else she might have gotten up to away off there in France… a woman alone with a rubber horse.

Tents like the one the Stebenses were erecting were not the dome-shaped self-supporting marvels of today. They were heavy, straight-walled canvas affairs, with a roof pole supported by uprights resting on the ground at each end. Their entire structural stability depended on firmly anchored guy ropes front and back. For the back, Mr. Stebens managed to find a handy tree and tied the rear guy rope to that, but out in front there was no tree and he was forced to make the best of things by tying onto the supporting leg of Pendlebury's loudspeaker platform.

Darkness was just falling along the beach when Miss Prestoupoulious finished blowing up her rubber horse and was testing its firmness by sitting astride it on the ground in front of the Stebens' tent. Mr. and Mrs Stebens were inside the tent heating water for a nice warm "cuppa" on the Coleman stove. Perched high above them on his little platform, surrounded by microphones and switches, Pendlebury McNeish adjusted his souped-up public address system to the maximum possible volume in preparation for the flash of light from Hughie's "Battleship" island that would signal the start of the fireworks display.

Nervously, he eyed the tangled mass of wires strung about the van and draped across his precarious little platform, wondering just what the effect of this untried combination of over-powered amplification and huge loudspeakers would really be.

Down by Hjalmerson's ice house, the Norwegians and the Icelanders had set aside their preferred sport of fighting to turn their attention to the second love of their lives, boats. It was Barney Hjalmerson, wandering along the shoreline looking for a bush that could provide enough privacy for the unloading of a considerable quantity of used beer, who had stumbled across Joe the Baker's new Peterborough Lakeside, complete with its powerful new forty horsepower Evinrude outboard motor. Pausing only long enough to take care of his original mission, Barney rushed back to Hjalmerson's icehouse with the news. Every ice-blue northern eye that could still focus grew cold and hard. That huge motor challenged not only their traditional mastery of the waterways, but worse, they were in danger of being left in the wake of a Bavarian baker.

Hjalmarson turned to Einerson, Einerson turned to Johnsgaardson, Johnsgaardson turned to Thorlickson, Thorlickson turned to Ingebritson, Ingebritson turned to Williams, whose father was Welsh, but whose mother was a Finnebogason.

There wasn't a 'forty horse' to be had; in fact, nearly everyone used the same motor, the old dependable Johnson OK75, officially rated at 7.5 horsepower, but capable, at their finely tinkered best, of producing nearly 10.

Later when everyone was trying to piece together the events of the day, they would blame the idea on Williams who, after all, had foreign blood in him. But, in truth, it was an idea born of the laws of mathematics. If one motor produced ten horsepower, it was irrefutable that seven motors should produce an awe-inspiring seventy horsepower. No one ever tried to figure out whose idea it was to remove the mock Viking ship from the Polker's Icehouse wagon that had carried it in the parade, and lash it to the deck of Einar Einarson's old netpuller, but the effect was splendid. What was even better was that when the seven motors were mounted on Einar's old boat, they were completely hidden by the overhanging stern of the longship.

Darkness was just beginning to fall as the Viking ship, moving with deceptive stateliness under the power of only one of its seven motors, carried its load of horn-hatted warriors, about forty pounds of unauthorised fireworks and a considerable reserve of aquavit out into the bay.

Out on the little island that was to play the part of the besieged enemy battle cruiser, Joe the Baker and Otto the Bank were putting the finishing touches on the fireworks. Wooden racks had been constructed along the spine of the rock to hold the rockets. Along the shoreline, row after row of fire fountains sat ready to provide a visual outline of the fighting battleship. Near one end of the rock, on a low flat ledge nearly level with the water, two members of the Rotary Club, supervised by Hughie the Movie himself, readied strings of huge cannon crackers that would provide the gunfire sound effects. The racks for the rockets were full. Twenty-four tall cylinders, each trailing a tail of fuse, stood ready to go. Stacked horizontally like cordwood, another hundred and twenty or so rockets lay ready to replace the ones in the launching racks.

Anyone with any conception of how dangerous fireworks can be if not properly managed would have felt his hair stand on end at the sight of the rockets, bombs, fire pots, and crackers heaped together in the close confines of that tiny rock. But there was no one on the rock that knew anything about fireworks, so no one's hair stood on end. In any case, given the effect of Louie the Jay's bootleg whiskey, it is doubtful if there was a hair on the island capable of standing up under even the most horrifying of circumstances.

Darkness was just beginning to fall along the beach as Joe the Baker fumbled in his vest pocket for a match.

Up by the change house Anton Krzwyks from the Hungarian float was demonstrating cavalry sword drill to an admiring cluster of beribboned Ukrainian dancers when word passed through the crowd that the fireworks display was about to start. Everyone rushed for the beach, Cossacks and Tartars, Slovaks and Austrians dodged through the trees, racing to gain a good spot from which to view the fireworks.

Anton, attempting to get past the mob and lay claim to a good vantage point for himself, decided on a short cut. Still holding his sword at the high charge he veered left, and the fates took him directly through the line of the English tents.

The guy line Mr. Stebens had strung between the front of the Stebens' tent and the supporting prop under Pendlebury McNeish's broadcasting platform was perfectly placed to catch Krzwyks by the throat as he charged through, and it did.

The force of Anton's charge yanked the supporting prop out from under McNeish's platform and collapsed the Stebens' tent onto the Stebenses and the Coleman stove. Anton himself pivoted into the air in a graceful double back-flip, not actually a complete double back-flip, but about one and a half of one.

He didn't land on his feet but came down out of the sky head first with his sword still extended ahead of him, to land like a huge javelin right in Miss Prestoupoulious' lap. The sword, just missing some of the more treasured bits of Miss Prestoupoulious' anatomy, passed between her thighs and skewered the rubber horse. Krzwyks wasn't the only thing to land there. As the broadcasting platform collapsed, the microphone, still turned up to the highest volume that Pendlebury's electronic genius could achieve, landed in Miss Prestoupoulious' overcrowded lap, just ahead of Krzwyks.

Something like the flatulent sound made by the air escaping that punctured horse might have been heard from time to time in the Corona Hotel beer parlor of an evening, but never so fierce or so sustained. The anguished gobbling and gargling coming from Anton's tortured throat may have been heard before, perhaps as some Bengal tiger tucked into his unfortunate evening meal. No doubt the world had been subjected to the sort of scream pushed forth by Miss Prestoupoulious on some horrible occasion of pillage or rapine, but never before had three such sounds been pressed onto the world in concert. McNeish's microphone caught it all and multiplied it a thousandfold.

Amplified to a level never before dreamed of, that obscene, heart stopping, antediluvian chorus brayed out over the darkening waters of the bay at a volume not even anticipated as necessary for Judgement Day. It was a blood curdling, marrow chilling trump that sobered Vikings, silenced Frenchmen, disorganised Germans and wilted the upper lip of every Englishman for miles.

Even Hughie the Movie out on the island thought that Pendlebury McNeish had gone a bit far in devising an opening fanfare for the fireworks display.

As that horrible sound rolled across the water the effect was instantaneous. With one huge roar every motor on the lake leapt into life. Boats, big and small, charged the rock in the bay from all angles with firework "cannons" blazing. The "battleship" on the rock was not long in getting its defending fire into action. At first, with the boats circling more or less to the left like skaters on a pond, it looked as though the whole thing might just come off. But no one had anticipated the maelstrom of waves that the combined wake of four dozen boats would produce.

Firing platforms on the pitching, plunging motorboats were no longer level. Rockets were being launched at all kinds of angles. Some went straight up and then turned to plunge in flaming fury on the boat that had launched them. Others roared off horizontally, leaving a trail of fire in their wake as they menaced island and boats alike.One stray missile managed to touch off the pile of spare rockets stacked on the island and, in moments, the whole bay was ablaze. "Star Shells" and "Burning Blossoms" and "Midges Sky Fountain Whistling Tracers" deluged the dry shingles on the roofs of lakeside cabins with red and purple fire. Some started mini forest fires in the tall trees along the beach, and whole rows of tents were bursting into multicoloured flame.

The uproar was so great and had reached such a pitch so quickly that everyone's attention was drawn away from the Viking ship, which had moved out into the bay and was even then turning with stately if unsteady grace to join the attack on the island. Down inside the old netpuller that bore the Viking hull the Johnsgaardson brothers began methodically starting motor after motor, shrieking with the wild-eyed grins of true berserkers as they jammed each throttle wide open. Suddenly, the longboat was on the move. Picking up speed at an incredible rate, it tore through the water, shedding oars and shields, some with Vikings still attached, as it charged toward the pandemonium on the island. The plan had been to steer the boat by shouting directions down to the Johnsgaardsons tending the motors, but no one had reckoned on the overwhelming noise the combined engines would produce.

In any case the Vikings still left on the deck had their own problems. A stray rocket had landed in the middle of their contraband store of extra fireworks. Belching a now all too real breath of fire, the dragon boat, completely out of control and covered in flames and smoke, roared right up and over the sizzling island. Jean Joseph Pierre Jesus LeGrandnezes' Carlyle Special, which was just passing by at the time, was sliced neatly in half by the smoking long ship as it headed for the beach.

With his head still buried deep in Miss Prestoupoulious' offended lap, Anton Krzwyks took a second, or perhaps two, to go over the options open to him. Considering how the Stebenses would surely interpret the present location of most of his upper body, and interpreting the clamour that he could hear even through the padding of Miss Prestoupoulious' thighs as that of a community already rising in outrage, it was clear that flight was his one and only hope of salvation.

With a mighty tug Krzwyks yanked his sword from the dying horse and his head from between the legs of the outraged teacher, who was by this time shrieking randomly in Greek, English and French. Leaping to his feet, Anton fled toward the beach, his sword still held at the High Charge in trained reflex.

Behind him, the collapsed tent had caught fire from the Coleman stove, but this did nothing to deter the charge of the Stebenses to the rescue of their ward. Completely entangled in blazing canvass and bellowing Anglo Saxon oaths not heard since that bad day in 1066, the Stebenses, Mister, and Mistress, pursued the fleeing Hussar through the trees.

On the beach, mothers dunked smouldering offspring in the lake and fathers flung leftover Limeaid onto burning tents and cabins. The whole maddened crowd surged this way and that in a desperate effort to escape the continuing rain of fire from the bay. What happened next must surely account for many a behavioural quirk that surfaced in the general population in the years to follow. Into the terrible scene of fire and panic Krzwyks, pursued relentlessly by a flaming tent , burst out of the trees just as the fire belching longship roared through the shallows and right up onto the beach. With all seven motors churning it threw up a huge tail of dirt and gravel like some prehistoric dirt bike and charged on across the campsite.

First the Stebenses, tent and all, were picked up on the serpent prow of the longboat, then Krzwyks in his turn was swept off the ground in mid-flight. The grand tableau that followed only lasted for a moment but was burned into the memory of everyone who saw it.

The Viking boat, spewing fire and flame in all directions, smashed across the campground with Anton, sword still held high, impaled on the prow with the Stebenses, and their flaming tent wrapped around him like a huge toga. I said the tableau was short-lived and it was, ending abruptly against the side of Cotton Charlie's new truck. The wreck of the Viking boat and the remnants of the truck blazed merrily long into the night, watched by the singed and smoke-blackened Vikings and the equally singed Stebenses who had been extracted from the wreck.

It was in fact quite a while before anyone calmed down enough to recall the sword- bearing figurehead the ship had worn on its death charge. It was some time after that they finally located Anton Krzwyks. The force of the impact had launched him into the air and through the window of Maundie's Lakeside Store where he had landed in the ice cream freezer. When they finally extricated him from the jumble of crushed Eskimo Pies and Revels, he had stiffened up considerably and had assumed a strange blue colour. Every one thought he was a goner. The Stebenses were heard to mutter that it served him right. But Mrs. Prystyp Mykelnetlicoff and Mrs. Boyar Pelstrycknichuk, two ladies possessed of the huge bosoms and mighty hips that bear witness to a heritage of the Steppes and familiarity with the cold, undertook to thaw him out clasped between them.

Prystyp Mykelnetlicoff was sure the Hungarian was taking longer than he needed to thaw out, pillowed, as he was between Mrs. Mykelnetlicoff's imposing breasts, but everyone put that down to the historic distrust between the Ukrainians and the Hungarians. Mrs. Mykelnetlicoff told Prystyp that she would thaw out her Hungarians any way she pleased.

Cotton Charlie and the Vikings who could still walk, looked for Hughie the Movie all that night, vowing a very public and horrible end to that man and his plans for all time. There were some who claim Hughie spent the night under Hjalmerson's dock, breathing through two soda straws. Others were sure he had been spirited away by the lady who took tickets at the theatre, and who was thought to be sweet on him. Anyway, by the time he turned up two weeks later, the killing urge had somewhat worn off.

The next First of July we had a tableau of Champlain landing on the shore of the St. Lawrence done by the members of the Figure Skating Club and tastefully illuminated with battery-powered lights supplied by the "man from the mine."

Mizzus Yer Honour

THERE WERE SOME GREAT FISHING LAKES WHERE WE LIVED. Truth is almost any lake you went to in those days was a great fishing lake. Lake Athapap could produce from its terrifying cold depths lake trout bigger than the most optimistic of fishing guide books said they should be. Schist Lake, with its reef-strewn, boggy bays was home to some of the longest, most prehistoric looking jack fish any one could ever hope to catch. The pickerel that lurked along the rocky shores of Tin Can Narrows and Eight Chain Bay were maybe the tastiest in the country. There were so many fish that it seemed you could fish forever without reducing their numbers.

So when the proposal was put forward to promote our lakes to the Americans it was received, at first anyway, with great enthusiasm because it was generally accepted that sport fishing was going to bring a wave of prosperity to the town. Hotel owners thought secretly of raising their room rates. "Wong's Golden Gate Cafe" no longer seemed classy enough as a name for the town's major eatery. Names like "The Copper Lode Dining Salon" were considered. Big John Kipper even thought a second gas pump might be necessary. It was a given that the Baker's Narrows Lodge was about to make a fortune renting rooms and boats to the Americans and selling them fish hooks.

Well, the Americans came alright, but they came in half-ton trucks they called "pick-ups," each truck loaded with gasoline, motors, food, beer, tents, stoves and enough fishing equipment to make the Bell Hardware's spring order look like a sample. Behind each "pick-up" they towed at least two boats, sometimes three piled one on top of the other, and every available space in those boats was packed with more beer and more fishing gear. They drove right past Kipper's gas pumps and right past the new tackle displays in the hardware store window. They didn't even stop at the Corona for a beer, let alone a room, and, without a how-de-do, used the boat ramp at the Baker's Narrows Lodge to launch their equipment. Clusters of tents sprouted all over the lake with flotillas of assorted aluminium boats hauled up on the beaches in front of them and the shore sparkled with empty beer cans.

No one was making any money. What was worse, coffee conversation in the Golden Gate Cafe after the weekends began to reveal that even the most wily and successful local fishermen were starting to find it hard to come up with the sort of impressive catches they were used to. The locals were getting resigned to glumly standing by the government dock and watching their American guests loading cooler after cooler of fish into their "pick-ups." As the summer wore on, however, and one after another of their favourite fishing holes proved to be fished out, a certain snarliness began to manifest itself along coffee row and in the change-house lunch rooms.

Some times in life there are a lot of things going on at once. Individuals are busy planning their own little games, completely ignoring what a "tangled web" the world of mortals really is. Every once in a while, though, if the gods get bored, they'll start to fool around just for fun, pulling at a string here, loosening a knot there and all the little plans and strands in the community start to get tangled up. Things that you never would have thought had anything to do with other things begin to crowd each other and you can't really predict what the outcome will be. This is pretty much what happened to the election of the year that Dewdney's boathouse burned down. It was pretty plain afterwards, of course, but nobody could have predicted it at the time...

Our mayor, Two Bob Bobdinsky, was up for re-election that year, and more than a bit worried about his chances because of the American fisherman thing. It had been Two Bob that had pushed for advertising in the American fishing magazines. "It will bring a whole herd of Yankee fishermen up here and those guys will all be stayin' in the hotels, and drinkin' beer in the beer parlor, and buyin' gas and fish hooks.

It's gonna be a gold mine." Well, like I said, they came alright but the outcome wasn't doing Two Bob's election chances much good. There was even grumblings in the Corona that maybe the deputy mayor, Gunther Volkstein, should be given a whack at the mayoring job.

The "man from the mine" and Two Bob drank most of a "forty pounder" of rye one weekend trying to figure out a scheme to get Two Bob's train back on the track. The mine liked Two Bob. Things went smoothly with him in the chair and they weren't at all keen on Gunther who was, after all, an employee and, what was worse, a union man. Gunther had appeared in our town somewhat mysteriously from Europe. He was never too specific about what part of Europe, although he was always quick to point out that it wasn't from Germany. He had been hired by the mine's machine shop the day he applied, precision grinders were rare and grinders of Gunther's craft and accuracy were rarer still. It was said that when they asked him if he could machine a block to within a thousandth of an inch, he asked "Which side?" When they didn't understand he explained that the measurement was a line. A line had thickness no matter how thin it was and he needed to know if they wanted his work to fit the inside, outside or middle of the line. He got the job.

He applied the same sort of thinking to the town council and Mayor Two Bob was secretly very happy to have him do so, for loopholes and errors in the city solicitor's by-law drafts never got past Gunther's near maniacal demands for perfection in all things. That Gunther wanted to park himself in Mayor Two Bob's big chair as the mayor didn't trouble Two Bob too much. Gunther's dour perfectionism was handy for by-law drafting, but not the stuff of a mayoralty contest, although it had to be admitted that Gunther's persistent campaigning was beginning to win him a respectable level of support in certain circles.

Staples Dibson's troubles were less threatening. In fact, he was taking steps to deal with them even before that fateful summer. Staples owned the local newspaper and was also its editor, most of its reporting staff and, with a little help from his wife, the circulation department. For some time, Staples had been dissatisfied with the headlines that topped the front page of the *Daily Staple*. A good headline should have people buying the paper just to find out what the head-line was about, even if there wasn't too much in the way of real news. A good headline should hint at mysterious things and it should have rhythm and a newspaperish sort of melody. The book on headline writing that was part of the correspondence course that Staples had ordered from The Chicago School of American Journalism was particularly concerned with melody. "The poetry of the front page" they called it. Staples was determined to put these theories into practice in the *Daily Staple*. It was not as easy as it sounds because headline poetry, unlike normal poetry, rhymes the first letters of the words instead of the last. Some of Staples early efforts were not too bad...

"FISHING FANATIC FILLETS FORTY POUNDER"

was his best effort so far, but still it lacked that "big hook" that the Chicago experts called for, the hook that would make people buy the paper to read the rest of the story. Every night, after the shop was closed he would sip his evening rye, study the book, and then try his hand at a headline or two...

"CURLING CHRISTIANS BIG CONCERN
FOR LOCAL PASTORS"

was not even close. Even so, Staples was not a guy to give up easily. It was just a matter of application and practice. He wrote practice headlines every night and had to admit they were getting better and better. He particularly liked...

"WATER WORKS WON'T WASH"

...referring to the annual rejection by the council of a water system for the town. He wasn't quite ready to try the new headline style on the *Daily Staple* itself just yet, but he continued to work hard at his practice headlines. He did feel that he was beginning to master the art. It wouldn't be long before his new skills would be contributing nicely to the circulation figures.

Laura Langmuir had her own fish to fry. Actually, Laura Langmuir was really Lettie Lobchuck but, during the train ride from her home town of Pelly, Saskatchewan, she had decided to give herself a whole makeover, including her name. This was not uncommon in our town. Isolated and remote, it attracted the adventurous, the ambitious and the dreamers.

It also attracted a certain number of people who, for one reason or another, needed to start over, especially in the name department. Lettie had studied Pitman shorthand in business college and could type with commendable accuracy and speed, but these were not really skills in high demand in her small farming community. Lettie's other problem was that, although she certainly was able to attract any young man that interested her, none of the young farmers in the area could even stir the slightest spark in her well-upholstered chest. Lettie's mother summed the problem up neatly: "Lettie, you got a body would make a grown man cry, but you marry one of these shit scrapers around here and you'll wear it out hauling slops to the hogs." Lettie knew she had to get out. When her uncle Slobodian wrote about the opening for a secretary with our town council, she packed her bag and was on the Friday sleeper. On Saturday morning Laura Langmuir got her first whiff of smelter smoke as the porter handed her down onto the stool that made the last step onto the station platform. She got the job just before noon, and by two she had discovered that Mayor Two Bob Bobdinsky was not only single, but belonged to the Greek Orthodox church. By suppertime of her first day at work, she had her goal firmly in mind. The wife of a mayor of a smart mining town would never have to slop no hogs.

Gunther Volkstein had his own devil to deal with. He wanted Mayor Two Bob's job so bad he could taste it. Two elections in a row he had come pretty close with the help of the union and the undercover support of a few businessmen who thought Two Bob was spending too much money on frivolities like fire trucks and side walks.

Gunther had convinced himself during the two previous election campaigns that he had a pretty good chance. On both occasions, however, and just before voting day a sudden flood of advertising, newspaper articles, interviews on the local radio station, even once a picture article in the provincial paper, had given Two Bob a sudden boost that took him back into the mayor's chair.

Gunther suspected, well, he was certain, that the "man from the mine" might be quietly helping Two Bob out, but there was never any proof. Heading into the third election of his short political career, Gunther was still sitting in the deputy mayor's chair, trying desperately to think of some way to move himself over into Two Bob's big chair at the head of the council table. And now, a second preoccupation was causing more wrinkles in Gunther's big square forehead. He had fallen hopelessly in love with Laura Langmuir, smitten beyond salvation the moment she opened her shorthand notebook and crossed those lovely legs that had been painted brown with a black stripe up the back to look like silk stockings.

Two Bob and the "man from the mine" met discreetly at Two Bob's cabin on the West Arm to talk about the upcoming election. Both agreed that if the fishing thing could just be resolved, Two Bob was a shoe-in. If catches continued to dwindle though, and Two Bob remained identified with the policy of bringing the Americans in, there was a real likelihood that Gunther Volkstein might just become the new mayor. And that outcome neither Two Bob nor the "man from the mine" found very appealing.

Athapap Lake wasn't the only lake around of course; the country was a network of lakes, most connected by small creeks, and there were lots of fish in those other lakes. Lakes like Trout, Big Island, Aimie, Mikanogan and Tartan, boasted enough fish to satisfy all the locals forever. The problem was that most folks had their boats and their boathouses on Athapap. True, Mikanogan Creek did lead from Athapap into Big Island Lake, and once a boat could be gotten through the rapids in the narrow gorge at the foot of the creek, you could move from there into all the other lakes with ease. It was that gorge that was the problem.

The water surging through the constricted channel made it nearly impossible to get a boat through and into the calmer reaches of the upper part of the creek. At one time it could be done with a lot of rope and muscle, but now a tall, jagged pillar of rock stood smack in the centre of the channel and nothing could get past it. That obelisk-like barrier of stone was the result of a failed attempt to widen the little channel in the creek. Powder Phil Sugarman had spent the better part of the winter quietly amassing a large quantity of dynamite by putting a stick or two in his lunch kit whenever he thought the underground shift boss in the mine might not be watching too closely. There was a deep crevice in one of the rock walls that formed the sides of the channel and it had been Powder Phil's plan to stuff that crevice with the purloined dynamite and bingo, a wide channel. But either the crevice had not been deep enough or Phil's lunch kit had been too small because all that happened was that a hunk of the wall had moved right into the middle of the channel sealing the entrance to the creek as effectively as a gate. It was a tall slender needle of rock with a sharp jagged point at the top, defiantly sticking up into the air right in mid stream. It was promptly named "Phil's Finger." Someone even painted that name on the rock itself.

About half way down the bottle of rye, the "man from the mine" quietly pointed out that if the folks could get their boats up past Phil's Finger and into Big Island Lake, they would be fishing in areas not infested with "You-Alls." The odds on Two Bob's re-election would improve considerably if that could be made to happen.

It didn't take long for them to hit on John Makook. John had a well-deserved reputation as a welder and mechanic, the kind who could find a solution to the most intractable of mechanical and engineering challenges. The "man from the mine" hinted that if John were to approach the mine for materials that he wouldn't have a whole lot of trouble getting permission to rummage through the mine's scrap iron heap and there were always odds and ends of cable around. By the following Wednesday, John showed Two Bob a sketch of a simple man-powered hoist that could lift a boat over Phil's Finger and plop it down in the creek above. By Friday, a portable welding outfit loaned by the mine had been floated over to the mouth of the creek and John Makook, his head in a black welding helmet, was making the sparks fly.

The election was only three weeks off by the time Makook was ready to demonstrate his marvellous contrivance. On the rock above the gorge, opposite the offending finger of rock, John had constructed a pivoting metal arm that could be swung out over the calm water below the obstruction. A cable attached to a hand-operated winch would be attached to a waiting boat. When loaded, the boat would be lifted high into the air, swung right over the rock obstruction and lowered gently onto the surface of the pool above. The winch was fitted with a lever-operated brake to lock the boat in its suspended position while it was moving over Phil's Finger and to enable the operator to control the rate of descent into the creek above.

The only real drawback anyone could see to the machine, which was simple and elegant enough, was that the hoist was out of sight of the upper pond, a location made necessary by the fact that there was no dry ground in the gorge itself. Whoever moved a boat up the creek using Makook's hoist would have to have a partner above the gorge to tell him when to start the lowering process. This was not deemed to be much of a problem since fishing was a social business and almost no one went out fishing alone.

Two Bob was, by this time, pretty conscious of the importance of even a few votes and so, at the next council meeting, a formal ceremony to inaugurate the new hoist was proclaimed. It was not by accident that it was scheduled for the weekend before the election. A good crowd was expected, as there was no shortage of disappointed fishermen wanting to escape the fished out lakes below the gorge. Two Bob volunteered his new Carlyle Special to be the first boat officially over the obstacle in the creek. Staples Dibson could be relied upon to be there with his news camera. As the builder, John Makook would be given the honour of hoisting the boat with the windlass and releasing the brake to settle it gently down into the pond above the gorge.

The arrangements seemed fine to every one until, much to Two Bob's dismay, Gunther Volkstein volunteered to be the one who would stand on the rock above and signal John when the boat had been safely swung past Phil's Finger and could be lowered into the creek. Two Bob's political alarm bells went off like the gong in the firehouse. To let his potential rival for the mayor's chair be seen to be directing things, and to put him in a position that would permit him to make the grand opening something less than a tribute to Two Bob himself, was unthinkable.

Frantically casting around for a solution to Gunther's all too transparent attempt to finesse him out of the glory of solving the fishing problem, Two Bob had a sudden inspiration. Or it may have been a god out for a little fun that drew his eye to the trim figure of Laura Langmuir, primly perched near the clerk's table with her shorthand notebook on her crossed knees.

"Well, you know, there has been a lot of work involved in getting this boat hoist thing done. Miss Langmuir, here, has done a lot of letter writing and note taking above and beyond her regular work. I would like to see her standing up on that rock right alongside the deputy mayor... show the council can appreciate the work of the fairer sex... maybe Gunther could whisper to her when to yell out 'lower away' or something."

Well, if this had been one of them Greek plays, there would have been a bunch of singing Greeks in the background, lined up along the wall of the council chamber singing, "Don't do it, Two Bob. Don't go that way, Two Bob. The god's are treacherous, Two Bob. They'll grease your toe rubbers, Two Bob!" But of course there wasn't any Greek chorus, there were hardly any Greeks in our town at all in fact. Too cold I guess; they all lived in Toronto or somewhere.

The day of the grand opening of the "Mikanogan Creek Boat Lift" was a lovely one, lovely as only a northern summer's day can be. Below the gorge, at least twenty boats were bobbing around on the water, waiting a turn at the new lift. Two Bob's beautiful mahogany Carlisle Special was manoeuvred into the slings that John Makook had made from a couple of hunks of old conveyer belt from the mine. Laura was perched as pretty as a picture on the top of the cliff and standing right behind her was the Deputy Mayor, wearing his best fishing stuff. John Makook was at the winch, which was already taking the weight of the mayor's boat. Staples Dibson had found a good angle for the picture of the boat at the time when it would be suspended in mid air making the perilous passage over Phil's Finger. The "man from the mine" was not there, of course. It would never have done for him to take an open part in the town's affairs. The mine manager and his wife had been invited though, and their boat was one of the ones in the bay.

Everything seemed to be set and the mayor waved to Laura and Gunther to signal John Makook to start hoisting. If anyone had taken a close look at Gunther Volkstein, however, they might have called the whole thing off. His hands were trembling, beads of sweat were popping out on his shiny forehead and his mouth was opening and closing as if he was trying to say something that just wouldn't come out. The problem, of course, was his proximity to Laura Langmuir. Her perfume seemed to surround him in the warm summer air. Her silky hair was lifted by the light puffs of breeze from the lake and blew across his fevered face. That same warm wind was impudently pressing Laura's silk blouse against her in a most revealing way. Try as he might, Gunther could not get his eyes to rise from her softly rounded shoulders to take up their task of monitoring the progress of Two Bob's boat. And so, that's how it all happened. Just as the boat was at its most perilous part of the crossing, suspended in the air above the jagged needle of rock that Powder Phil had pushed into the middle of the creek, some mischievous god summoned up a puff of wind that set the Mayor's boat swinging. Laura took an involuntary step backward, right up against Gunther's heaving chest.

Gunther was a man of iron self control. Had to be, working to the fine tolerances of his trade. But this time he watched helplessly as his arms, as though they had a mind of their own, lifted themselves up and wrapped Laura Langmuir in a hug that included some parts of her not usually open to the public.

Her reaction was immediate and loud.

"**LET GO**! " she yelled and John Makook, interpreting her outraged cry to mean that a prompt descent was needed, yanked open the brake and down came Two Bob's boat right on the point of Phil's Finger. That cruel rock made short work of the delicately fitted planks, and artfully crafted frames of the bottom of the hull. In a moment, what had been one of the most beautiful boats on the lake was a gutted wreck impaled above the swirling water on an obscene point of rock named after a dynamiter's digit.

That night, after writing the article on the happenings at the boat hoist, Staples Dibson settled himself down to do his headline writing homework for the Chicago correspondence course. His assignment was to do headlines about a fictitious riot of iron workers, but it wasn't but two or three inches down the rye bottle that Staples started to toy with the day's events. **"Boat Bottom Dealt Blow"** was discarded as soon as he wrote it down. **"Mayor's Mahogany No Match For Rampaging Rock"** also ended up on the floor, as did **"Boat Bottom No Match For Phil's Finger."** The story was too good not to have an eye catching headline in it somewhere and Staples alternately wrote and refreshed his "rye and ginger," each draft coming a little closer to achieving the "poetry of the headline" the course outline had promised. It was late when he staggered off home, leaving his last and, he thought, his best effort lying on his desk. It was his custom, once he had reviewed the news, to write the real headline for the next day's paper and leave it on the print shop bulletin board for the type-setter who came in the early hours of the morning. It was either the rye or the meddling of the gods, but this time he forgot.

When the layout man and the typesetters came in and found no headline pinned to the board, they looked around and found what appeared to them to be headline for the day's paper lying on Dibson's desk. It only took moments to set it up. Soon the presses were humming. By six o'clock, the first bundles were delivered to the Club News on Main Street, just in time for the men going on day shift and coming off graveyard shift to pick up their copies.

Staples Dibson sometimes drank a bit more rye than was called for, but he never missed the morning train. No matter how late the night before might have been, Staples would be at the station for the six-thirty departure of the Winnipeg train, making notes of who was leaving, and why, and sometimes picking up tidbits of out of town news from the train men. It had always been his habit to pick up a couple of copies of his paper from the Club News on his way from his home down to the station since the newspaper office was somewhat off the most direct route. This morning as he walked along staring with horror at the headline to the main story, he realized with a sickening lurch to an already precarious stomach just what must have happened. Without missing a step, Staples continued his walk to the station, but this time, instead of chatting with the crowd on the platform, he mounted the steps himself and found a seat on the third car between the diner and the mail coach. He slouched well down in his seat and covered his face with the newspaper. About fifty miles out of town, the conductor found him there and, although it was a bit unusual, Staples was well known to him and he sold him a ticket to Kelowna.

You got to hand it to Two Bob Bobdinsky. He must have known it was all over, but he did make what was later agreed to be a gallant try. As soon as the beer parlor in the Corona Hotel opened that morning he stopped in to buy a round and chat with the boys as he often did. The raillery was just too much. Every which way he turned, someone was waving the paper at him and making some kind of remark. He tried the Royal and even went down to the Richmond where he nearly got into a scrap with Barney the Barber. Staples, he soon found out, had fled. Later in the morning, when Laura saw him sitting alone in his office, head in his hands, staring at the front page of *The Daily Staple*, she thought it best not to disturb him. She had read the masterpiece of a headline Staples had created, as had all the rest of the town, before the morning blast whistle blew.

"PHIL'S FINGER FRAGS BOB BOB'S BOTTOM!"

Oh, as a headline in the true Chicago style, it was a dandy all right, poetic and just vague enough to invite purchasers of the paper to find what it was all about. It was simply bursting with rhythm and journalistic flair, but it was also the end of Two Bob's political career. Two Bob had always kept the interests of the mining company in mind and they didn't forget him. By Tuesday, the mine had called to say how much they needed him to accept a position in their Montreal Metal Refinery and by Friday, Two Bob was on the train.

Gunther got himself elected by acclamation. Laura, who knew a winning horse when she saw one, had managed to convey to the new Mayor that she wasn't all that upset by his attentions.

Every fall the Rotary Club staged their grand Harvest Thanksgiving banquet. Absolutely nothing grew in our town because of the poisonous smoke from the smelter, but most of the citizens had come from places where there were harvests and the tradition was well accepted. When Jimmy McWhortle, the Master of Ceremonies, got up to introduce the head table there was a polite round of applause for his honour, Mayor Volkstein and an even more enthusiastic burst of hand clapping for his new wife.

Also at the head table a little, toil-worn old lady, whom Laura had introduced as Mrs. Lobchuck, the companion of her youth, sat with her bowed head covered by a colourful, hand-embroidered babushka. She sobbed happily into a handkerchief decorated with equally colourful embroidery as she listened to the Master of Ceremonies introduce Laura Volkstein nee Langmuir as:

"mizzus yer honour"